Fever
In The
Blood

Fever
In The
Blood

ROBERT FLEMING

Datina
BOOKS

Kensington Publishing Corp.
http://www.kensingtonbooks.com

DAFINA BOOKS are published by

Kensington Publishing Corp.
850 Third Avenue
New York, NY 10022

All Kensington Titles, Imprints, and Distributed Lines are available at special quantity discounts for bulk purchases for sales
promotions, premiums, fund-raising, and educational or insti-
tutional use. Special book excerpts or customized printings can
also be created to fit specific needs. For details, write or phone
the office of the Kensington special sales manager: Kensington
Publishing Corp., 850 Third Avenue, New York, NY 10022,
attn: Special Sales Department, Phone: 1-800-221-2647.

Dafina and the Dafina logo Reg. U.S. Pat. & TM Off.

First Dafina mass market printing: May 2006
10 9 8 7 6 5 4 3 2 1

Printed in the United States of America

For Cheryl, Ze'ev, and Ava,
who gave me my life back when the lights went dark.

"In all of us lodges the same fuel to light the same fire. And he who has never felt, momentarily what madness is, has but a mouthful of brains."

—Herman Melville, author

"I pity the race, for the Woman is the enemy of Man, and his hate for her is uppermost for his survival, is the name for her: whore, bitch, gold-digger, mule, to kill her, to kill wife, mother, aunt, grandmother, to poison the sap in the roots to bear false testimony, to deny, to make sterile all fresh and new life."

—Sister Zubena, poetess

Chapter 1

FALSE ARREST

There was blood on my hands and I had no idea where it came from, how it got there. You know how they arrest black boys on a whim. Needlessly. So they collared me, on a bum beef. Murder, no way. I don't think I killed anybody. I really don't remember.

Being around white folks doesn't seem to be everything it's cracked up to be. It's not a picnic. Ask them if you think I'm lying. Something is wrong. Something is wrong with me.

About this blood on my hands. Where did it come from? I don't know where it came from. I loved death. Killing. My grandma told me that something was wrong with me and I agreed, even when I was a kid. The first corpse I ever saw was not human. It was my dog, Felix, which I buried behind our apartment building in Brooklyn. The pooch, a black mutt, was named after Felix The Cat, the cartoon. A dog named for a cat. I considered that ironic, the name. I was six. I killed Felix, choked him to death with my bare kiddie hands, until its eyes rolled back in its furry head.

Wore my father's work gloves, no fingerprints. Didn't leave a trace.

When I next thought about the dog, it was early evening, and my father, my real father, was asking me about the mutt. Once I kill something, I never give it another thought. It's on to the next thing, just like in life.

"Where's that goddamn dog?" the old man asked, snarling. He wasn't really that old, just fifteen years older than my mother. Moms was in her mid-twenties at the time, looked like a young Diana Sands, the actress. But ink black with smooth skin like satin.

I lowered my head in a mournful expression, pure Shakespeare, and lied with a straight face. "I don't know."

Somebody should have stopped me back then, nipped me in the bud, before the bloodlust really took hold. Before I knew the thirst. No one did. I was an apprentice killer. No monster sprouts from the dry soil fully grown, fully developed. Every tragedy takes time to stretch to its complete length, gaining power and force with each passing hour. That was how it was with me.

A person, especially a young black boy, who has spent so much of his life internally, inside himself, in his own head, is frightening, even to himself. One incident changed me forever. Maybe I was nearly ten. A neighborhood bully teased me about my father's profession before his friends, his homies. He taunted me about my Pops being a drug pusher. What I didn't know was his father was a laid-off bus driver. This boy teased me, then he bitch-slapped me to the ground. Everybody laughed, he slapped down the runt.

Quietly I got up, blood leaking from my nose, brushed myself off and walked a few blocks to my house and got a butcher knife. When I returned to the scene of the crime, the crowd of kids parted like the Red Sea before Moses, leaving the bully standing there in this circle. The power. The fear in his eyes. Without saying a word, I stepped up to him and slashed him the length of his face, along the cheek. The blade struck once more and I marked him across the forehead. Everybody ran, screaming and carrying on, damn, he fucked him up.

"He's covered with blood," one kid yelled. "You could have killed him."

I looked down at my soaked trousers, drenched with his blood, and saw that I was hard. My dick was as hard as a diamond. His folks called the cops and that was that. Someone ratted me out. I rubbed my hands on his face, the color of it, the red, and waited for the law to come for me.

To my old man, it was just a case of "boys will be boys." Testosterone running amok. His thing was not to back down. Be a man. At all costs. Moms did not say a damn thing when he slapped me for letting a boy steal my lunch money, for being a punk. Be a man. Get mad. A man gets mad. Show some backbone and kick that boy's ass. Don't come home crying or I'll kick your ass.

The old man was full of macho beliefs like that. Never let a female shame you or a dude make you "lose face." If other men saw you crying or whining, they wouldn't respect you. Get hard, get tough. Never let anyone know what you're feeling inside. Get hard. Use your pain to make you hard. Never let your voice betray you. It's a guy thing. Be a man.

My current round of troubles started late this afternoon when an unmarked cop car pulled up sharply at the curb as I walked casually along 125th Street, the main commercial artery of Harlem. The avenue was packed with people. I was high. Two blunts after breakfast. Primo shit. Maybe I had just killed someone. The kill was so fresh that I couldn't remember it. The rush from it still lingered with me so I paid little attention when the tires of the prowl car screeched to a halt just inches from me.

Nothing could snap me out of my vile mood. Then the voices kicked in and the officers barked at me, waving their guns. Get the fuck over there against that car. Keep your hands where we can see them. Don't act a fool. This can go easy or hard. I let it go easy.

A crowd gathered to watch them shove me into the black-and-white city issue, striking my head on its roof before getting me all the way inside. Listen, nigger, your job right now is to not give us any trouble. Understand, black boy?

We didn't go to the police station. Maybe because I looked so out of it, they took me to Bellevue, for loonies. Maybe because I was screaming full tilt at the three female mannequins in a shop window a half hour earlier, they took me to Bellevue. They must have seen the blood on my hands but they didn't say anything until later.

Once in the nut ward at Bellevue, I sat there staring ahead, lost in my own world, my glazed eyes locked on the wild geometric patterns only I could see in the drab wall paint. I didn't belong here. Still, I felt the sensation of having my head pushed underneath water. All around me was a sea of disorder and chaos, nutville, but I felt strangely calm and serene. The place was a damn zoo. I didn't belong here. I wasn't like the rest of these fruit cakes. The young wolf chained. I sat quietly, cuffed hands folded in my lap, no telltale sign of agitation or nervousness. A rock.

The holding room for dangerous cases like myself was not that large, almost bare, very antiseptic, with thick mesh on the windows. Several policemen mingled with the hospital staff, keeping a watchful eye on the captives. I was never too verbal. I sat quietly in my chair; I gave them nothing.

Whenever someone came into the room, I smiled politely at them, completely tame. A disheveled woman, hair all over her head, stared at me across the room. Occasionally, she wiggled her hips suggestively and ran her tongue around the rim of her thick lips. Like she wanted to go down on me or something. Most women would say that I'm quite handsome for a twenty-year-old black man, wiry but rugged, just over six-foot and very fit. I don't eat a lot of junk. One of the cops ragged on me about the length of my hair, my short Wyclef Jean dreads, called me a fairy and a potential jail bridesmaid. My smile widened with his every word. I don't trust them because I know bad things can happen to a black man in custody, like that brother they busted out his back door with the toilet plunger. Sick puppies.

"Edward Michael Stevens, is that your name?" asked this one cop who looked like John Candy, the dead fat comedian.

"Correct," I answered. I didn't volunteer any information.

The whole bunch of them resembled Dick Tracy clones, Keystone Cops, circling me like buzzards on dead meat. I didn't like their stares. Every black man I know has had a run-in with these fools, not knowing what they're going to do next, whether there was going to be "an accident" of some kind. He resisted arrest, he went for a knife and we had to shoot him.

"Something's not kosher with you, Buckwheat," a plainclothes cop with a red Irish face said. "You've been up to something, boy."

They watched my eyes. Two of them moved their

chairs closer to me. Close enough for me to smell the lunch on their breath, meat with a beer chaser. I sat there, smiling. Then the questions came in a flurry, so fast that it was hard to follow who was doing the asking.

"Why were you yelling like that on the street? Are you psycho or something?"

I remained mute, still smiling.

"Are you on any kind of medications? Under a doctor's care?"

Not once did I lower my eyes. Staring right back at them. But not one word and that was frustrating the hell out of them. I finally figured out what it was, the nuts bit. Everybody has a thing about crazies, wackos, the folks minus cards in their decks. Here I was: the boys in blue with Sambo. What if Buckwheat ran amok? They felt unnerved by my eyes, my detached manner, my silence, my sense of cool, and all of them felt it. It.

Something menacing, something frightening, something disturbing but barely repressed. Like I could break out and go off the deep end at any moment.

"Where do you live?"

My grin answered for me. Bellevue. Where the elite meet and greet.

"Do you live at home with your parents? Do you work? Are you still in high school?"

I was their prisoner, wasn't the first time either. The last time was in Brownsville, Brooklyn, four months ago, after a ruckus in a parking lot. Man backed into my car or rather my father's car, and tried to drive off. I went ballistic on his ass. I wasn't high but I wasn't going to let him diss me like that. Just drive off. I punched him out, stomped him some, and somebody called the law. The cops arrested me, didn't say shit to the other guy because he looked like he was white, a light-skinned

Puerto Rican, threw me on the ground, and handcuffed me like I was Dillinger. They wanted to do a Rodney King on me but there were too many people and you never know who might be carrying a video camera. People, most of them out shopping for the holidays, stood around, watching the bust go down. They cheered when the cops jerked me to my feet, my arms ripping open from the cuffs, and slung me into the car. DUI. They read me my rights, joked a lot, and took me to jail.

"Why am I here?" I asked quietly, returning to the present. My captors chose not to answer me, instead they chatted among themselves.

"Why the hell am I here?" I shouted. My voice could probably be heard out in the hallway and everybody turned and looked at me.

"Don't get fucking cute," John Candy whispered close to my ear. "Mr. Stevens, you were acting strangely, menacing the public, so we got a call."

"That's bullshit. I was minding my own business."

"How did you get the blood on your hands, Mr. Stevens?" Officer Candy asked, kneeling in front of me. I wanted to kick him right between the legs. Damn, was I tempted.

"I don't know, cut myself maybe." I stared at the cops who stared back with open disdain.

One of the other men stepped up on the side of me, out of view but close enough for me to feel his presence, his malice. "Whatcha mean you don't know, Buckwheat? You know how it got there."

I glanced at my hands, dried blood in the palms and on the fingers. I recalled an old memory. "My dog got hit by a car and I carried him home. He died. I didn't get a chance to wash my hands."

The Keystone Cops huddled, talking in whispers,

motioning wildly. I couldn't make out any of it. A
member of the hospital staff joined them and the conversation became even more animated. One guy wanted
to hold me overnight, another said he didn't want to do
the paperwork, and John Candy insisted he could make
me talk.

I couldn't take my eyes from the blood on my hands.
Blood. I wanted to wash my hands in the worst way, feel
suds on them, wash them over and over as I did back
when the slaughter took place, back when I first bugged
out, back when the Congressman first rescued me. Wash
them over and over, which I often did at home, over and
over. Forty, even fifty times every day. Sometimes I went
through three bars of soap a day. Sometimes I felt like
I could never get them clean, no matter how much I
washed them. There were times when my hands bled
from so much rubbing and wiping, the ribbons of bright
red blood running down over the porcelain into the sink
drain.

"Dog, my ass," John Candy said in his wicked voice,
grabbing me under the chin. "I'm not going to ask you too
many more times. Where did the blood come from?"

"Hell if I know." I was tired of their bullshit.

Before I could say anything else, Candy's hand met
my face and I tumbled back in the chair, hitting my head
on the floor. The hospital guy rushed over yelling,
"None of that in here!" My face vibrated and the familiar flash of blinding white light followed the
thunderclap sound. In the background, the gibberish of
the cops and the nutville crew sounded like the madcap
crooning on one of those shitty Xavier Cugat cha-cha
records that my stepmother loved so well, the sound all
speeded up real fast. White noise. Static.

They yanked me up to my feet and pushed me back

into the chair. I smiled warmly at them like a small kid about to give a short Easter speech in church before his family and the entire congregation.

"Where did the goddamn blood come from?" Candy pressed. "Who did you fucking kill? Where's the damn body, perp?"

Another slap but I took this one, sitting perfectly still. My head didn't hurt so much this time. I was the Chosen One at the mercy of the Philistines, Christ in the hands of the Roman guards, Joan of Arc held at the pleasure of her molesters, Charlton Heston in the clutches of the talking apes. Tupac in the gun sights of his assassins. But I was strong; I did not falter.

"Where did the blood come from?" Candy repeated and was about to pop me again but someone grabbed his hand.

A line of blood flowed from my left nostril into my mouth but I didn't wipe it away.

"Why am I being held in a psychiatric ward, gentlemen?" I decided to speak.

"Where did you get the blood on your hands?"

I could be just as stubborn as them. "Why am I here? I'm not crazy."

Candy stood over me, glaring down at me. He wanted a piece of me so bad. "You're real cute, Buckwheat. When the officers asked your identity uptown, you gave them some off-the-wall remark. I forget what you said. It's here in the notes. You said your damn name was Joe Tex. But that's not your fucking name."

I smiled at them again. "I can answer any way I want."

Something Grandma once said to me came into my aching head. "Honey, in some seasons, madness is among our kind in full bloom. You don't have to look hard to see it." That's heavy but she was always saying stuff like that.

Nutville. Once Pops walked buck naked out into a snow-storm, did a couple of snow angels, not even shivering, until a neighbor yelled out the window at him. Then he came inside, acted like nothing happened.

"What were you doing earlier today?" Candy asked. "Where did the blood come from?"

I didn't answer. I watched my hands, my bloody hands, folding and unfolding them. Another tall white man entered the room, someone with authority and rank because the others straightened up at his appearance. He had a gray face and chain-smoked the entire time, saying nothing but listening to the others. He occasionally coughed a phlegmy cough, deep in the air sacs, like he had minimum lung capacity.

"We can have a wacko skele like you locked away in a place like this for a long time, a very long time," the tall man finally said. "We're not buying this crazy act. You know something and we're going to stay on your nigger ass until we get it out of you. Understand?"

"Can I have a cigarette?" I asked.

John Candy nodded, reached in his breast pocket and produced a pack. Camels. I took one in my cuffed hands and placed it into my mouth, and the fat man fired it up. The tobacco smoke felt hot and comforting as it entered my body and exited from my nostrils.

"What have you been up to, boy?" Candy started on me again.

I thought about the white man calling me crazy, bent, sick in the head. Shit, white folks think all niggers are crazy anyway. Maybe they are right. Living in this country can drive you crazy. When I thought on it, I was more mad than crazy, angry, enraged. I had every right to be. The homeboys had a term, *crazy mad*, someone over the top, beyond the limits of sanity and beyond the zone of insanity as well. This fit me sometimes. Sometimes I didn't care about a damn thing. That term fit a lot of people in the Hood. However, being mad, even crazy mad, was a useless emotion unless put to use. I put it to good use. I had been crazy mad for a long time, mad at the world, mad at the family I lost, mad at the family that found me, mad at myself for getting caught. I should have washed the blood from my hands right away. I bugged out. But the cops had no body, no evidence, and I would be more careful next time.

Suddenly, another cop in uniform entered the room, interrupting the interrogation, and whispered at great length with John Candy and the tall man. I could tell by their expressions that whatever they were being told did not sit well with them. John Candy's chubby cheeks reddened and he slammed his fat fist hard against his thigh.

I knew exactly what the deal was. "So you assholes found out who my father is." They wanted to beat the smug look off my face but couldn't.

"We can't hold him," the uniform said. "The guy's old man is that bigshot spade congressman. Congressman Stevens. The Congressman called somebody downtown. The boy's out of here. Somebody at One Police Plaza sent word that he walks and walks now."

Immediately I stood up and held out my cuffed hands. The cops, including the tall man, argued with the uniform, who kept shaking his head, no. John Candy glared at me once or twice during the powwow. Suddenly, their meeting finished, the cops left the room without saying anything, no apology, nothing. I asked the hospital staffer where the restroom was and went to wash off the blood, thinking that the cops might try to get a lab sample just in case. They blew it.

Twenty minutes later, I was sitting in a cab, humming

Queen Latifah's "The Evil That Men Do," en route to
my apartment and a rendezvous with the half-filled cup
of mango sorbet in my fridge. I was sloppy this time. I
would not be next time. For some reason, a quote by this
Samuel Beckett dude I read in my English class a long
time ago popped back into my head. It went: "The
major sin is the sin of being born." Damn right.

Chapter 2

GRANDMA TIMMONS'S HOT TRUTH GUMBO

One thing you can always expect when you're a murder suspect is a quiet, efficient police escort. They're always there, lurking to the right of your shadow. I don't know if they bought my fable of carrying the bloody dog or not. I really didn't give a fuck.

Keeping an eye on the unmarked car in the background, I went all over the city, even to some sinister places just to make the cops uneasy. But I did a lot of normal things too. Went to the hardware store on St. Nicholas Avenue for a length of rope, putty knife, pliers, and some nails. The car was still there. Went to an exhibit of the artists Charles White and Jacob Lawrence at the Studio Museum. Strong, dark, emotion-filled works. The car was not far behind. They stayed on my ass, especially this one Detective Bradley, short, chunky black guy with piercing brown eyes and a walrus mustache. He was right there in the car when I went to the Fairway off 125th Street for grape juice, fruit, spices, toilet paper and oregano for my visit to Grandma Timmons.

She asked me to pick up a few things. The car waited patiently in the dim light under the bridge for my exit from the store.

I remember Detective Bradley poking a long finger at me before I was released. "Niggers are the worst threat black people have. Remember when President Clinton said awhile back that violence for white people too often comes with a black face."

"What the hell does that have to do with me?" I was really being a smart-ass.

He was adamant. "The president was talking about predators like you, but you're even worse than that. You prey on your own kind. I will get your ass. Count on it."

"You have nothing on me," I said.

The detective said violence was commonplace in the Hood. I was not yet a grown-up and he knew it, offering an olive branch between us because he respected my stepfather, the Congressman. No one wanted to get on the wrong side of the politician. He tried to understand me but there was no understanding of the warped mind my family had nurtured in me. I was totally fucked up.

"What goes on in the head of a young man like you?" He narrowed his eyes at me.

"You talk like every one of the adults talk," I said. "We didn't create this world. We're just trying to live in it. It's not like the place when you were kids. Everything is all screwed up. You made the world violent. You made the world crazy."

He was stumped at how much sense I made.

"The world glorifies sex and violence," I explained. "Sex and violence are sold everywhere. We're even violent in our homes. I was not born in money. I was born poor with guns, crime, poverty, alcohol and drug use, and violence. My parents died as a result of violence."

"Who were your real parents?" he asked, scribbling on a notepad.

"That's none of your business," I smirked.

"I'll find out. We can find out anything. Maybe that is the reason why you have an attitude. Like you don't give a damn. What they need to do is lock your ass up and throw away the key. Once you get inside, then you'll change your tune. Yeah man, they'll make you into a bridesmaid in no time. A jailhouse bitch."

I stood up. I couldn't get away from there soon enough.

Two nights later, the lovely Xica went with me to see the film, *Shine*, at the Loews on 86th and Broadway and we watched it while eating hot buttered popcorn and overpriced candy. I loved her because she was the first girl I knew who had a stud in her tongue. She said she drove the guys nuts, sexually, and had a few girls on the string too. She wore her hair wild, all over her head, and had a Japanese tattoo on her neck. The characters said: *honor* and *respect*. For a couple of days, she had been bugging me about seeing the movie, saying it had hidden meaning for her, but she wouldn't tell me what it was.

Xica cried quietly when the pianist as a young boy was abused by his oppressive father, a man trapped by his own demons. I think she was abused by her aunt. Her mother, a junkie, had dropped her off on her way out of town going to New Orleans and her father was absent so it was left to her aunt to raise her. The woman was jealous about Xica since she had this wicked body of a vixen, all curves, and baby definitely had back. Back for days. Righteous ass.

"You never cry," Xica said. "That movie broke me up."

"Hey, I don't see how it was strange about what the old man did to the boy," I replied. "People do that kind of thing and worse every day. I didn't see anything shocking or painful about it. I've seen worse shit and endured worse."

She laughed. "Hard-hearted man. Lots of thick callouses on your soul, right?"

"You got to be hard if you want to survive," I said. "The world ain't about being no softie, no chump. You know that."

"Maybe, but how could someone do that to their own flesh and blood, knowingly hurt them like that?" she asked in that low coyote rasp of hers as we left the theater. "That's why people should need to get a license to have kids."

"I know a lot of bastards shouldn't have kids." I lit a cigarette for her.

She went through cigarettes like mad. "It's about sex with most folks, the babies are just the by-products, a mistake," she said, between puffs. "Look at these shorties living out on the streets, easy prey for anybody with a dollar. Nobody gives a damn about them. It's all fucked up if you ask me."

I noticed a white man pivot slightly to catch a glimpse of her shapely ass, the J-Lo roundness of it, as we moved past him. When I narrowed my eyes at him, he nervously looked away.

The other thing I like about Xica is that she tells on herself. Totally honest. Anything. She was telling me about living with her aunt and uncle. They have two daughters, older than she is. She said the uncle feels them up on their butts and touches their breasts and they don't seem to mind. Every time her uncle gets her by herself, he starts to talking about how he feels close to her, almost as if she is his kin. When they kiss and they do often, he has begun to not kiss her on her cheek but wander near her lips. Like lovers do.

"Oh shit," I said. "That's wild. So what do you do?"

"I don't want to hurt my aunt because she took me in and all that," Xica said. "But I'm getting feelings for him. He talks to me and shit. I feel safe with him."

"So you want to do him?"

"He talks to me, honest adult talk, and he doesn't bullshit me. I'm scared because I don't want to back up and shit before we get down and it's about to happen. If we aren't careful, it is going to happen."

"Would you fuck him?"

"In a heartbeat. I was in the shower and he walked in, big as you please. He had on these yellow boxers and man, he had a bone on him. I was wet. But I played it off like I didn't notice. See, I love my aunt very much. She has been like a mother to me and I don't want to fuck that up."

"What do you think she would do to you?" I took the cigarette from her.

"She'd fuck me up, period."

"What does your uncle say? He's probably worried and shit."

"Hell, yeah. He thinks that I will let him fuck me and then I will tell her. I told him that it would be real foul for me to do that. I would never tell her, never."

I walked her to the curb and another guy was peeking at her ass. She caught him and frowned. "My aunt would never want to have anything to do with me again. She's waiting for me to make a move. And I'm not going to do it. But the feelings are there. You can feel it. She senses it whenever we come into a room. She speaks to me as little as possible, unless it is just necessary. And that's cool."

We walked for awhile without saying anything. Silence was something I specialized in, expertly mute, and any female involved with me had to expect large blocks of dead space in any conversation. Xica didn't mind the gaps of quiet. But then she was always the first to talk.

"I tried to get you on the phone the other night," she asked. "It was after two. Where were you that late?"

"Oh, just out walking. Couldn't sleep."

"I don't understand how you can function with so little sleep, Eddie. That can't be good for you, not sleeping. If I don't get at least seven hours of sleep, I'm a wreck and not worth much the next day. I don't see how you do it."

I liked being weird, odd. "Yeah. Well, it must be something biochemical in my head because I've always been like that. My mother and grandmother were like that too. A family of insomniacs. I guess it's in the blood."

She stroked my arm and felt my bicep. "You ever think about taking some pills or doing yoga or something like that? Because it'll undermine your health. Eddie, it really will."

My mind was somewhere else, like on the first time I met her on the street near the Apollo Theatre walking with her little niece, a pixie of a little girl, and now how it blew me away to see how many pairs of shoes Xica had in her closet. Probably the only other people who had more shoes than this girl were my dead mother and Imelda Marcos. Females with serious foot fetishes.

The other time I was at a snow-and-slumber party on Grand Concourse in Bronx, cocaine and beds, a bunch of people at it, and I was just strolling around in the hall checking the doors. Door number two. Door number three. Everybody was doing the nasty. I went inside and plopped down next to a bed where two girls and a guy were naked and ready for action. Every now and then, I would reach out to cop a feel on a tit and a butt cheek, and they were totally uninhibited like they didn't even know I was there.

I recognized Xica doing a sixty-nine, lapping up the honey between the other girl's smooth thighs while the brother was rocking her world, his heavy balls plunging under her ass. She reached around, checked his condom, and moaned to let him know that she was good to go. He was thrusting his hips like a pile driver, filling that tight space as I waved and went out. I thought about staying and joining them.

"Not sleeping will make you sick, Eddie," she repeated to snap me out of my reverie.

"Let's talk about something else," I said, watching the cars zoom past and bicyclists weave in and out of traffic. "This will depress me if I keep yakking about it. What's up with your job hunt?"

"No dice."

"Didn't you have a sister?"

"She's nothing," she said. "All she wants to do is sex. Boning."

I knew everything about women. "In the end, it's always about sex with females, who's got the biggest meat, who can last the longest, who gets them off."

"What is it with you and sex, Eddie?" she asked. "You act like it's something sacred. Like it's something holy. Sex ain't nothing. You make too much of it."

The memory of my mother, of what she had done, had tainted my morals. Women were whores. Black women grew up too fast. "I guess so. Sex is serious business. It's not to be played with. If you just hop in the bed with anybody, after awhile it doesn't mean anything. It should be special."

She laughed again. "So if a woman enjoys sex, what is she then?" She watched my face for a reaction.

"A whore," I said quietly.

Suddenly, Xica stopped and pointed at a gray unmarked automobile, a Chevy, parked slyly between two delivery trucks. "Look, Eddie, there's that car again. You know, the one that followed us around when we left my place yesterday."

I nodded, knowing what was happening, and shot a quick glance in that direction. Yes, it was there, my shadow. My cop buddies.

"Who are they?" she asked. "What do they want?"

"Me, I guess. I had a beef with them a few days ago over some stupid bullshit and they've been on my ass every since. You know how they do us. You don't have to do nothing to have them all over you."

Did I want to tell her the truth? Could I trust her? Would she put it in the street? I knew I must be careful with females because they love to chat and oops, the rabbit would be out of the hat. One thing I learned from my Pops was that you never let anybody know all of your business anyway, never. There must be secrets. A real man had secrets, plenty of them. Secrets.

We quickened our pace, with her almost trotting to keep it up, moving through the late evening crowd. Everybody was in a testy mood. Giving off much New York City attitude. Snarling. Pushing. The two streams of bodies walked lockstep along the sidewalk like two subway trains hurtling in a whir on opposite tracks against the flow of the other. And the unmarked car was still there.

We crossed the street, going against the light. I figured we couldn't lose them if we tried, but it was worth a shot. At the parking lot, I gave the attendant, a short West Indian man, his money and walked over to my car. The brand new Jeep Grand Cherokee Laredo 4x4 bought for me by the Congressman as a birthday gift. Bright red. Cherry. It came fully loaded with air, CD player, small fridge, dual air bags, sunscreen glass, everything. A boy and his toys.

Once out of the lot on the street, we turned north on West End, picking up speed to slip our police escort in the crush of cars heading for the West Side Highway and the frenzied drive uptown. The cops stayed on our tail for much of the way. But we shimmied into a hurricane of yellow cabs and let them do our work for us, starting and stopping around our pursuers until we got a chance to disappear in the distance. The Jeep handled well in the demanding traffic.

"When are you going to see your Grandma?" Xica asked.

"I'm going there after I drop you off," I answered.

I chuckled to myself when I recalled Grandma Timmons's first meeting with Xica, the regal aging monarch and the restless upstart. The old Creole woman sat completely still in her book-cluttered apartment, giving Xica the serious once-over with her X-ray vision. It was as if she could see into your very soul.

Finally, she motioned for the younger female to come closer so she could use her voice to full effect. "What kind of name is Xica?" Grandma Timmons asked, sipping from a steaming cup of hot burdock root tea.

"I didn't like my birth name so I changed it to the name

of this Brazilian woman, who used her womanness and magic to gain her freedom from her Portuguese masters," Xica explained. "Xica represents something like that for me. Freedom."

Grandma grunted. "How are you a slave, girl?"

"Just being a woman in this male-dominated society makes you feel like a slave," Xica said theatrically. "White men think all we're good for is sex, white women believe we should be carrying a dish or watching their babies, and black men think we should be their mothers and take care of them. The entire world is afraid of the black woman. Nobody wants to gives us our props. You're a woman so you know what I mean."

Grandma Timmons shook her head as if she was addressing an unruly toddler, then she turned to me. "Mr. Eddie, you've got folks worried about you. I hear you stay in the streets, never at home. I have my sources. Where do you go at night when you trot off by yourself?"

"I go hunting." I laughed to give the truth a deceptive spin.

"Well boy, it's not good to be alone so much. Folks are worried about you, worried about staying to yourself. That's no good."

Anytime I visited Grandma Timmons, I expected the third degree, the probing questions, the searching looks, the sense of coming under the microscope. A wiggling bug with a pin jabbed through its middle being scrutinized by a single cruel eye. I knew she cared about me, probably was the only person who really did, but I resented her keeping tabs on me so closely. In a way, I hated that she wanted the best for me. I'd rather she was against me like the rest of the world, then if the killing urge hit me, there would be no remorse. No guilt.

It was starting to get somewhat chilly when I stopped

the car in front of the old red-brick pre-War building on Amsterdam and 143rd, which housed Xica's cousin's two-room flat, complete with fake Art Deco décor, fold-out Queen-sized bed, leafy plants, stacks of fashion magazines, piles of jazz and hip-hop CDs, and photos of Thelonious Monk, Odetta, and Miriam Makeba on the walls. A hip crib. We kissed soulfully for three beats, touched each other's arms and hands, and then she was gone. Xica was nobody's woman. She was a free spirit.

It was starting to rain for my long trek to Grandma Timmons's place in Mount Vernon. On the way there, in the rear view mirror, I noticed the familiar cop car changing lanes trying to tail me in the homebound rush.

Grandma Timmons's neighborhood was so quiet and serene compared to where I hung my hat, the constant wail of ambulance and police sirens in Harlem totally absent here, along with the ever-present boom-boxes blaring salsa and rap songs. The cop car stayed close. I circled her block for nearly ten minutes before I found a suitable spot to park. Out of habit, I removed all valu-ables, including the detachable radio, and secured the steering wheel with the anti-theft bar, although the area seemed tame.

This was what I loved, the smell of Granny's house. I never knew what aromas awaited me when I visited Grandma Timmons's small two-story house. It was either the succulent smell of down-home cooking or the tantalizing fragrance of freshly cut flowers neatly arranged in vases throughout the rooms. Today, it was the delicious, head-spinning scent of boiling caramel, something that immediately triggered childhood mem-ories of dipping apples into a large pot of bubbling sweet goo. A wave of gentleness came over me as she took my hands in hers and planted a loving kiss on my cheek.

"How are you, Mr. Eddie?" she asked, adjusting the strings on her apron. "Ain't seen you in awhile? What have you been up to?"

"I'm good, keeping out of trouble. What are you cooking?"

The old woman smiled and guided me toward the living room. "I'm making candy apples for one of the booths at the neighborhood bazaar. I don't mind helping out if it's a good cause. They're trying to raise money for a new playground and sports equipment. You know, the city cut back on its funds for recreation, so this is a good thing to keep the kids out of mischief."

I followed her into the living room, which seemed smaller each time I visited. When I was a kid, the place seemed cavernous, so full of fun and mystery, so unlike the tiny rat hole where we once lived in Brooklyn. She offered me a cup of mint tea and I accepted. With surprising agility, she turned and disappeared toward the kitchen. I noticed her battered bicycle leaning against a wall in the hallway. It reminded me of how athletic she still was, even in her eighties. She rode her bike through the town whenever weather permitted it, doing errands, visiting sick friends, and using the exercise to maintain her vitality.

"Are you still painting?" I asked, thinking of her striking portraits, landscapes, and still lifes that lined the small upstairs studio, full of jars of paint brushes, crushed tubes of color pigment, and canvases.

"Oh yes, I try to get in at least two or three hours a day at the easel," her voice came from the next room. "You got to stay busy. My painting and my flowers keep me young."

She soon returned, holding a teapot and two cups. "I believe in staying on the move. I'd rather burn out than rust out. One of my girlfriends in Mexico City sent me this wonderful reproduction of a Diego Rivera painting of two peasant girls. Simply wonderful."

I looked at that painting, which was not framed, and nodded my approval. Some things I knew about her past. I knew that she studied art in Mexico City way back when, working as an assistant with the fat Rivera on several of his murals. She treasured those times with the moody, brilliant genius, especially during his controversial stay in New York in the 1930s. When I was a child, she explained the work of the Mexican greats to me: Rivera, Kahlo, Siquieros, and Orozco. Her house was filled with these art books and many afternoons were spent going through them, talking about form, texture, color. I loved our afternoon trips to the museums where she would walk slowly, stop near an artwork, and point out its various strengths. We discussed her brief career as a painter out on the West Coast, her inability to sell her work and make a living. Then she got married and the babies came.

"Hey, that's a new picture there of you, right?" I directed her attention to a framed photograph of her on the mantel as a young girl dressed as a boy in a dark suit, clutching a top hat. In the background, shadowy adults were milling about, clad in different costumes and masks. It had a Mardi Gras feel to it.

"That was taken a long time ago at a masquerade ball," she said, smiling, pouring out the tea into the cups.

"You look just like Mama . . . the pictures of her when she was young. Or rather she looks like you, Grandma."

Grandma Timmons sat down in a chair opposite me, shaking her head mournfully. "Your mother was just a magical child, truly magic. Everybody felt it whenever they were around her. But you know something? I never felt she was mine, not like some parents do. She was always her own little person. So headstrong."

I laughed to myself. She asked me what was so funny.

"Nothing really," I said. "Tell me more about my mother. She was such a mystery to me. She never talked about herself, her past, her childhood. Nothing. When she was killed, I felt that I really didn't know her at all. She was very close-mouthed about anything personal. It was as if she was concealing some dark secret about her life and was afraid it might get out."

She crossed her legs at the ankles. "Eddie, a lot of colored folks are like that, keep their inner selves away from their kids. They're only comfortable giving their children just enough knowledge about them to let them know that they're human. Colored folks, by and large, don't discuss feelings and the like. We sing about them but we don't carry on about them like white folks."

"And Mama? What was going on inside her?"

"I don't think anybody knows that but her. I'll tell you this. Your Mama, my daughter, was deathly afraid of dying poor, afraid of not having what she wanted. She made a lot of mistakes and the first one was getting tangled up with your father. That man was trouble. I saw that the first time I laid eyes on him. If your Mama had gone on to college like I told her, none of this would have happened. She loved excitement. She loved the nightlife."

I sipped the sumptuous tea. "Did you judge her for that?"

"No baby, I didn't," she replied. "It's not for me to

judge anyone. I'm not God. I think we spend too much time judging one another. I only turn away from those things that are cruel and hurtful to others. My daughter was grown. She made her choices and she had to live with them. She knew what those people in that life were about and she brought them into her home."

I was seized with confusion. "But Pops got her into that junk. He's the one who got her mixed up with drugs and all that. And the riffraff. I blame him."

"No, no, no," she answered, wagging her finger at me. "Your Mama could have walked away anytime she wanted. She told me that she couldn't go back to the straight life, the square life. I told her to leave long before anything happened. She told me she couldn't do a nine-to-five, wasn't in her program. Plus she believed your Daddy was going to strike it rich and they'd go away somewhere and start over."

"We didn't live like we had money," I grunted. "We did without a lot of times. Where did the money go?"

"I asked her that. She told me they spent it. I asked on what and she answered that was none of my business."

My headache suddenly kicked in. It had been throbbing since that incident with the cops and wouldn't go away. Dull ache. I stared at the floor for a moment, the pain in my head rising a notch. Headaches were my pals since I was a kid. Really bad ones.

"What's on your mind, Eddie?" she asked. "You look puzzled about something."

"I don't get it," I said. "They were fools, Grandma. I get so mad sometimes just thinking about what happened. They didn't have to die that way. You just don't know. I get so many dark thoughts, ugly thoughts. I hate her for what she did."

"Why her and not him?" Grandma's eyebrow wrinkled.

She reached over and patted me on the arm. Comforting. "You shouldn't. You have to let it all go and move on with your life. You can't let their deaths destroy your life. You're young. You have to put it behind you."

"I'm angry," I said.

"Who at?"

"Women." I itched for a cigarette. "The old man didn't deserve that and neither did the girls. They were just kids, babies. The bitch was responsible for them getting killed. She couldn't keep her legs closed."

Grandma slapped me viciously. "Don't ever let me hear you speak about your mother like that. You hear me? I'm not playing. I will slap the taste out your mouth if you do. You hear me?"

I took it like a man. I thought back to the funeral of my parents. Grandma Timmons didn't cry at the funeral and neither did I. I was numb. We stood there in that church, the gospel choir singing badly behind us, holding hands. I was eleven. I was never a crybaby but the deaths of my family, gunned down like dogs, overwhelmed me with such anger and grief. It was a living thing, this rage, a physical suffering that crowded its way into every corner of my life. I knew I'd never be the same. You never recover from stuff like this. I hated them for leaving me alone. I hated the men who stretched my mother out on the carpet before my pleading father and my trembling sisters and took turns raping her. All four of them, before shooting her in the head. Before shooting all of them in the head.

Grandma Timmons saw the tortured look in my eyes. "Honey, we all have disturbing thoughts, thoughts so ugly that we can't tell anyone about them. But it's no good to harbor them inside. It's no good to do that. They'll tear you apart."

I rocked back and forth to comfort myself. "I get so mad sometimes. I hurt, hurt so bad, and that makes me want to strike out at the world. Fuck the world."

She rubbed my shoulder tenderly, ignoring my profanity. "I know, baby, but anger is no good. It just shortens your life, eats away at you like a cancer. In the end, it'll make you its puppet, make you do things you wish you hadn't."

"Do you think I'm weird, crazy?"

She laughed and gulped some tea down. "Lord no, no more than anybody else. You've just had a rough time. Everyone goes through something that shakes them to their foundations sooner or later in life. These are the tests of life, the things that either makes us stronger or ruins us."

"Everybody thinks I'm nuts," I said.

"Who is telling you this mess about you being crazy?" she asked. "Is that head shrinker woman the Congressman's got you going to see? They should have left you with me. Said I was too old. What do they know?"

The pain in my head was pounding like a big bass drum. "The Congressman treats me like I'm a wacko. And my therapist says I'm troubled, whatever that means. I know I have a bad temper and sometimes I act nutty. Remember they used to give me that stuff, Ritalin, in school, to quiet me down? I hated that. The other kids used to tease me a lot about that."

"Yes, I believe that's what messed your mind up in the first place. Got you confused. I told your stepmother not to do that. She told me you were uncontrollable without it. Damn fools. Hell, anybody would act out if they saw what you saw. No child is supposed to see anything that terrible."

Something so terrible. The men burst into our apartment, with their guns drawn, punching my parents

around. I hid in a crawl space where I saw all of it.
Where's the money, bitch? Where's the stash? One of
them held a gun to my younger sister's head and put
his hand under her dress. My other sister was so scared
she peed herself. My father ran toward the guy molest-
ing my sister and another of the thugs knocked him to
the ground. He crawled on the floor, trying to get to
the man who kneeled before my sister, unzipping his
pants. He was trying to put his thing in my sister's
mouth. The others kicked my father. My mother just lay
there, her eyes wide and frantic. Where's the money,
bitch? I couldn't get those images out of my head,
couldn't get them out. No matter how hard I tried.

I didn't realize there were tears in my eyes or that I
was shaking so violently until Grandma Timmons put
down her cup and hugged me. I was eleven again, stuck
in that terrible nightmare all over again. My head hurt
so much. Right behind my eyes. She stroked my head,
murmuring poor child, poor child. I covered my face
and cried into my hands. Cried full out like a dam had
burst inside me or something. The tears wouldn't stop.

Her touch felt good. It had been so long since anyone
touched me like this, so lovingly, so tender. I leaned into
her caresses like an abandoned tabby. For too long, I had
felt like nobody gave a damn about me. For too long, I
had wanted to die, to disappear, to vanish to a place
where I wouldn't hurt anymore. Because I knew if this
went on for too much longer that I was going to do
something bad. Hurt somebody or myself.

"Why don't you stay the night, Eddie?" Grandma
Timmons said. "You can't drive home in such a state.
You're too upset. You can sleep in the guest room."

She helped me to my feet, led me upstairs to the
room. I couldn't stop my body from vibrating, couldn't

stop the pounding in my head, couldn't stop the pictures in my mind. After I laid across the bed, she rubbed my neck and back, speaking softly under her breath. She whispered, "Let it go, let it go baby, let it go."

All I could think: either I will hurt somebody. Or myself.

Chapter 3

THE BITTER HEART

Genuine sleep eluded me during that restless night. An old childhood habit of putting on a light during the darkest night hours returned to me but I still got only a minimum of rest. I closed my eyes, and tried to quiet my chaotic mind. The madness. The pictures never stopped. I tossed and turned, screamed and pleaded while the nightmares replayed in full color, filling my head with terror.

Getting up to lock the guest bedroom door, I pulled my two joints out, licked them to moisten their paper, and set one off. Benny said it was the bomb. Would make me see stars and shit. I was thinking it was PCP, angel dust, getting dusted. But I didn't give a shit. Not about anything. I let the smoke ease out my nose, gentle and slow, metallic smell. I sat on the bed across from myself, talking with myself, speaking in two different voices. Two selves. Me and my shadow self. Identical yet distinct.

A knock on the door. "Eddie, what is that smell?" Grandma Timmons called. "You're not smoking dope, are you? Tell me you're not smoking dope."

I answered, pinching my nostrils. "No, I'm not. Just chillin'."

"Boy, I better not catch you smoking that mess in this house," the old woman shouted. "I mean that. Open this door."

"I'm tired, just let me lay down," I replied. "Okay? Please." I heard her walk down the hall, her steps heavy and weary. I was hit by sudden, violent fits of nausea, puking right down on the floor, between my feet. My legs wouldn't let me stand. I couldn't get my balance, wavered, tried to get to my feet but slipped head first in my oily retch.

The room began spinning. My other self started to talk. How did they get into the house? How did they get past the locked doors? And the alarms? And the Dobermans and the pit bulls? Shit. Cant figure it out. They were on Pops and the boys before they could grab their guns and fire. On their asses. The fellas dressed to the nines, adorned with a pair of shades, going to play for the blood and guts. Moms stood there, pleading and moaning, going on like she knew the dudes. "Don't hurt them. Just take the cash money." No way. They wanted to go for the splatter, hurt somebody, put some metal on some flesh. Pops called one nigga a fuck and dared him to mess with him and the other guys laughed. They shoved each other as Pops' boys realized that everything was serious as a heart attack and said whatthefuck the nigga wanted to die. They started punching him, kicking him, spitting on him and saying the boy was a punk. He got one shot against one dude's head, but he got hit again, and five fists smacked in the face and then another and he went to his knees.

I could see it. I could see it as if it was a replay on a NFL game. Slow motion.

Someone yelled at Moms and asked her to give him some head. Come-on bitch. Don't be stuck-up, let's party. Nigga won't mind, right? Man you can give us the bitch or mebbe one of the youngbloods wanna bend over and give me some ass. Some tight shit. Ain't never been fucked with. Pretty soon Pop's pleading with them, don't do some shit y'all regret. Them babies, come-on man, please. You dudes gonna get in trouble. The dude Moms knew grabbed a dirty rag and wiped his mouth and then his crotch. She knew what he wanted, wanted some young trim, pussy with the seal still on it. Those little girls.

I could hear him say fuckyaself, my older sis, and asked she had ever played with a man's thing before. Played with it until it spit. Pops shook his head, no, don't. Don't do that. This was Mom's dude, I'd seen them fucking, he fucked her bent over the sink, his fingers directing her quivering butt cheeks, snapping like a whip until she couldn't breathe, until she almost passed out.

He teased Pops, this wasn't about a stickup, a heist, no it was about something else. Claiming Pops' pussy. The old bitch and the two girlies. I hear your bitch's a good hump. Bitch wear a nigga out. I could see Pops panicking cause he knew what they were up to, and he tried to run for his piece, his 9mm, but somebody tripped him and he went sprawling on the rug. He tried to pull himself up but they took turns kicking him, in the belly, in the head, in the groin. All between the legs. He screamed, cried, pulled himself into a ball, knowing they were going to tear them open, rip them apart. He couldn't do shit. One man slapped him in the face with the gun, sending him against the wall, and onto the knees. The man put the gun to Pops' temple, smiling as if he had a prediction of the time to come, pulled the trigger finger and splattering bone and blood onto the plaster.

The other self silenced. Something was in the room. I could feel it. When I pulled my head from under the pillow, I saw my mother, my dead mother all ashen gray, standing near my bed. She stared into my face with red, burning eyes and walked closer and closer until I could smell the dirt and decay on her. Her hair was matted with twigs, bugs and dried blood. My heart raced so fast that I thought it would burst from my chest. I closed my eyes again and wished for her ghost to leave. But when I opened them, the spirit was still there, hovering in the air, its feet not quite touching the floor, and her throat was bloody and torn. That's when I screamed and screamed.

I cried out, howling and ranting from the fears. My screams must have waked up the entire street. The ghost vanished by the time Grandma Timmons arrived with soothing words, a gentle smile and a calming touch to rock and cradle me into an almost placid state. A glass of warm milk did nothing to stop my shakes. Still, she stayed with me until I dozed off.

The following morning, she was up at the crack of dawn, preparing breakfast. Grits, scrambled eggs, salmon cakes, wheat toast, and orange juice. I slowly showered, groomed myself, and thought about what was obvious and hidden about my family. Our evening talk yesterday posed new questions for me about the role of my mother in the butchering of the clan that horrible day. I was determined to get to the bottom of it all at the breakfast table with Grandma Timmons.

"Did you sleep well the rest of the night?" Grandma Timmons asked as soon as I entered the kitchen. "I didn't hear you up there?"

"No, I woke up not long after you left but nothing else happened. I never sleep and when I do, I have the worst nightmares," I said. "I would love to get a full night's sleep. If I sleep three hours a night, I'm happy because then I don't feel like I'm about to snap all the time."

She wore her wire rim glasses this morning, the better to see the wide pan of browning salmon cakes, their aroma intoxicating. Her quick gray eyes inspected me during a smooth turn of her head while she moved as if walking through water from the oven to the kitchen table. An expression of worry flashed across her face. I imagined I looked like hell.

"Can I ask you something, Grandma?"

"Yes, but don't get too heavy before breakfast. It'll spoil your appetite and you need to eat to keep up your strength. Go ahead and ask me what's on your mind."

"You think Mama hated us?" I asked reluctantly.

"Why, baby? We went through all of this last night. What more do you want me to say? Your Mama did the best she could."

One thing you could always count on was that Grandma Timmons kept repeating the same things. Forget the past. Don't talk about painful events and they will go away. I felt a sudden uncontrollable urge to laugh at myself, my head dusted and all, but I didn't. There was an uneasy silence in the room. I needed answers, real answers.

"Eddie, don't talk about anything unpleasant," the old woman said.

I ignored her, thinking of my mother's nightly meetings with men at local motels. "Mama never said she loved me unless she wanted me to lie for her. She slept around and wanted me to lie to Pops for her, saying she was off with this girlfriend or another. He slapped me around because he knew what I was doing. He knew I was lying for her. Then she'd kiss all over me in public like she was the perfect mother, a show for folks in the streets, but once we got home, she acted as if I didn't exist."

Grandma Timmons poured the juice into the glasses. "Eddie, she didn't hate you. She was just distant sometimes. When she was little, she was strange just that way. Very cold. Closed in on herself, with her feelings."

We sat down and said our prayer of thanks. The old woman sliced a piece of the salmon and put it in her mouth. She watched me carefully while she chewed.

How childhood can warp you for life, twist up your insides like a pretzel, force you to spend the rest of your days trying to undo what has been done. Don't parents know the power they possess over the wee lives entrusted into their care? The bastards. I loved Moms more than breath itself but she was no damn good. To the core. A Queen bitch.

"Remember that time when Mama took me when I was real little to the shopping mall in Queens and left me?" I asked. "She just let my hand go and walked off. I was so small, so scared. I still have nightmares about that."

"I know." She bowed her head, ashamed.

"She wasn't worthy of being your daughter, let alone my mother," I blasted her.

"She had her shortcomings. That stunt she pulled there bothered me for years. What she did was wrong. Boy, we had to fight like hell to get you back from the child welfare after that foolishness. They paraded you around like a prize monkey. It was all in the papers and on the TV. I don't know what was on her mind when she did that."

I drank the sweet juice, surveying her over the top of the glass. "Do you think she regretted what she did?"

"Yes, honey, I think she did. You don't remember this but the police arrested her, charging her with abandoning you. I believe she was telling the truth when she said on TV that she was sorry and wanted you back. I chewed her out for what she did. I let her have it. She didn't hear a word I said. I think she loved being in front of all those reporters and all, in the limelight. We watched it here, your Cousin Earle and Aunt Fell, and the girl looked right in the camera and said: 'I miss him and I love him. I'll do whatever I have to do to get him back. I want to give him a big kiss and tell him that I'll never do it again'."

Now the food was sticking in my throat and turning rancid in my stomach. I felt sick but I needed to hear more.

Her eyes served as a stethoscope. I believed she could see my palpitating heart through my shirt, hear its flutters and thumps. Electrical disturbances of the cardiac system caused by betrayal and rage. I begged her to go on and tell it all.

"Please go on, Grandma," I pleaded.

After a forkful of grits, she went on with her revelations. "But Eddie, don't put the blame all on her. That no-count husband of hers had a hand in it. Count No-Count. He never liked you. He preferred the girls over you and treated them like princesses. Whenever he talked to you, he was always putting you down. He slapped and cussed you in public. I didn't like that at all."

I chimed in. "I expected no less from him. He wasn't shit no way. But she was my mother. She should have stuck up for me. I looked to her for love and support and there was none."

"Watch your mouth, boy. You know I don't allow that kind of talk in this house. I don't care what you say in the streets but that doesn't go over here. Understand?"

I forced down more food. "Sorry."

"Why don't you put some of those ill feelings on him," the old woman said defiantly. "He was in the wrong just as much as she was."

"I don't want to talk about him," I answered, squinting my eyes. "She's the one who hurt me most. She was my mother, the woman who pushed me out into the world. She should have known better. A mother should love her own child no matter what. Even animals do that much."

Her voice became stern. "My daughter, your mother, had her faults but it's wrong for you to pin everything wrong in your life on her. You're grown now and you've got to take responsibility for what you do and how you act. It's like colored folks yelling that they can't get ahead or act decently with one another because of what white folks did to them during slavery. That was then and this is now. We can't afford to use that as a crutch, just like you can't with this tragedy. Also, I don't know why you can't see that it was that fool of a father of yours got his family killed. Him and that drug dealing mess."

I knew what I knew. "You don't know what Moms did."

"What did she do? What did she do that he didn't do?"

She knew what her daughter did. "I knew two of those guys who killed Moms and Pops and the girls. I told the cops and they didn't do a thing, said it was drug-related and that was that. But Moms was running around with one of the guys. He used to come by and snort coke with her while Pops was out. And one time I walked in on the two of them. She whopped my butt so bad that I couldn't sit for a week."

Another long silence. We picked at our food, listening to our forks hit the china and swallowing the long gulps of juice.

"You don't look too well," Grandma Timmons said. "What can I get for you?"

"Nothing, I'm cool," I replied.

My mind exploded with swirling images, sounds, bits and pieces of lurid hallucinations. I no longer cared to hold my rage. Or my demons at bay. The face of the woman I'd killed not that long ago flashed before my eyes for an instant, her bloody pleading face, her hands with their crisscross of deep wounds, the red torrent on her neck.

"Boy, are you okay?" the old woman asked. "Why are you trembling so? Answer me, Eddie. What's wrong?"

"Mama was a fucking bitch," I said coldly. "I'm glad she's dead."

Grandma Timmons glared at me, shaking her fork in my face.

Fuck Moms and her too. I stood up, slammed the chair against the wall. I looked at her angry expression. Why was she so pissed at me? For a second, I imagined Grandma's body covered with stab wounds, sprawled on her stomach on the black-and-white tiles on the kitchen floor, face staring lifelessly at a table leg, blood flowing from countless gashes in her dark flesh. The knife was on the sink. It was within reach. The impulse came without warning as it often did. I could easily kill her. I must leave and leave now.

"Excuse me. I got to leave for a minute . . . the bathroom. I'll be right back." I didn't look at her when I spoke those words.

However, I didn't go to the bathroom. Without a backward glance, I walked quickly out the front door of the house and down the path of blooming flowers to the street and my car. I didn't think I would make it. Her voice was in my ears, asking me not to go. I ignored it. Her life was at stake. Once inside the car, I grabbed the steering wheel tightly with both hands and bashed my head hard down on it, again and again and again, trying to knock the cries for blood out of my mind. Grandma Timmons came out of the house onto the walkway, still yelling. I couldn't make out what she was saying and didn't care to know, as I put the key into the ignition and pulled away from the curb. She was spared.

Chapter 4

WHEN THE
MOANING STOPPED

I've been a naughty boy. The newspapers ran a story two mornings after my visit to Grandma's house telling me that Victim Seven had been found, even if she was somewhat worse for wear. They found her body, which they labeled Jane Doe, in an empty lot, wrapped in trash bags and covered with cardboard. Just as I left the bitch. She tried to fight back and I had to show her who was boss. The articles went on to say nobody had missed her, not her family, not her boyfriend, not even her coworkers.

How many people in this vertical city disappear and nobody even notices their absence? The stab wounds were random, the papers added, appearing everywhere, in the neck, chest, arms, and legs. One wound was delivered with so much force that her heart was penetrated to her back and a massive head gash revealed a sizeable portion of the brain. I never realized that I hit her so hard but she was struggling. She was not going out easily. All she wore was a torn, blood-soaked blouse, a watch, and an Egyptian ankh made of mahogany. Her pants or dress were missing.

It was a dress, a tight short one that left nothing to the imagination. In fact, I swear I could smell her privates as soon as she got into the car. It was as if she had just finished having sex and went out in the streets looking for another dick. I knew her kind, never satisfied with one man. Always on the hunt for something new. Like Moms. Right? Moms was always looking for something new, another man, another huge dick to take the place of Pops' limp one. Drugs can do that to you.

Grandma Timmons said I should not blame Moms for everything wrong with me. Then who should I blame? She said I should think about the good things I remember about Moms. Like what? Okay, Moms had beautiful eyes, light brown, the kind that could make you forget your hurt. That's the only thing I can summon up about her. Moms was a schizo. She could be sweet one minute and a bitch the next. What did she say that one day that broke me down: I'll be old soon and you'll regret you had not been more loving to me, I won't always be here, you have no idea what I've given up in this life for you, Eddie. You have been trouble for me since the day you were born. You ruined my insides and stretched me out of shape down there. No wonder your father never wants me. I should have aborted your little nigger monkey ass. I should have killed you in the womb. Did you know your Daddy started running the streets after I had you? He said he couldn't feel me down there when we made love. Said I was too big now.

Moms wanted me dead. DOA in the womb. Shortly after that, I looked up the term in the dictionary for killing your mother: *matricide*.

Two days ago, I walked into Victim Seven, kinda like a pickup. I was polite. I was friendly. I was emotionally available and attentive. They love that.

"Let's eat there," Victim Seven said, pointing to a restaurant on Broadway near Columbia Presbyterian Hospital, across the street from the old Audubon Ballroom where Malcolm X was shot. The place had cheap meals so that was alright with me. It catered to the locals and hospital staff, not the gilded tourist trade like the famed Sylvia's or Copeland's.

It was late so there were only a few people on the terrace. We took a table inside. I suggested it for the sake of privacy and she bought the idea, thinking of the romance to follow.

"I don't understand why you don't have a steady girl as pretty as you are," Victim Seven flirted, constantly pushing a few strands of her camel-hair weave out of her eyes.

I looked her over: brown skin, average build, height, and looks. She had junk in the trunk. Lots of ass. She was dressed to show it off. Dressed like a slut. On the prowl. Like me. Two hunters.

"Nobody wants me," I finally said. "I'm an oddball."

"No, you're not, pretty nigger," she smiled. "I have a good feeling about you. We've talked for almost an hour and you haven't said the word, bitch, once. That's a first for a black man."

That remark alone sealed her death. Like a cat with a cornered mouse, I wanted to take my time with this one. I was prepared to go with the flow of the night. If the opportunity to reap her life arose, then I would take it. If not, that was alright too.

"Waiting for Ms. Right, huh?"

"Maybe. You never know."

as I ended its life on the plate. "Don't worry. I'm tame. I've had all my shots and I'm neutered."

She liked the dog analogy, all men were dogs. We laughed again. Little did she know she was chosen, that I'd heard her inner voice whisper: *kill me kill me kill me kill me*. Any doubt about her membership on my list of redeemed whores was erased when I saw the flickering pale amber light around her body. Her aura. It was low like someone on the verge of crossing over to the dark beyond. She wanted to die. In less than thirty minutes, I granted her wish although she changed her mind at the last moment and wanted a reprieve to live. Tough shit.

The entire time while I was killing her, I kept seeing a close-up picture of the girlfriends I knew in my head. And Moms. I heard the females laugh in the distance behind me. I tasted my blood in my mouth. When we walked down the rocky slope under the bridge, I put on my gloves, keeping my eyes on her leading down the path. The river smell was strong. I sneaked up behind her, grabbed her and struck her head on the ground. Then it was on. I stabbed her repeatedly. I killed her, simple as that.

Chapter 5

COMPLICATIONS

The cop car followed me back from the East Village where I went to an afternoon showing of Antonioni's *The Passenger*, involving Jack Nicholson pretending he's a doomed gunrunner in Africa, wearing the cloak of false identity until he meets the fate of the original target. I sat in a diner drinking several cups of coffee. Black coffee. I felt dull and needed to be perked up. Finally, I dragged myself to my apartment, retrieved my mail, nothing but bills for the most part.

Yesterday, I never stopped to even glance in the mailbox, although I knew there were some official papers coming from Unemployment Compensation, from my last job. They didn't come. I worked as sales help at a music counter of Tower Records. Jobs came and went with me. I changed them like most guys changed underwear. I was lazy. No big thing.

All I got was a postcard advertising the Congressman's appearance at a bookstore on Lenox Avenue that following afternoon and another card with Dinah

Washington caressing a mike in mid-song at Newport 1959 on its cover, complete with message:

Thanks again for all your thoughtfulness, the caring and sharing this week. I cannot tell you how much you have brought to my life. The petty annoyances are so much easier to handle and the serious conflicts more worth the effort. You give me hope about so much. Xica.

The Congressman. Congressman Franklin Delano Stevens. He represented all that was wrong with the black upper class: arrogant, snobbish, near-sighted politically, isolated, misinformed, and acutely conservative. My stepfather never saw life as a creative act; it was a means to make money and acquire power. Everything else in the sphere of things was second-rate: hobbies, familial ties, petty emotions; only fund raisers were matters that held real weight.

Strangely enough, the Congressman, my name for him that he hated, saw himself as the second coming of Adam Clayton Powell without the so-called liberal baggage. He was Harlem's answer to the Republican right. A conservative African-American JFK, the press said. The Congressman could be perversely witty, utterly charming, quirky with an oddball humor, knowledgeable in most political issues, but ruthless in the exercise of his power. The man, however, was a great actor, a superb communicator, and his skills with a hostile crowd were legendary. I learned much from him about the art of shutting down the emotions before doing a disagreeable task. Blank it from your mind and do what you must do, the Congressman loved to say.

When the Congressman asked you to do something, there

was no debate. You did as you were told. I appeared on time
at his appearance at the Harlem bookstore, dressed in a dark
suit, dreads pulled back and tied. There was very little parking around the place where he was promoting his new book,
Speaking Right From the Hip. He was winding down his
multi-city book tour, TV and radio appearances, and mall
signings nationwide. All of this activity was coordinated to
coincide with his latest re-election bid. And he loved it. The
man loved the media attention.

I barely found a seat in the back. Many people were
standing along the walls, some near the doorway or in
the aisles. The store was packed. It was a racially mixed
crowd, with a sizeable number of whites who approved
of his maverick nature and staunch right-wing leanings.
More whites were moving into his district, buying aging
abandoned brownstones on the southern fringes of the
community, and they loved him. But African Americans
loved him too. See, he had them fooled into believ-
ing that he was a God-fearing man. That he loved the
church, especially black churches. He consistently
drove home that blacks were a God-fearing people and
that they only strayed when they followed their bestial
nature of the jungle. Those are his exact words. A true
black conservative.

The massive crowd was shouting his name when the
Congressman strode boldly into the room, followed by
the entourage. Bodyguards bracketed him as he walked
head-up through the throng, touching an occasional
hand, making eye contact with old friends, and smiling
triumphantly. His handsome brown face was split with
a frozen smile.

Applause died out after a brief introduction of the
eternal candidate by a dotty white woman, a Republican
operative from downtown, in a gray business suit. The

Congressman never said he was a Republican; he would say he was Independent. Although he said he was an Independent, a man who answered to nobody, there was a lot of GOP money and muscle behind his re-election bid. His opposition tried to score some point with that fact but it was lost amid the politician's control of the black neighborhood newspaper and local officials. He would do whatever he must do to win.

The Congressman stood at the podium, still smiling, glancing at the notes taken from his pocket. His ramrod stiff stance highlighted his well-toned body, tight with gym-honed muscles, dressed in a dark blue Bill Blass suit. He cleared his throat and started in the smooth firm voice that caused people to think of the canned voice-overs used to sell cereals, headache medicine, and bug sprays.

"Someone the other day in Indiana asked me if I was truly an Independent in my political thinking," he began in his radio announcer voice, a rich baritone. "You know I was helping another African-American Congressman candidate to get elected. Anyway, I wanted to turn to this man and say why don't you read the book, but I didn't."

Someone laughed and the Congressman paused to let the moment pass.

"What I did say was this," he went on. "We as black people cannot afford to be tied to the Democratic Party or any political party. We must support those who support us."

That brought more applause and he waved his hand to silence it. He loved manipulating the masses, the power of persuasion.

Now he leaned on the podium, locking eyes with the crowd. "It is time for political reform. It is time for us to throw out political correctness. Correct for whom? We must be willing to buck the party line, whether it is theirs or our own. We must return Harlem to the people and America to the people. We are a part of those people. Washington must learn its responsibility to us all. The rules that apply to us as citizens must also apply to the politicians, to the people who serve us. They are not above the law."

The Congressman was very adept at turning any situation into a campaign rally. He knew how to work a crowd, to mold their moods, to sway their thinking, all with an earnest look and sincere words. It was theater to him.

"The power of Big Government must be controlled," he said very quietly. "How can any one of us be truly free if government has no limits? We must be empowered. Big Government's power to tax and spend must be curtailed. We must be able to prosper as individuals. The rewards of real economic growth must not trickle down to us, for we must be permitted to participate fully in America. Pennsylvania Avenue must acknowledge the real needs of Main Street. And it definitely has to acknowledge the needs of 125th Street as well. The American people are decent. The American people are fair. The average citizen, regardless of race or religion, wants to make a difference in the life of this country. Right now, there is a national outcry for change. Yes, we want peace and prosperity, but we want ethics and morality as well. There is a need for greater personal responsibility by those who lead us. We need a Washington establishment that is pro-family and pro-God."

There was a surge of clapping among the crowd. Suddenly, a black man clad in African garb stood up.

"Brother, I respect you, but all of that stuff you're speaking sounds like yak-yak-yak to me and most of the people out here. What does any of that mean to us? Why are you or any of the other so-called African-American leaders relevant now to us as a race?"

This was when the Congressman was at his best. He loved open debate, being challenged by what he considered inferior minds. Sometimes he swatted them away with a superior retort. Sometimes he cajoled them with a sugared, long-winded reply. He knew the power game like most husbands know the pattern of moles on their wives' bare backs.

"I'll tell you why I'm relevant," the politician answered. "About twenty-two percent of Black America doesn't know what a job is. About seventy-two percent of black children are living in poverty. For every four black men in college, there are another ten in court or locked up in prison. These facts and more are the reason why I am relevant. Both Mr. Carter, my opponent, and our current president have failed us. Carter knows I delivered the goods in my first term. And by the way, they are Democrats. Kennedy failed us. The Great Society programs failed us."

"You sound like a Republican," someone in the crowd shouted.

The Congressman chuckled briefly. "Republican equals conservative. I'm conservative but I'm Independent. Conservative. Is that such a bad thing? Even a conservative like Nixon captured forty percent of the black vote in 1960. Look what the Republicans did in winning House seats in 1994. They didn't do that without black help."

"Weren't Bush and Reagan racist?" another black voice shouted out.

The reply was swift. "How can I answer such an absurd question? They were Americans and acted accordingly."

"What about our poor?" the voice followed up. "Conservatives like Bush and Reagan devastated them by cutting money to our programs. They tried to undo everything we fought for during the civil rights era, including affirmative action. They didn't give a damn about us and neither do you. None of you care about the poor. What about that?"

The Congressman walked to the edge of the stage and removed all emotion from his words. "Is this the so-called underclass we hear so much about? Let me say this and you can call me a lawn jockey, an Uncle Tom or whatever. I'm tired of hearing about these people who wish to have others do for them what they should be doing for themselves. Nobody talks about the black middle class who work hard, maintain their families, and play by the rules. What about them? I'm sick of the worst of us representing who we are. What do they contribute? The world judges us by this wretched element of our race. This is not fair. Do you think it is fair?"

Some of those vocally agreed with him, cheering him on, while others yelled their disapproval. The Congressman was in his glory. News photographers snapped shots of the more agitated members of the crowd. More publicity. He loved being a political lightning rod.

"And these are the same people who are bringing so much suffering to our communities," the politician railed. "Why should we protect them? Why should we coddle them? Just because they're black? I say no. They are robbing us of too much of our potential, our youth, our human capital. Killing our young people, destroying property with graffiti. Robbing, raping, and killing. Their useless, thoughtless behavior is hurting all of us in a way the so-called white man never could. Think about that, please."

"What should we do with our poor folks?" an old black woman asked, pressing the point. "I'm on Social Security and Medicare. I see in the papers that y'all up there in Washington gone let all that fall down. You cut the welfare and food stamps. It sounds like if you had your way, you'd let us starve, just to get rid of us. What is your plan, Mr. Congressman?"

He held up a copy of the book. "I address all of that. Read pages 101 to 105 in the book."

Some people, mostly whites, laughed. Several of the blacks jeered at the remark, shouting to answer the question, Uncle Tom. "Don't give us more of your double talk." They hissed at him and shook their fists in his direction. The room was getting tense and the store representative sent for more security staff just in case things got out of hand.

"There is no reason why we as blacks cannot get where we must go," the Congressman continued. "But we must not waste time. We waste time moaning about ethnic and racial differences and preferences, quotas and Affirmative Action. We waste time by tolerating black victimizing black. Our young men have become the biggest threat to life and property in our communities. Our kids can't speak proper English and we want to teach them Ebonics and cripple them in the job market place. What kind of madness is this?"

An African-garbed brother sprang to his feet. "Who speaks for us? Where are our leaders? I repeat, some of you side with Whitey every chance you get. Like on the Affirmative Action issue."

A laugh sent the Congressman back on his heels. "That's crazy. Affirmative Action should be about fair play. If we fail, we should fail. Why should we expect to be given something we did not earn? You tell me that."

While more security personnel filtered into the crowds, forming a phalanx, my stepfather decided to antagonize the militants and radicals in the gathering even more once he realized that TV camera crews had arrived. He paused, screwed up his handsome face in feigned deep thought and walked back to the mike.

"Blacks are a conservative people," he said solemnly, putting the statesman's edge in his voice. "Blacks are not a beggar people. Very little of what's killing us has to do with the so-called white man. Why can't we teach our own people, feed our own people, employ our own people? We were once bold, self-reliant, and proud. These are the things that enabled us to survive slavery and hard times. Where are those qualities now when we need them most? We should have never been nor should we become that which we despise. We have always worked, struggled, and strived. When did we become lazy and criminal?"

A white man got to his feet, waved his hand, and the Congressman pointed his way. Something akin to a groan went through one section of the audience.

"Thank you for recognizing me, Mr. Congressman," the white man said in a nasal Don Knotts-Mayberry voice. "I think, as many whites do, that the civil rights movement was an unqualified success. It didn't fail. All we need to do is to look at the black representation on Wall Street or in Hollywood and Washington. Blacks are everywhere, working hard and not asking for a handout. What is your opinion of this?"

"Aw, sit down, white boy," a black voice yelled. "Nobody wants to hear that bullshit."

"You're wrong, I want to hear it. As your congressman, I need to listen to everyone and I think we as Americans might be better off if we started to listen to one another on a number of domestic issues. We as blacks must stop isolating ourselves. Get into the mainstream. Assimilate. Be a part of things. I'm tired of this Blame Whitey syndrome. We, not Whitey, are teaching our people to be victims. There is no racist conspiracy. We are our own worst enemy."

Someone shouted that whites, not blacks, were bringing dope and guns into our communities. And what about the CIA and the Contras bringing crack into the inner city? A loud roar went up from the crowd. The Congressman responded by waving the statement down, glancing over at the store representative in an indication that he was finished with the Q & A portion of the program.

"I think we've become too hypersensitive about everything to do with race," my stepfather said before stepping away from the podium. "When did we become so thin-skinned? Thank you for coming."

The applause for his performance was more than I expected. He waved once more to the crowd and disappeared in the swarm of security personnel. The store representative announced that the Congressman would be signing books in the large reception room downstairs in a few minutes. More clapping. Some catcalls and booing.

Before I could slink out of the store, one of my stepfather's operatives grabbed me by the arm and alerted me to the man's firm request for a brief audience. I would meet His Eminence in a side room for a few minutes after his meeting with the media. Another female aide ushered me to the hallway near the room where the Congressman was effortlessly fielding questions from the press. I looked inside and listened. It was always an honor to watch a true master of his craft at work.

"For those who didn't hear this question," he asked, "why didn't I attend the supposed summit on black-on-black crime in Washington with Jesse Jackson, Minister Farrakhan, and Representative Maxine Waters?" he repeated. "The answer is an easy one. I wasn't invited. No one wanted me to be there. I'm too much of a loose cannon. Too independent. However, I'm glad to see we realize that something must be done to curb the high level of violence and crime in our communities. Or our problems will do us in."

He waved for the next question that I didn't hear. The noise was constant. His response was typical Stevens.

"Separatism is back. Isolationism is back. Both things can hurt us as we as a race go into the twenty-first century. We need to participate in the game, not go in a corner and sulk. No, what do I care if they call me a race traitor or house Negro. I think they need more black people like me involved in Beltway politics. And yes, I think guilty white liberals have done us more harm than good. I try not to use the L-word in vain."

Some laughter. He finally looked over my way and acknowledged my presence. One of his publicity staff motioned that one more question was it, noting that the Congressman had a busy schedule before him.

"Is it a neck-and-neck race?" a reporter asked him. "Do you think you will win?"

"No doubt," the politician smiled. Then he posed like a victorious boxer after a tough championship bout, the classic Stevens smile and warmth in action. A blinking halo of camera flashes paid tribute to his charisma and charm, and he basked in their glory. Finally, he nodded, motioned to his bodyguards and walked toward me.

"Where the hell have you been?" my stepfather asked

me immediately. "I've been trying to get a hold of you since this nasty police business. Where were you?"

I didn't look him in the face. "Around, at Grandma Timmons."

He shrugged. "That crazy woman. Now what is this shit about you having blood on your hands? What did you do? Cut or shoot somebody? I want the truth. I don't want any surprises in the newspapers."

"I did nothing. I cut myself. They stopped me because I'm black. You know how they do young black dudes."

He shrugged again. His voice was lowered to a whisper. "I don't want any trouble from you while I'm running this campaign. I've got enough fires to address. I want you to be on your best behavior between now and election day. Do you understand?"

I shook my head but there must have been something contradictory in my eyes because he glared at me and moved close to my ear. "Be a good boy. Don't do anything foolish. You don't want to get me mad. Understand?"

I nodded more humbly this time. He smiled that Colgate smile of his. I figured he knew people were around and could see us.

"Aren't you seeing that head shrinker today? Thought so. Do you want a ride over there?"

My inclination was to spit in his face right then and there or to smash him with my fists or a chair until he was bloodied and motionless on the floor. Asshole. Pompous asshole. I hated the way he talked to me. Like a slave, a subject of the realm, a maggot. By the time he finished laying down the law with me, telling me how to act, I was steaming mad as hell. For a moment, I thought about how much pleasure I would get in fucking up his campaign. I was so mad that I zoned out and missed the entire last part of his put-down until he pinched my cheek painfully and scowled: "Now, get the hell out of my sight." Then the Congressman turned imperially and walked away. Elvis has left the building.

Chapter 6

MIND OVER MATTER

Later that night in my apartment, I woke up drenched in sweat, like I do every night, completely unnerved. I couldn't seem to get my breath, the air wheezing in my lungs like an asthma victim in seizure. I paced the floor of my room until I tired, then I sat on the edge of the bed with my head in my hands. Then I made my first mistake. I knew something was wrong with me.

I looked into the mirror. I was eleven, on my way home from school. Some black boys walked up to me, started yelling at me, cursing, and then they sucker-punched me. Two of the older boys held me down and a third got a paintbrush and a small can of paint. I kicked at them. I struggled and fought but they subdued and painted my face with white paint. Some nigger you are, the boy said as he painted around my ears.

I pushed away the mirror, because I could still see myself as the pale colored boy. If I ever told the old man what they had done, he would have crucified me. I believe all men have this macho streak. They hate a punk. I recall a teacher, a woman in her forties, she had a solid build, a Coke-bottle figure. I was real wet-behind-the-ears. A tyke. She always smoked Luckies, her hand held just so, and the bright red lipstick would be on the crumpled cigarette. I liked her, her attention for me, her ready smile, and her letting me bum ciggies. She flirted with me, kissing me on my cheeks, sharing sexual secrets, and pausing to place her fingers in my crotch.

"You know what the word, taboo, means?" she asked me one day.

"Really bad, punishable by prison," I answered. She laughed so hard that she honked through her nostrils. Like a duck.

She told me a joke that ended with a question. "Do you want to fuck me?"

"Yes," I replied but I didn't know whether it was a trick question.

I met her about four blocks from the school at a gas station. She had a Volvo, the humped back kind. The gas station attendant looked at her open cleavage, her puffy breasts pushing out over the thin fabric of her blouse, and checking out the really hot-looking attitude of a vixen. To make a long story short, we got blasted on shots of Jim Beam and a joint at her place. The alcohol and the weed had me going. I would have done anything she wanted. She got my pants off and wrapped her lips around my dick. Sitting on top of me, she mounted me, telling me I was big for my age, and did a quick, rhythmic snapping movement on me. As a snake dancer would do. She wanted to stick her fingers up my ass, said it would make me come. I told her no.

"Did you know the head of your dick swells when you're about to come?" She laughed, grabbing it. "It's cute. And you're cute."

She enticed me into a torrid relationship lasting for

two months, treating me to dinners and gifts. I trusted her. She helped me with my homework. If I did well, she'd give me a treat, a blow-up or hand-up or letting me do it doggy-style. She liked that. Her man, a Cuban cook, supposedly liked anything to do with perversity. Including the rear. She was married for three years. Just as quickly as we began the affair did it end. She rushed me out of her apartment one afternoon, said her old man was returning, and that was that. At the end of the semester, she moved and went to Miami with her Cuban husband.

When I told my head shrinker about the teacher, she said the woman took advantage of me. The doctor explained sexual abuse of children was nothing new and that one in four girls and one in six boys will be sexually abused before they turn eighteen. She said plenty of boys and girls get abused because we lived in a modern age so smitten with sex. Young folks were treated as sex objects in ads and on TV.

"She was my first," I said to her. "I didn't know she was married until the husband appeared later. I thought I was in love with her. She called all the shots. I had a junior high school crush on her. She convinced me to have her and her girlfriend in bed. I did her and she had her face between her friend's legs. I was in total shock. I was beside myself. I felt helpless and knew there was nothing I could do. They even shaved my pubic hair, like a little boy."

"Please don't be graphic," the shrink said. "What does it make you feel about women? Do you resent them?"

I knew something was wrong with me. I didn't answer. Lately I couldn't remember whole blocks of my life, entire weeks and months, stuff even since the killings of my folks.

"Do you think you need psychiatric care, Eddie?" She folded her arms.

"I don't know," I said. "Maybe, maybe not."

But the fact of the matter is that I could hear them now, the press, everyone, saying why didn't his parents see this coming, even the Congressman and the Missus. With my background, coming from a drug-dealing criminal family, they could see that I was going off the deep end. I was abused, tormented, and neglected as a kid and I never got over the shit. I was broken inside very young, the hurts accumulating, and I never healed. Like so many young black boys, I never talked much about what was done to me, not the worst of it. I hid the damage from everybody as best as I could.

Shit, my step-folks said they loved me but they didn't treat me like they did. They broke my heart, my spirit, my will. They reminded me that I was from the Hood, of poor beginnings and the projects, and inferior. I wanted them to love me, desperately. I needed them to love me. Instead of beating my ass and yelling at me all the time. They blamed me for all of the bad things that happened to their marriage.

Maybe the arteries in my brain were hardening. Hence the memory loss, like a big eraser steadily in motion, all the scenes of joy and happiness zapped out of existence. The blood cut off and the brain withering from lack of nourishment. In the last few weeks, I've had these blackouts where I find myself somewhere else. Walked into traffic the other night, just opened my eyes and cars were coming at me in a blur and I didn't know how I got there. The other day, I sat in a café downtown and stared at a glass of water for nearly an hour. Nothing could have forced me to drink it. I knew it was poison. Toxic. Something wasn't right with me.

As a protective measure for his campaign, the Congressman arranged for me to meet two times a week with a shrink to unburden my soul. I wished he could have hired somebody black for me to see. I spent so much time on the couch when I was in my teens. I was beyond reach of a talking cure. My stepfather felt the trauma of what was done to my family must be addressed, those were his very words. Still, not one of those shrinks ever got through to me. It was a game. You must give him credit. He did hire two shrinks back when the incident was still fresh. But it was a game. They had no idea of what my life was like. They talked the jargon the shrinks did, the search for the unconscious, the easing of repression, and the assaults on inhibitions.

The real deal was that the shrinks wanted to make me over in their image, sorta like God doing His bit with Man, like silly putty. The Dr. Freud routine. Can the cause of this profound disturbance be traced back to your childhood? Dumb question. Hell, walk through the Hood in any city and you see a lot of damage being dished out to kids.

My father, my real father, was a hustler. You wouldn't ever find him talking this kind of shit. He knew the score, the real deal. He told me that the most cursed, hated thing on earth was the black man. What he said was that everybody and everything was against the black man, even the black woman. If you check out the rap videos or the lyrics, you can see what he means. Snoop Dogg once said: "Bitches ain't shit but hoes and tricks." I watched how he dogged women, included my mother, because he felt like it. From the time when I was very young, he'd whisper to me that black women were taught to feel that black men were not worth a damn, weren't shit, and that women could do better without them.

"Don't think with your dick, son," he said, hugging me. "If you do that, you're lost. Women are pussy or cash. If you go against that, you're a chump. Don't be soft around them. You'll be the pussy then. I don't want any son of mine being a faggot. Game them bitches before they game you."

Maybe that's why he dogged them so much. I never knew what kind of a past he came from. They said Pops was hell on the broads when he was young. He didn't talk that much about his real family, not my father. He lived in the moment. I wondered how many black men felt the way he did, that he was no better than an animal, just like the white folks did. If the women felt like he said, how were we as men supposed to survive, how were families supposed to survive, to love each other right, and make real families like other people did?

Probably that was why we could not make the same progress as other people who got off here from the boats and did big things for their children and families. Everybody got a slice of the American pie except niggers. We hate each other, that's what, men versus women. Pops was right.

"Girls, don't you ever count on no damn man 'cause they ain't shit," Moms would tell my younger sisters right in front of my father. "Always be able to take care of yourself. Ain't no man lower than the black man 'cause every other man can do for his family. Your father's a damn disgrace."

Moms treated the girls alright but she was very hard on me. She usually ignored me, never had a kind word for me, or beat me for the littlest thing. One day, I was riding the subway when I saw this mother, a young black woman about twenty, slap her little boy, who was about five, hard across the face. He didn't flinch. He just stared at her with cold, distant eyes. The white people on the train frowned, embarrassed by the show of force. Some of the other mothers nodded and smiled.

I sat there and listened to her tell the little boy: "You're gone be nothing just like your damn daddy." How many times had he been slapped like that, heard those cruel things said to him, been humiliated in public? I winced when I heard her say those things because my Moms had said the same things to me so many times. Imagine what that little boy will be like in another ten or twenty years. Imagine how he'll treat women.

When you go to school, you can see the kids, especially the boys who have been raised like that, and know that they will come to a no-good end. I could sit in class and pick out the young brothers who would be dead in two years, who would be locked down, who would end up killing somebody. I guess you could do that anywhere where young black kids are in school in this country. Maybe this all goes back to slavery. One thing's for sure, this isn't all about the white man and his hate for us. This is about us. How we treat each other. How we love each other. Or don't.

Chapter 7

THIS, THAT,
AND THE OTHER

For over two years, I've been saving newspaper clippings of what parents do to their kids, the cruelty, the vicious things. Yesterday, I cut out the story of a five-year-old boy found roaming the streets of Brooklyn at four A.M. after his mother left him alone to go to a party. She was charged with endangering the welfare of a child. She told the cops she needed a break from parenting. And where was the kid's old man? Poor choices. In another one, a father forced a ten-year-old boy to deal crack from a scooter. He was busted. A twenty-year-old Trenton woman was charged with dumping her baby in a trash bin on the coldest night of the year. A five-year-old Harlem boy was discovered with four bags of heroin in his jacket, the child of a teen parent living with a girlfriend. Damn.

Check this out. Another story had this seven-year-old girl in the Bronx whose grandmother poisoned her with a mixture of vinegar, ammonia, cayenne pepper, and olive oil. She said the deed was done to purge the girl of devils. The old woman tied the kid up and taped her mouth shut so she couldn't spit it out. Females.

The Congressman usually sent a car to take me to the shrink. At one sharp in the afternoon, delivered like a package. He knew me pretty well. I might start out for the shrink's office and get waylaid by some other activity. Anything. He also knew that I might go one or two times, then quit or go for a month straight and not go back.

The name of the new shrink was Dr. Almut Schmidt. Real German. Berlin, I think. Frau Schmidt greeted me at the door with a mannish handshake and a steely glint in her light blue eyes. You knew she was strictly business. All stiff. That Nazi thing. Very Nordic. Blonde, tall, sturdy, and in her late fifties. Dressed in a dark gray suit. I guess the Congressman figured he'd try something new. The Third Reich approach. She laid down the ground rules immediately, no questions about her, anything she wanted to tell me would come without prompting. If she had her way, she wouldn't talk at all, only listen.

"Questions are never discreet, while answers are, sometimes," Frau Schmidt said, sitting ramrod stiff on a chair across from me.

"Who said that?"

"Oscar Wilde," she said, smiling coldly. "So you have a little problem with rage and violence. Yes?"

I sat with my legs crossed. "I'm sure that the Congressman has filled you in on what's happening. I don't need to add to any to that. He thinks I'm sick. Sick in the head."

"Sick how?"

"Sick, nuts, wacked." I wanted to smoke again.

"Are you sick in the head? Is that how you would de-scribe yourself?" She was looking at my dreads, which were tied up in an odd ponytail, then she wrote some-thing down.

"I think I'm cool," I replied.

"Do you really think so, Edward? I see a very tired young man before me. There are deep circles around your eyes and your face appears fatigued. Are you really handling everything okay?"

I closed my eyes for a moment. "Yeah, there are days when my nerves are on edge. But that shit happens with everybody. Yeah, I get jumpy. I get tired and I can't sleep. But that's because I'm worked up."

"Worked up? Is that another way of saying depressed?"

Frau Schmidt mumbled under her breath, shifted her weight in her chair, and came at me again. "Do you sometimes feel like pulling the blankets over your head and not leaving your bed?"

I smiled at her, leaning forward so I could smell her body aroma. But she had none. Not even the smell of soap. "Yeah, I've felt that. Who hasn't?"

"Your father says you become enraged almost instantly," she said. "True?"

"I'm moody, I guess."

"I know about your background, your family before Congressman Stevens, your criminal past," she said. "Is that what makes you angry? Violent?"

"It has nothing to do with my past," I snarled. "If someone did something to you, you must strike back. Everything needs retaliation. Nobody wants a punk. If you get mad, you take them out. No problem."

"Do you think about death?" Her lips turned down in a scowl.

"Hey, I don't care about dying," I replied. "In the

streets, you better shoot first. It's like war. Like they say, 'I'd rather be judged by twelve, than carried out by six.' But hey, if it happens, then cool."

"I do some work with the public schools, volunteer work," she said, "in the disadvantaged areas. I think young people always overreact. Put a lethal weapon in their hands and add the high emotions, then you have trouble. Teen adrenaline. The prime objective is not to stay alive. Most young people have seen someone die or lost friends or relatives. They do not see life as permanent."

"I feel that way too," I laughed. "I live in the moment."

"I know society doesn't make it easy to be young," she said. "But you have to respect yourself. Society wants you to grow up fast. This is not a caring society."

"Damn right." I picked at a hangnail. I was dressed in all black. Black everything. "I've got to get mine. No one matters and no one gives a shit. In an atmosphere like this, violence, madness, and everything is acceptable."

"Do you have close friends?"

"Not really," I said, looking over her head at the numerous accreditation plaques on the wall. Harvard. Some screwy place in Vienna. John Hopkins School of Medicine.

"Why do you segregate yourself from others?"

I tried to read her face but she gave me nothing. Her Prussian game face. "I'm comfortable with my isolation. One thing I learned from my real father is don't trust people, anyone, and he said that meant him as well. People will fuck you over every time. Those were his words. Distrust is normal. Well, that's me. I'm down with people but I don't trust them for shit."

"What leads you to believe distrust is normal?"

"I think everybody I've ever trusted in my life has hurt me in some way. Not the bastards in the streets. You

expect that. But not even with family and blood rela-
tions, I never let down my guard."

She mumbled again to herself and wrote more scribbles
on her notebook. "The depression. Do you have . . . or have
you ever had crying spells?"

"No."

"What were you thinking about when those tears
came?"

"No, I never cried. I might be sad but I never cried."

"What was it that needs fixing? Do you have any
idea?"

"Not normal, abnormal."

She changed her voice tone, more friendly, more neu-
tral, and asked me something that I had hoped not to
face in one of the beginning sessions. "If you're so sick,
why would your father, Congressman Stevens adopt you
after the killing of your family? He didn't have to do
that."

"Know anything about American politics?"

"Yes, I know some things about it."

My hands turned palm up and offered my answer as
the only solution to her question. "Publicity. The Congressman is a career politician and he knows all the
tricks. A vote is a vote is a vote. My tragedy was good
publicity for him back then. Now he wishes he could get
rid of my ass."

"You really think he's that calculating," she started
yakking but I cut her off.

"Damn right. The Congressman is only concerned
with power, his career, and the limelight. Not necessar-
ily in that order. He couldn't give a shit about anything
else."

Frau Schmidt shook her head. "I'm missing something
here. How could adopting you be good for his career?"

"It was all a publicity stunt," I said firmly. "What happened to my folks was all over the papers and the Congressman was running for re-election, a tough race, just like he is now. So the bastard sees an opportunity for a boost in the polls. The Good Samaritarian vote. He turns up one afternoon at the foster home where they were keeping me, with every damn reporter and cameraman in the city. The next thing I know he's got me by the hand, leading me into this explosion of flashbulbs, people shouting questions, and the Congressman yelling something about 'a fresh start and a new beginning.' The woman who ran the home had been paid off. The city agencies rushed the adoption papers straight through and soon I was on the campaign trail with him, at his knee like a pet chimp. A mascot. He's a great actor. He played the loving father role like he was born to it. I was the poor little nigger waif from the crack dens. He was the Great Black Father, the Savior. The Pure Pol and the dirty little dope orphan. It all made for good press. The public ate the shit up. And he won the race easily."

She coughed and stopped writing. "What about you two, afterward, the relationship after the election?"

I stifled a laugh. "Bastard soon dropped me like a hot potato. He kept me locked away so I wouldn't embarrass him. Sent me away to private schools where I kept getting kicked out. He never talked to me or nothing. He igged me big time. I became invisible."

"Do you think you've always felt that way? Invisible."

"Yeah, like that cat in Ellison's novel. Or Claude Rains in that old movie. Just a pair of pants and some shoes moving quietly across the floor with nobody in them. Transparent."

"You ever tell him any of this?"

"Why should I? He doesn't listen to anything I say. I don't exist."

She went back to writing in the book with frenzy. "But you do exist. You are here, right now. That invisible element. Did you feel invisible as a child?"

"When I was little?" I asked only to buy time.

"Yes, when you were with your biological parents?"

She was making me restless, uneasy with these questions. It would be easy to derail all this digging. Think psycho. "I guess so. I don't want to answer any more questions. I'm starting to get a headache again and soon the voices will come back. They always come back when I'm under a lot of stress."

Her eyebrows arched up. "What do these voices say?"

"It's too early for me to tell you that. We'll go there when I know you better."

The pencil was going like crazy across the page. "Why? You can't be afraid of a breech of confidentiality. We talked about that upfront. You have my every assurance that I'll indeed keep my word. I need your complete trust for us to move forward."

"Who is paying for these sessions?"

"You know the answer to that. Congressman Stevens is paying but that does not mean he will ever learn what is discussed here. We already talked about this too."

"He is a powerful man," I said. "He has ways of getting what he wants. I know this man. I've seen him in action and he gets results."

She made strong eye contact with me. Her eyes locked with mine. "Oh no. Be assured that I'd never speak about anything that is said in this room. Trust me."

"Sure. Next you'll say some Freud shit like the adult part of your ego is in conflict with the infantile part of your self and you're seeking a libidinal relationship with your stepmother. Just words."

The pencil stopped. "Your stepmother? This is the first time you've mentioned her."

I rocked back and forward. "Right. Ms. Chocolate Zsa Zsa Gabor. All fluff. Totally bush-wa. She doesn't even sleep with Mr. Wizard anymore. The bitch sleeps in a separate room with these two tiny poodles. Damn dogs. I bet she's getting a little on the side from somewhere else."

The phone rang. Frau Schmidt stood and apologized that she'd have to take the call since her assistant was off sick. She walked over to her desk across the room and lifted the receiver with a yank. Her back was to me. I could only hear brief snippets of what she said since she lowered her voice to a near whisper. She spoke in German: ". . . guten tag . . . ja . . . ja . . . ja . . . zum flughafen . . . das ist zu teuer . . . was vedentet das? Nein . . . nein . . . wie weit? . . . ja . . . sonst noch etwas? Vitamintabletten . . . sie solten emen spezialisten aufsuchen . . . ja . . . ja . . . bitte . . . Ich habe etwas im ange . . . bitte . . . danke . . . auf wiedersehen."

Nothing is worse in life than being ignored. This pissed me off. Damn Nazi talk. This was my dime, my time.

"Now where were we?" she started up again.

"Let me ask something," I interrupted. "Do you think a white therapist could really understand someone from a different cultural background? Like a black person. Wouldn't she miss all of the things that are specific only to that culture or race?"

She sat up completely rigid, as if I had slapped her. "Why would a question like this come up now?"

"Just answer the question. Wouldn't a black therapist

be better suited to deal with someone who looks, talks, and thinks like her?"

She was quiet. Like a statue, granite and cold.

"What?" I moaned. "That doesn't answer my question."

"I don't believe that I'm not capable of providing you with some options to your emotional dilemma because I'm white," she said. "All I ask is that you give me a chance."

"Listen, I know what I don't want," I said in a voice that said I meant business. "I don't want to end up in some nuthouse. Once you go to those places, people never deal with you the same way again. You're cursed with this nut label. They treat you differently. They treat you like you're permanently crazy. I don't dig that."

"Edward, this takes us back to the truth issue? Do you find there is an imbalance in your relationship with people?"

I shook my head. "It's a waste of time to get involved with most people. You have nothing to offer them and they have nothing to offer you. I keep to myself mostly. I don't miss much. I know the world doesn't revolve around me."

"Is this because of what your father said to you?"

"No, hell no. And he is my stepfather."

"You must understand that parents are humans too," she said in that heavy German accent of hers. Colonel Klink. "They are human with all that implies. They have flaws. They often love their children but they don't like them at times."

"That's bull." She was making me madder.

"Parents can become angry at their children sometimes," she went on. "They don't know how to deal with a child that is not helpless or dependent. I imagine you were that as a child. Right, Edward?"

"Whatever you say, doc," I wisecracked.

"Maybe it is something that reminds the parents of themselves, this thing they see in their child. Am I right? Maybe this is the way it was with you, Edward. Maybe they see something in you . . ."

"I am not their child," I shouted.

I jumped up from my chair, said to Frau Schmidt that I had enough of this chitchat, and I was out of there. She called to me a couple of times, then stopped. I walked to the elevator and rode down to the ground floor. Bought a *News*. Then I walked out into the chill of the spring sun, laughing all the way, and caught a cab uptown.

Chapter 8

THE CHECKERED PRESENT

Like everybody, I looked forward to the weekend, a chance to unwind, to kick back and chill. The past few days had been quite productive for me since I had killed once in eight days, an easier task than I thought possible with the ongoing police shadow on me. I tried to stop myself but I couldn't. Maybe that chat with the shrink triggered something. For three days before I went out there, I was thinking real hard about Pops, my real father, and why it didn't work out between my mother and him.

I remembered coming home late afternoon and he had the drapes pulled and the apartment was completely dark.

I cut on the lights and he told me to turn them back off. In the seconds before I switched them back off, I saw he had been crying; his eyes were bloodshot. "If she goes with her damn men-friends, you kids are going to stay with me," Pops said in a weak voice. "That's final. You-all aren't going nowhere. Understand?"

"Yeah, sure," I answered. I had never seen him all busted up like that. All emotional. I wanted to run over and hug him and say everything will be alright. But I didn't. Pops never liked that kind of display of affection. Hugs and kisses were out.

Once I touched my father's face while he was asleep on the sofa. Just lightly. It was the only time I remember any real tenderness between us. I felt uncomfortable doing it as if I had betrayed a private code between us in some way. Men never touched or showed any softness. Not real black men.

He woke up, squeezed my hand and bent it back until I thought it might snap in half. With icy contempt in his stare, he looked deeply in my eyes like a killer, he whispered, "Get your punkass away from me and don't ever touch me like that again as long as you draw breath."

Oh yes, Pops could be chilly, ice cold. I remember when we lived on Snyder Avenue in East Flatbush where he was dealing crack, reefer, and heroin. He called H "boy." One of his teen dealers came in and told him that he had killed a woman's eight-year-old girl because the young dealer gave the mother some drugs and he wanted his money. The dealer got tired of carrying her so he strangled the girl and hid the body in a weed-covered lot near a supermarket. The girl was wearing only her nightclothes.

"Your beef was with the mother, not the child," Pops said, then whispered to his enforcers who left with the dealer. The room was full of people, who knew he wasn't playing that shit. Justice was swift. The dealer turned up dead, shot twice in the head in an alley behind a Chinese laundry.

Pops had five locations in East Flatbush, Bushwick, and East New York. It was like a cell, with a core of forty regulars, very organized and integrated, controlling the product from start to finish. He oversaw the processing, packaging, marketing, and accounting. An old Haitian woman kept track of sales with an electronic money counter. Pops once paid for surgery on a cyst on her ovaries and for her two daughters to go to college. She was fiercely loyal.

The soldiers, armed with nickel-plated .38s, were extremely businesslike, no nicknames, no uniforms. They could earn $3,000 in a night, 25 percent of the gross from the sale of 530 $25 bags of crack peddled. They too were loyal. The teen soldiers were the couriers, only taking orders from an adult overlord of three units of four dealers. The adult overlords answered to Pops, who knew that the teens would be treated more leniently for drug violations. The overlords would be responsible for seeing that the soldiers be returned to the streets quietly. The oldest of the young soldiers was sixteen.

"Hey, the kids never have to worry about jobs and their families are taken care of as well," Pops always said, making sure that their families were treated properly. "I treat my folks right. I'm the original trickle-down economy here."

We, Pops and I, would sit in the car, a new Jaguar, and watch the troops work the corner. It was high art. They would work in teams of two, one—a juggler—slaps the hand of the buyer with the cash from the car and drifts away and the other—a holder—would pass the dope. Clockwork. The transaction would take only seconds. Pops would nod in approval.

On other days, we would drive up to one of the factories where the thousands of dollars worth of coke in its raw form would be cooked. The apartments, which would be rent-free, usually belonged to relatives or girl-friends of the overlords. Pops also paid them a stipend for the amount of the product cooked. A supervisor was also on hand to make sure that the drugs weren't sampled. Sometimes the girls turned tricks on the side in one of the bedrooms.

"These places should be efficient like an assembly line run by General Motors." Pops laughed, watching two cooks cutting the powdery cocaine by blending it with baking soda, increasing its bulk and weight. One cook would weigh it on a triple-beam scale, put it in a test tube filled with water, then slide the tube into a small boiling pot of water.

Three cutters were responsible for slicing the hard-ened crack on trays with razor blades, packaging each chunk or rock in a tiny plastic bag with the stamp of a smiling old black man. I teased him that the old man looked like Uncle Ben, the nigger from the rice box. He said it resembled Uncle Titus, who was a pimp on the cold streets of Chicago. He was the dude that hipped Pops to the Life. Since Pops wasn't the Mack, he had to settle for the Salesman of Joy and Bliss.

About four months before Pops was murdered, one of his Bushwick apartments was stormed by a rival drug gang, killing everybody in it. Six people, including a toddler and a pregnant woman, were murdered. Each victim was shot once in the head at close range and the pregnant woman was also shot in the belly, killing her and the unborn baby. One of the teen soldiers went to the apartment, peeked through the peephole and didn't hear anything. An enforcer got there and unlocked the door, discovering the grisly murders. An anonymous call was placed to police after the apartment was thor-oughly cleaned out of drugs and weapons.

Then two weeks before the killing of my family, another house in East New York was torched. Neighbors tried to awaken the tenants with loud knocks on the door and windows. They could see the people running around in the rooms, aflame, waving their arms. Three people died and two others were critically burned.

"They want me out, they want me out," Pops said, starting to carry two pistols with him at all times. "Somebody is trying to take me down. I'm paying off. The cops are cool. They want me out. Be careful out there. I'm serious."

A week before the killings, Pops was passing out five dollar bills in the parking lot in the Pink Houses in East New York with a crowd of kids around him. Small kids. When someone started shooting at them, police quickly arrived but three kids were killed and the old man was wounded in the arm. One of his enforcers was also dead.

"They almost got my monkey ass," Pop joked as they patched him up in Brookdale Hospital. "I've got nine lives. I used six of them."

When Pops was under pressure, it was really hard on us kids. And I imagine with Moms too. But then he could be almost sentimental. It was a real mixed signal and totally messed up my head. "I've been just as much of a parent to you kids as she has, so I demand respect," he said, all choked up. "I've been here with you guys when she's been out in the streets sleeping around and nobody knew where the hell she was. You kids will stay with me if she goes anywhere. I mean that."

He was asleep on the couch three nights after that. When I came into the room, she was standing over him with a loaded gun. The .45 Pops kept in the dresser in the bedroom. I could tell she was thinking whether to

shoot him. I pleaded with her not to do it because she'd
go to jail and we'd end up in a foster home somewhere.
She turned like a zombie, face emotionless, and walked
to their bedroom and closed the door. Never said a
word.

Their marriage stopped working a long time before
they were killed. I don't know whose fault it was. Who
could you blame when they were doing the same
things? At least that was what Aunt Fell said. Pops
couldn't control her, he wanted to, but he couldn't. She
said what she wanted and did what she wanted. He tried
to watch her, calling her all day to check on her if he
was out. He wouldn't let her work or have close girlfriends. He kept her away from everybody, or tried to.

They fought like cats and dogs, anything went during
their brawls. My mother did things to provoke him. It
was like fighting aroused her in a strange way because
after their knock down-drag-out battles, they'd go into
the bedroom. And you could hear them moaning and
groaning for three city blocks. Her face would light up
after he gave her black eyes and bruises. Then she
would fuck his brains out and the two of them would be
okay for a few days. Soon the cycle started all over
again.

One night she came home late, drunk and smelling
like sex. Pops was sitting in the living room doing a deal
with a few of his friends. Everybody could see and
smell what she had been doing. His buddies started
laughing at him. He lost face. Before anybody could
stop him, he began hitting her with his fists, hard body
shots like a boxer would do. She didn't go down. It was
incredible. He yanked her by the hair and slammed her
against the wall. Somehow she got a bat and threatened
him with it and he laughed at her, said she was bluffing.

She whacked him real hard against the chest with the bat and he fell over, spitting up blood. The cops came, he went to the hospital and we stayed at Cousin Earle's for a week.

Every time after they fought, they separated but soon the apologies and gifts would come and before you knew it, they were back together again. I couldn't figure it out.

Aunt Fell told my mother she should either get help for the marriage or go to a battered women's shelter. But Moms said no. When my aunt asked, "Why did she stay, was it because she loved him?" My mother replied, "no." Then why? Moms winked and giggled like a schoolgirl: "Because the sex is so damn good."

Chapter 9

EVERYTHING FEMININE

Saturday night. When the night moves along the dark and dangerous streets, we walked amid the groups of people chugging 40s, crack fumes apparent, thieves trying to sell their hot wares and whores patrolling the curb for quick johns and dollars. Xica and Sakia had been lovers before I broke them up, but my girl sometimes went back for a little taste. I don't mind. Girls are like that. They can go for the beef or the yam. The punani. I just didn't want her messing around with any dudes. Definitely taboo. The girls talked about Yolanda, one of their sisters, who got stabbed just because she liked girls. Some brothers stepped up to her, called her a fucking dyke, and shot her. That was that.

"My Aunt Fell calls them bulldaggers," I said. "Did you know her well?"

"Sakia used to go with her," Xica said. "When is the wake?"

"Thursday, you going with me?" her friend asked.

"Yeah, girl, no doubt," Xica replied. "You heard about Paulette?"

"No." Xica, Sakia, and Paulette grew up together.

Xica scowled at her friend's plight. "Paulette went buggy. She got knocked up by this dude, older than her uncle, and he wanted her to get an abortion. Her mother convinced her to have the child. She was an only child and her mother wanted a baby around the house. When her father found out, he flipped and threw Paulette out. The girl didn't know anything about a baby and had to go to a shelter. Babies are expensive. So she started turning tricks at the Holland tunnel, got busted twice, and now they want to take her baby away. She totally flipped out. She's in Bellevue. Absolutely mad as a hatter."

"Oh shit, Paulette was the most logical, common-sense girl we knew," Yolanda said. "Not flighty. Not flaky. Totally had her head on straight."

Xica wanted to rock Saturday night. We knew she knew some wild people. She got off on exhibitionism, and anything crazy. She hugged Sakia, kissed her on the lips and said they'd get together on Thursday. As she watched Sakia walk away, she smiled and winked, approving the curvy bottom on her friend.

"Let's get wild," she said. We got in her car, a Plymouth, and went downtown.

On this night, we visited an underground club in the East Village with lots of Latinos, blacks, and some whites. The music was jamming. A young crowd. Through the fog and cigarette smoke, guys and girls writhed to the techno soul beat of Goldie, grinding against sweaty bodies on the electric pulse. Some of the females had their breasts exposed. I was Xica's victim. She wanted to seduce and ravish me before the crowd, which was worked up to a sexual fever. There was a dance-off with four couples in the center of the clapping fans. One girl tore her man's shirt away and began sucking his nipples. Another girl mounted the fella like a horse, rubbing her crotch on him. The other couple were shy, afraid to go for it. A surge of claps and hoots emerged from the crowd when Xica kneeled, undid my pants and put me into her mouth. I was so fucked up on coke and weed, it didn't matter. She was wasted on pills. The girls loved it. The guys cheered her on, stomping to the music.

I was totally embarrassed. After we left, Xica couldn't stop smiling. She thought it was funny. She smiled at me wickedly as I entered her apartment on Lenox Avenue, covered with sweat. When she moved to unbutton my drenched shirt, I stepped back instinctively and then allowed her to strip away my wet clothing.

"That was foul," I said angrily. "Totally fucked up."

"Why? Because I wanted to have fun."

"Fun at someone's expense," I replied. "You don't care about anyone but yourself. That's it. Don't you think about anybody else?"

She went into the bathroom, could hear her turn on the water in the tub. Upon her return, she twisted another joint and fired it up. She didn't say anything. I knew what she was thinking. I was a crybaby, whining, whimpering. Twice she said, I don't know how you could be so uptight especially when you had the father you had. Everybody knew my old man. I took the joint from her and proceeded to get my head worse.

Finally, the water in the tub was hot. Xica steered me into her tiny bathroom where a fine mist of heat coated everything, including the large mirror above the sink. Feminine items were displayed with their labels facing out, in easy reach. I looked down at the bathtub that was filled almost to the rim with bubbles. I turned toward her. Her head was still covered with those ridiculous tiny curls that I loved to caress.

"Get in," Xica said. "I'll wash your back and any other place you can't reach." She poured more of the bubble stuff into the water.

I waved my hands, no. "They'll call me Peter Pan."

She laughed, screwing the top back on the bottle. "You're funny. If they hassle you like that, you can use me as a reference. I'll vouch for your masculinity."

In so many ways, she was everything both of my mothers were not. There was something sweet and tender about her. Softness. Accessible. "Xica, where do your folks come from originally?"

"Detroit. Motor City."

"Why did you move here?" I tested the tub water; maybe it was too hot.

"We moved to the Apple about five years ago. Daddy got laid off from Ford and couldn't find work so we came here. He's working at some factory out in Queens. I moved away from home about three years ago."

Her voice came now from the other room. She went for a fresh washcloth. "Part of it was the tension of watching my father look for work. He's had it rough here. It's a drag for people to get a job when they reach my father's age. Fifty is considered ancient here in the states. In other countries, they honor age and respect people when they get gray hair. Everybody dreads getting old in America, especially women. Because at forty, a woman is thought to be over the hill. I hate to even think about getting old."

"I try not to think about the future," I said, taking off my underwear and climbing into the tub. "The present is difficult enough."

When Xica finished lathering my back and head, she

told me to stand up and turned on the water from the showerhead to rinse me off. I tried to step out but she gently pushed me back into the tub. Her hands were strong as they scrubbed under my arms, across my hairless chest, over my butt, and between my legs. She liked that part. I flinched when she drew the cloth near my privates. Sensing I was getting more irritable by the minute, she wrapped it up quickly and reached over to get a towel. The towel felt comforting on my head as she rubbed it dry.

The windows were open in her living room and the twinkle of the night lights in the city gave everything a picture postcard look. The Naked City. I could hear the sultry voice of Cassandra Wilson coming from the apartment next door, pure and strong.

"Want to drive out to East New York with me?" Xica asked. "To Kwame's place."

"What for?" I frowned.

"Eddie, it's not even that late. It's two-thirty at night. Just a few people getting together. Kwame asked about you last week. Said you stay to yourself too much."

"What's wrong with that?"

"It's not good to spend too much time alone," she said. "I don't know how you can stay cooped up in that roach trap where you live. You should get out more. People like you. They miss you hanging out."

Everybody always wanted something from you, even if it was your time. I had things to do. "Why should they be so concerned with me? I don't bother anyone. I mind my own business and they should do the fucking same."

"Are you going to move?" Xica asked. She hated the SRO where I stayed.

"You sound like the Congressman now," I said. "He says it reflects badly on him that I live like that. He wants me to move into Lenox Terrace, says he has a connection over there who could set it up for me. Lenox Terrace where the black bigshots live. Fuck that shit. I feel more in my element over where I'm at."

She was disgusted. "He's just trying to be helpful. That place is below you and you know it. There's nothing in that building but losers, people who have given up on life and want to wallow in their defeat. Eddie, you're not like that. You still have a chance to do something with your life."

When in doubt, shut the hell up. That was what I did when she kept on with this babble about my moving into a more decent residence. We sat in silence during most of the ride to Kwame's crib out in East New York, with her whistling some hip-hop tune I didn't recognize. Xica wore one of her more outrageous outfits, too short and too tight. She teased me about how plain I dressed. I stared at her.

"Eddie, you're awfully quiet," she said, steering her ancient car between a parked cab and a creeping van. "Don't sulk. Let's have a good time out here. Alright? I wasn't trying to start any trouble. Don't take it that way."

Xica's body was a thing of wonder. She was constructed like a thousand black women, the classic African shape, marvelous breasts that jutted out with a glorious sense of youth, narrow waist, and hips that cried for childbirth.

"Is my ass too big?" she once asked me. "I don't want to end up like my mother. Her behind is so big that it leaves a room five minutes after she does. I hate that."

"You have a pretty ass," I wisely complimented her, lighting a cigarette.

"Must you do that?" she said, frowning.

A pause. "Yeah, tell me something," she went on. "How come you never stay over, Eddie? Where do you go at night?"

Questions spook me. Curiosity killed the cat. "Don't start on that again. I told you before; I get restless. I just ride around. I like the night. It soothes me."

"I miss you in my bed," she pouted. She missed my tongue.

Her words never penetrated me. All this love shit. I didn't need it. I didn't need anything from anyone. She kept talking but I was somewhere else, in my car on the night streets, prowling. Watching the female shadows wiggling those asses on the sidewalk. Advertising. Bitches. Whores. Appealing to the worst instincts in men. Damn, make them put some clothes on and act like ladies. My eyes burned into the darkness, seeking something fresh, a newer thrill, seeking a life for reaping.

We pulled into the parking lot of the housing project, checked the car for anything that might lure a thief, locked the doors, and got out. Kwame's building was across the street, a fourteen-story cage full of poverty, grief, desperation, and worse. Mostly young brothers hung out near the doors, watching the foxes, smoking blunts and drinking 40s, or plotting some bogus get-rich scheme. The rest of the inhabitants stayed the hell out of their way. Locked down in their apartments. Their prison cells.

Now Kwame and his crew were the kind of folks that President Clinton talked about in his 1995 "racial healing" speech when he said: "Violence for white people too often comes with a black face." None of these dudes had jobs or wanted one. Kwame was a criminal roughneck. Gang-bangers, drive-by shooters, strong-arm robbers, dope dealers, and carjackers. In a way, he was like me. He came from a fucked-up background, from bad blood, from a family nurtured on slaps and kicks. Something to be feared and locked away. It was a blessing that most of the black people were not like us, bruised and twisted, hurtling toward the boneyard without any hope of grace and redemption.

The apartment was full of ne'er-do-wells. Xica loved to slum. She liked to mix with these bad brothers because it spiced up her life. A wicked sense of danger. Like she was Nora Charles from that *Thin Man* movie. Mixing with the outlaws. The bad boys.

"The truth is that the government wanted Tupac and Biggie dead," Kwame said, taking a hit from a fat blunt. "They knew the brothas were marked, knew when they was going to get capped, but they didn't do shit about it. It's another conspiracy. I'm serious."

Everybody in the room, except me, agreed with him. I didn't say a damn thing, just sat there and watched. The place was a real pig sty, with clothes thrown all over, week-old pots and dishes in the sink, piles of the *Post* in a corner of the living room, and a backed-up toilet that reeked.

"All of the brothas that might know something are locked up," Jojo piped up. "They put them away so they don't have to deal with them. Shit, they can't even vote after they go up. Neutralized. And meanwhile, the sistas are getting over, getting stronger and stronger, and thinking they don't need us no more. It's a plot just like that AIDS shit to destroy our communities. Right, Xica?"

Xica nodded and smiled, avoiding the question. "I can smell it. Good herb."

"A man is no good to a woman if he's locked down," Monifa said. She was Jojo's lady and went to night school.

"Shut the fuck up," Jojo roared. He was tall, bald, and a junior perp. "What do you know about anything? The black man is an endangered species. Whitey knows if we get our shit together that we'd be a real threat to his program."

I didn't say anything.

"The only time a black man can get over is if he allows them to set him up as a freak or some circus clown like Dennis Rodman or Ru Paul," Kwame said, drinking some malt liquor. "Or like the Wizard of Odd, Michael Jackson. The white man let him ride high for a minute then trapped his ass up with some boy pussy. Dumb fool."

"That might change now that he's married with a kid," Monifa said. "When you throw in a kid, people change their opinion of you and let a lot of shit slide. Look at what it did for Madonna."

"Michael Jackson rented that womb and everybody knows it," Jojo said. "The world knows that. That white bitch don't live with him. He lets her know when she can come and see the brat. Check that out."

"We're the scapegoats for everything in America," Kwame said. "Look at the Susan Smith shit. All she had to do is cry a nigga did it, killed her kids, and they were rounding up brothas from coast to coast. That's why nobody wants to be black."

"Even Tiger Woods did the shit," Jojo interrupted. "I'm one-third everything else but nigga. Then this white man told him not to bring fried chicken and collard greens for dinner next year and the boy freaked out. Did you see him on Oprah?"

"That's cool because we know who Tiger is and still love him," Xica chuckled.

"What you say about that, nigga?" Jojo said to me.

He was talking to me but my mind wasn't in the room. The next thing I knew the fool was up in my face, shouting at me, pawing my clothes. He acted like he wanted to whip my ass. Maybe it was the chronic that had him acting like he had no sense. But that was no excuse.

"This punk makes me nervous," Jojo said, his hand wringing my collar. "You too fucking quiet. I don't like a nigga that don't talk shit. Say fuckin' something. Let us know your ass ain't brain dead. By the way, ain't your daddy a congressman or some shit?"

Xica jumped into the mix, trying to protect me from the ape. "Kwame, tell your boy about Eddie. Tell him he's cool. He's down."

I locked eyes with Jojo, letting him know that he had no idea who he was fuckin' with. That he could become a memory in a heartbeat. A ghost. Still, I remained mute and expressionless, drinking up their liquor and smoking their dope. Kwame offered me a hit off his pipe but I steer clear of that crack shit. They kept on talking, with Jojo occasionally glaring at me over his woman's shoulder. He acted like he really wanted a piece of me.

"You one sorry nigga, Eddie," Jojo shouted.

Monifa reached for cigarettes, shook one out, and I lit it for her. The dudes looked at me as if I had broke wind. She smiled a thank you and Xica rolled her eyes.

"Don't start tripping, man," I said, trying to calm him.

I was still in my own world. People were talking to me and my mind was off on four other things. You try not to lose your cool, your composure. You try not to get hyper. You try to show the positive sides of yourself, at least out in the world, in public. But in the end, it's all acting, a front, a pose. It's like playing a character, wearing a mask and no one knows the real you no how. That was when I heard the slap, loud like a gunshot or a car backfiring, and saw Monifa's head snap back. She screamed and pushed Jojo away from her.

"Fuck him and you too, bitch," Jojo mumbled.

He leaned forward, holding a beer bottle in one hand and pointing at me with the other. "Maybe you want to fuck her, chump. Did you know your bitch was playing your ass? Did you know that she was kicking it with that Spanish cat at that welfare place where she works?"

Shocked, I tried not to look at her. I focused everything in me on Jojo and what he was saying. If I went off on her here, it would not be pretty and he was starting to bug me.

Jojo was mocking, mean to the core. "Tell him, sweetheart. Tell him about how you hook up with Mr. Jon Secada after work at the Baby Grand, then slide over to his crib so you can do the nasty. That salsa long stroke . . ."

Jojo never finished the sentence. He never finished the sentence because I grabbed the beer bottle out of his hand, swung it around, and caught him with it across the face. It shattered and I brought the jagged glass back into an uneasy place under his chin.

He howled like a toddler deprived of milk. Punk bastard. A line of blood ran down his neck onto his shirt, forming red splotches, and he screamed that there was glass in his eyes. He kept yelling that he was blind, couldn't see. I knew he had a gun so I patted him down with my other hand. It was jammed in the small of his back, a .38 snub-nose. I pocketed it and shoved him to the floor where he curled up, crying.

Kwame glanced at his boy and shook his head. "They warned me about you, Eddie. Nigga, you crazy."

I laughed. "Right. Me and Martin Lawrence. Baby, let's split."

Xica didn't say a damn thing. She smiled woodenly at Kwame and Monifa, and followed me out of the place. We didn't say anything during the drive back to the city. There was nothing to say. The bitch betrayed me. I thought she was different. Xica was a skank ho. A whore. She had been caught with her drawers down, so to speak. I hated that I had been played for a chump. I had been decent to her. Fuck her. She dropped me off at my furnished room and nothing was said.

Chapter 10

SCAR TISSUE

All the experts will tell you the bust-up of a love affair involves a grieving process, the period of time when the healing of a broken heart starts. Roughnecks try to act as though breaking up is the easiest thing in the world, something that can be dismissed with a shrug and a wink. Not true. Some people will say it's time to truly go into your feelings. I withdraw. I shut down. I become numb.

Thinking back, to feel the rough edge of pain has never been foreign to me. I approach all the events in my life with a coldness, a lack of sentiment, understanding that I cannot undo that which has been done. The best I can do is to not give a fuck about anything or anybody.

Just like this Xica situation. It blew my mind when Jojo said that my baby was sleeping around, screwing somebody else, and I thought everybody was cool. All the slick talk, good wine, fine dope, romantic candlelight gone to waste. For what? I tried to be gentle and spontaneous in our relationship, doing little things for

her to show her that I cared. And my stepmother asked
me not long ago whether I was ever going to get married.
Why should I? It's a farce. We marry to not be alone, we
marry to make sure that our kids are not bastards, we
marry to be like everyone else, we marry to make our
families happy, we marry because we believe in mira-
cles. What's the point of it all? Love never lasts.

The following morning after Jojo's revelation, a letter
arrived and the clerk handed it to me when I returned
from breakfast at a nearby greasy spoon. It was sealed
in a pink envelope and smelled of lilac. I locked the
door to my room, lit a cigarette, lay across my lumpy
cot, and read it slowly:

Dear Eddie:
If you never want to see me again, I'd understand.
I thought about you last night, my sleepless night,
and how everything went down. What heartache
I've caused you! I've been thinking of some of the
things you said in the last few weeks about sincer-
ity, consistency, honest feelings, selfishness, etc.
I've tried to understand what I've done and why.
Right now, I can be thankful that you're still with
me in friendship (are you still my friend?) and that
the past events haven't completely poisoned your
impressions of me.

Believe me, I regret what happened. I'm sorting
through my emotions these days. The memory of
how deeply we loved is still strong. Words aren't
accurate to describe my feelings at this time. I des-
perately want to share myself the way I did with
you. Perhaps it's an exercise in futility, trying to
recapture something that may be lost forever. I

don't think our love should be lost. My love for you still runs deep.

If you could just find it in your heart to forgive me, to allow us to spend a little time together, alone and away somewhere, that would help us mend. I believe there is still something there between us, something quite alive. Doesn't it make sense to try and revive these feelings before time and anger kill them completely? That's what I fear. I know I lost you the moment Jojo opened his damn mouth. Nothing can ever make things like they were (or can it?). We've both grown from this, I believe, gotten more perspective and maybe more common sense. But we haven't stopped loving one another—at least I haven't stopped loving you.

I feel myself drifting toward painting a fantasy that may not be real. That's simple to do when I think of how we used to be. I fucked up. I really don't know why I did it. Call it weakness or fear or insecurity. Maybe I didn't love you as much as I thought I did. Maybe a person who sees herself as less than whole can't love—at least love one person. I've always been selfish and my needs always came first. You know that but you stayed. You saw only the best in me. You decided I was unlike the other women you loved. I failed you.

I want another chance. Think about it. Call me, please. Don't leave me hanging. Whatever you decide, I'll live with that.

Yours,
Xica

P.S. He was nothing compared to you.

* * *

Xica, Xica, Xica. What bullshit. The letter seemed to ignite in my hands even before I put a match to it. Smoldering ashes. My eyes became moist, my hands trembled, and my heart throbbed in an excruciating ache. She was just like the other females, the rest of them. How could I ever be with this bitch again?

A letter like this was enough to drive anybody over the edge. She gave me no credit for any kind of smarts. Once a fool, always a fool. The way I felt was not good. It fed the killing impulse within me. Everything's messed up. If I killed now, it would be sloppy, savage, and unnecessarily painful for whoever was chosen. The compulsion was building, rising to the pressure point, and there was nothing I could do to stop it from spilling over.

Chapter 11

THE BLOOD
BEGINS TO FLOW

Murder. Blood. Killing. When you kill anybody or anything, it is only because you stopped seeing the victim as human, as having any value of worth, any reason to exist. Once the act of killing begins, it cannot be stopped. A point comes where the decision to kill is made, the die is cast, and the breathing human being is transformed into a corpse. First mentally, then physically. Sometimes you think of holding the female captive for a few days, not doing anything to her, using her. Too risky. You feel so many conflicting urges and desires, but I get nothing from terror or torture.

So you drive around looking for another one, knowing where they gather or walk alone. You know where to dump the body, in an abandoned building or a trash-strewn lot, or even into the river. Sometimes it is best to pick them up in bars, let them get drunk so you can see their best nature. Like my mother.

On the subway, I sat in my dark blue suit, watching

for the signs that would tell me who was next to be chosen. My eyes scanned the faces, the quality of the clothing, and the bodies of the women who got on and off the train at rush hours. I looked for the fear in their expressions and the amber glow that said this was the one. The tainted aura.

Finally, a black woman pushed her way through the crowd to an empty seat, elbowing aside an elderly Hispanic grandmother, who was trying to position herself to plop down on the seat. The younger woman was dressed in a low-cut red blouse, tight black dress, and heels. She had slut written all over her. There was no handbag or briefcase in her arms so I assumed that she was not working a respectable job. She was a female who knew her body was her best asset and no doubt felt no qualm in advertising it. That sickened me. I realized immediately what I must do.

Walking several yards behind her, I watched her walk from the subway station, slowing her easy stride every few steps to give admiring guys a full glimpse of her large breasts, swaying ass, and long legs. Something in my head exploded in a burst of pain and my stomach tightened in an agonizing cramp as I trailed her for blocks until she wiggled her way across West 122nd Street, up Amsterdam Avenue past a row of rehabilitated brownstones. The woman stopped before her building, took a deep breath and walked up the stairs to its front door.

I monitored her movements from across the street. She went in and I quickly trotted behind her, hoping to reach the door before it closed but no such luck. I waited only a few seconds when a couple of kids tossing a baseball came out and I caught the door before it locked. She was on the stairs two flights above me, puffing heavily as her footsteps landed solidly during the ascent to her floor. I listened, careful as a hawk would in the darkness circling overhead his rodent prey, placing my feet down gently.

The woman was now at her door, fishing in her blouse pocket for keys as I moved slowly past her, acting as if I was walking toward a destination at the end of the hall. She opened the door a crack but turned suddenly when she felt me behind her. Her eyes met mine for a fleeting second before I shoved her inside and kicked the door closed. My gloved hand covered her mouth, cutting off a horrified scream. She knew she was going to die. She knew I didn't want her money or valuables. Instinctively, the woman leaped away from me when she saw the gleaming knife in my hand. Her lips moved but nothing came out. Finally she whispered, "Don't hurt me, please." Her eyes bulged with fear. She begged although she knew words meant nothing at a time like this.

I felt unnaturally strong, powerful, and invincible. No one was teasing me now. Nobody was judging me now. Nobody was telling me I wasn't worth a damn. I was master. I was in control. Now, at this moment, I controlled time, I controlled life. A black man in command.

"I want you to kiss me, bitch," I said, thinking of all of the women from my mother to Xica who had hurt me, all the black women who had destroyed a black man or a black child. Women who used their sex and their divine right to give birth as a weapon.

"Please . . . please . . . don't do this, please," the woman pleaded. "I don't even know you. I've never done anything to you."

I glared at her. "I don't want to ask again."

She continued to back away from me, moving

toward the center of the room. I glanced around her small, sparsely furnished apartment, trying to see anything that might say she was not alone. My steps to her left allowed me to block any chance of her running for the door. She was trapped and completely powerless.

"I don't even know you," she whimpered again. "Why are you doing this?"

"It's my job." I snapped my fingers. "Take off your clothes."

She said something else that sounded like: "Take the pussy if you're such a bad nigger." At least, that was the way my brain processed what I heard coming from her mouth. An insult, a dare, a diss. She yelled, gritted her teeth, and threw a heavy glass ashtray at my head. I laughed coldly and ducked in time to see it crash against the wall behind me.

"Are you going to fight me or are you going to give it up?" I asked her quietly, inching closer to her.

"Don't hurt me, brother," the woman said with a cry in her voice. "Look at your dreads. Aren't you a Rasta? They don't do this kind of shit. They respect women."

"Hair don't mean a damn thing," I growled. "I asked you for a kiss, skank bitch."

"If I give you a kiss, will you leave?"

When she said that, I knew why she had been chosen. My mind often played tricks on me, but the truth was I had been watching her for two weeks, stalking her, shadowing her. You never know who is watching you. I remembered her now. Victim number eight. On the subway one morning, I sat next to her, inhaling her cheap perfume, her fuck-me scent, and asked her the time. She ignored me. It was apparent from that she didn't have long to live. Slut.

Whore. The death glow emitted from the center of her chest. Dead woman walking. Wasn't original but I liked it. Clever.

"Do you want money? I'll give you all I have. Every cent. Just let me go."

"Go where? Besides, I don't want your money. I want something else."

Those words chilled her heart. She had no reply. Her terrified glance went to the windows, which were covered by pulled curtains, dime-store sturdy. Outside, the day was fading fast in a blood-red sunset, the perfect backdrop for the reaping. I lifted the arm with the knife slowly, with deadly purpose.

Victim Number Eight looked me straight in the eyes, grim and serious. "If you leave now, I won't report any of this to the police. There won't be any trouble. Just walk out now and I'll forget you were ever here. All right?"

I did a comic double-take, dropping my jaw open. "No shit. Will you forget all about it? I don't think so."

"I will. I promise." Her eyes were red and pleading.

My head said do it, finish this and go home. I felt the demon coming on. Full force once more. "You lying bitch! I hate lies and liars! My mama lied! Every woman I've ever known has lied!" Maybe a second ago, I could have left her untouched, walked away, went back to my dingy room and waited until this fever passed. But now . . . All she felt no doubt was a black shape collide with her neck, then her chest. A blur, then another blow, which sent her spinning around against a table. You stabbed me, she screamed in desperate panic as well as in surprise. The next thrust hit under her left armpit, pitching her against a chair, the following one into her back. Her entire body shivered. I loved her fear. I could feel the adrenaline rushing through me. Then the blade slashed down across her face and neck again. She crawled across the floor on all fours toward the door, unable to scream with a mouth full of blood, and I stepped on her hands, blocking her exit. She stared at me in wonder and shock. "Why? Why are you doing this? Why are you killing me? Why?" If I had the time, I would have explained everything but I had none. And neither did she. I would have answered: "Because this is what I do, bitch."

For a moment, she curled up on the floor but I yanked her to her feet by her hair and a change of expression went across her face when I hugged her like a lover and drove the knife hard between her store-bought tits. She moaned and pitched against me. My arms went sweetly around her waist to pull her tighter into my embrace, then I kissed her full on the lips. There was no passion in her smooch. Her fingers searched for my face, sightless, her vision starting to blur. I casually slapped her hand away and she slumped to the floor and I delivered the death stab to her heart, the harvest thrust. Then it was as if the world stopped. The apartment was strangely silent, not a sound.

Suddenly, the phone rang, two clicks, and the answering machine went off: "Hello, this is Janine . . . I'm sorry that I'm not in to take your call but if you'll leave a message after the beep, I promise that I'll get back to you." Whoever called hung up.

Calmly, I knelt beside her body, listening for that sweet breath, and it came. I felt so aroused. I was so hard that my penis was straining against my pants. Powerful. Then I lifted her soiled dress, pulled down her panties, and looked at the soft triangle of hair between her long, smooth brown legs. Lowly and gently, I knelt on all fours and lowered my face to her crotch and inhaled her scent. I remained there for quite awhile.

Chapter 12

WHAT HE WANTS

Waking up on the Thursday before Memorial Day weekend, I got a call from the Congressman, whose voice immediately said something was wrong. He was under attack from both his opponent in the congressional race and the media as well. At least, that was how he saw it. At an afternoon commencement speech at St. Anthony's University in downtown Manhattan, he publicly declared that his campaign was not going to be derailed by published reports alleging that there were contribution irregularities connected with his effort to retain his seat.

As he launched his tirade against the media, Lady Stevens, his fawning wife, sat next to him, along with the Speaker of the House of Representatives and two Republican bigwigs. He spared no punches as he turned the graduation into a political event. No doubt the organizers did not expect this kind of show when they invited him to receive a doctorate of Humane Letters before the hundreds of students gathered on the school's great lawn.

"The media says you should listen to us because we know and you don't," the Congressman said angrily. "Any talking head or person with a pen and pad is an expert. They feel the public needs its daily ration of dirt or it will channel-surf. The media says we know what you're thinking even before you think it. They believe only they know what you feel and believe. But they are wrong."

The students, obviously happy to see some real-life drama unfolding right before their eyes, cheered his every accusation. Their enthusiasm was not shared by the school officials who frowned and grimaced during the tirade. Some of them second-guessed themselves and wondered why they had not chosen Bill Cosby or Colin Powell, two popular celebrities for such an event.

"If we listen to the media, it says we just tell it like it is," the Congressman continued. "What they're really saying is that we couldn't possibly discover the truth for ourselves. Leave that to us, they say, because you're not that sophisticated or smart. Events and issues must be interpreted for you. They say the camera and the pen never lie. That's a lot of baloney. Yes, they say, we can look into a man's heart and tell you the true nature of his character. Every news story must have good guys and bad guys. Unfortunately, life is not that simplistic. They insist that you must be a criminal if you work hard and profit from your labor. Or as they like to say: the rich are not like you and me. Let me ask you this, our bright and shining future. Why have you gone to school if not to better your life and make a good living? How many of you went to school to be poor?"

Many students screamed a resounding NO! that shook the clouds, as they shook their fists at the people sitting on the stage in the packed auditorium. The young people enjoyed letting off steam after a grueling four years of studying, sacrifice, and test scores.

"I thought not," the Congressman went on. "The media wants to be the judge and jury of American life. They feel: the bigger you are, the more fun it is to bring you down. They believe Americans love to see its leaders and heroes topple. With this in mind, they spoon-feed us these degrading tabloid shows and supermarket publications that play havoc with the truth. Nothing is sacred. The media does not understand limits and doesn't believe there is such a thing as privacy. According to the media, the public has a right to know whatever they can dig up. That's madness."

The Congressman paused to let his words hang in the sky. He ignored the gestures from the school officials to cut his speech short and let his final arrows fly.

"We are thinking human beings," he said, holding his arms aloft. "We can be taught to look beyond the obvious to the real issues. We do not need these shabby behind-the-scenes exclusives or peeps into one another's bedrooms. We can get to the heart of a story without anyone's help. All of the news is not fit to be printed. They say you want and need this trash and that your life would be not complete without it. I say they are wrong. They say it doesn't matter to you if someone has been paid to lie about another person's life or integrity. I say they are wrong. I say they're wrong and I believe you feel the same way. Am I right?"

Again, the young people roared their agreement. The newspapers would later compare the commencement to a "delirious high school pep rally." I knew the man's moves and he could be real slick when he had to be. He was the master salesman, the master huckster, running his game with precision, style, and finesse.

"I'm not finished yet," the Congressman waved to

silence the shouts and cheers. "No doubt you've seen the attacks on my family and myself in the media. They say we don't make the news, we just report it as it happens. I say they're wrong. They say if you mess with us, we will get you if it takes forever. I say they're wrong. I'm not afraid of them or any living man. I answer only to the people I represent and God. I'm a fighter. I can take a punch. I don't need their scum. Is that the kind of world you want? I don't believe so."

The graduates went berserk, screaming and shouting their support of the wily politician. A master of melodrama, the Congressman bowed to them, pumped his fist once in the air, high-fived the class valedictorian, and found his seat next to the irritated college president. It took nearly five minutes to settle the students down before the ceremony could continue.

"It's all filth and contributes nothing positive to our society," the Congressman shot back before storming out. Reporters tried to interview him, running behind him shouting questions, but he ducked out the stage door behind the building where his limo was parked.

"Did you see what the bastards wrote about me in the papers this morning?" he now asked me on the phone the next day. "Everything in the articles was a pack of lies. They're out to get me. I'm sure of it. They're mad because I won't kiss their collective ass. Do you know what Tim Levin, my adviser, had nerve enough to say to me?"

I knew my lines well. "No, what did he say?"

He was totally hyped. "Remember what the media did to Nixon and Gary Hart. Remember what they've done to Clinton. I told the media to fuck themselves. This money business is something my opponent planted to sway the voters and the polls against me."

I never thought Mr. Slick would unravel under pressure but his seams were starting to show. He was unbeatable and he knew it. His aides were circling the wagons, under his command, for one last assault. Now Congressman Stevens was speaking to me on the phone in that ego-filled Napoleon tone of his, ordering me to accompany him tomorrow to the funeral of a thirteen-year-old Harlem boy gunned down by police. The boy was playing cops and robbers in a housing project when he was shot by housing police who thought his toy gun was real. The community was in an uproar. They were also ticked off at the Congressman because he was such a die-hard supporter of the cops. In his eyes, they could do no wrong. However, the Congressman was more concerned at present with his slippage in the polls with less than four weeks left in his campaign, and added to this stress was the financial scandal in the papers.

He sent a representative to the boy's family, offering to speak at the funeral. He also called the boy's parents, who were livid about the killing. His father was shouting into the phone that the cops could see that it was a toy. His mother explained that her boy would not point a gun at an officer, that he was not that kind of boy. The Congressman assured he would get to the bottom of this killing and there would be an investigation into the matter. Ultimately, the stubborn parents did not cave in to the politician's request, but they said he could attend the funeral.

"Our competition will do anything to silence me on the issues but I'll not go quietly," my stepfather explained to me during the ride to the Mt. Zion Baptist Church where the boy was to be buried with full community honors. "There is no way I'm going to hand this seat over to them on a platter."

I listened, looking out the window at the gray poor folks of Harlem shuffling aimlessly along the streets, their future bleak and their hopes diminished. I had been one of them, poor and hopeless, before my luck intervened. It was a matter of class struggle. Truthfully speaking, the Congressman wasn't really concerned about them. Even the white boys weren't concerned about them either. I wondered what they thought when they saw the Congressman whiz past them in his limo, all comfy in his power and luxury.

"What's the deal with the money business?" I asked.

"It's political hardball," he said crisply, brushing a speck of lint from the lapel of his Italian custom-made suit. "The papers tomorrow will say I embezzled for my private use over three million in funds from a group of five foster care centers in our community. It's all bullshit. Another lie."

This was something new. He was still the front runner, ahead in the race by a sliver of a lead, according to the polls. He was fending off torpedoes coming from all directions. He was accused of being a turncoat for trying to form a coalition with conservative Hispanic politicians. That was not done. The Harlem political establishment wanted to have more control over him, have him at their beck and call. Then there was a rumor of his role in a bribery deal to push through a deal for a casino ship on the East River with accompanying whispers of mob involvement looming large.

He looked out the tinted windows. "The bastards say a guy came to my office with an envelope full of money to buy my support. I wouldn't touch that tainted money. I'm in nobody's pocket, nobody's."

"Dad, I'd like to talk to you about something," I said, putting on the son bit to make him listen. "It's pretty

serious. I need to talk about it with someone. Someone
I trust."

He wasn't listening. He was preoccupied, wrapped up
in his own problems. The man was starting to look his
age, fifty, with deep lines and wrinkles in his forehead
and around his mouth, and darkened bags under his
eyes. The look of fatigue clung to him like the scent of
corruption. When I realized he was not listening to me,
I repeated my statement.

His eyes sparked for an instant as he searched my
face for meaning. "What the hell are you talking about,
Edward? You have plenty of people to discuss your
problems with, like that shrink I pay every two weeks.
Is she doing you any good?"

I could tell that he was not in the mood for anything
that wasn't directly linked to his campaign. My dark
secret was burning me up inside. If he could have talked
to me about my pain and confusion sometimes, maybe
the killings would stop. Maybe not. What was I thinking? He wasn't a father and never would be. He was a
politician. He was concerned with getting votes and sitting on the throne in his fiefdom in Harlem. He didn't
give a shit about me.

"Yes, she's great. We get along fine." I smiled weakly
and he touched me lightly on the shoulder. That was as
affectionate as he ever got with me. I could never remember a hug or a spontaneous declaration of love. Is
this how all fathers acted with their sons?

Meanwhile, Henry Sohn, his press secretary, read the
newspaper and called out the minutes to our arrival at
the church. We would be seated next to the mayor and
two area councilmen, the presence of power hopefully
enough to quell any potential summer rioting. Although
the minister officiating at the funeral was a known fire-

brand, representatives from the mayor's office had visited him two days before to warn him to tone down any inflammatory rhetoric in his sermon. Some minor arm-twisting. The usually publicity-hungry Reverend went along with the program, according to the Congressman, because he wanted to have some political favors to cash in later.

"That bastard struck again," Sohn said tersely, leaning forward in his limo seat to read from the newspaper. "Listen to this. The badly decomposed body of a Harlem woman who disappeared last March after an office party washed up yesterday near the boat basin near West 79th Street on the Manhattan shoreline. The corpse was found at noon, dressed only in a blouse. The victim's dress had disintegrated during its time in the water. The coroner's office said there were definite signs of foul play but withheld any further comment pending an autopsy and toxicological work. A spokesman for the medical examiner's office said the victim died from a heavy blow to the skull, leading police to believe that it may be the work of an elusive killer who has claimed the lives of nine young women in almost a year."

"Damn, they must nail the SOB pretty soon," the Congressman mumbled. "I've got enough problems without a madman running around scaring the shit out of my voters. Remind me to light a fire under the asses of the mayor and the police chief. This has gone on far too long."

Suddenly, something struck the window on my side. It sounded like a rock. Then there was another thud and another.

"I think we've arrived, sir," the driver said, looking a bit nervous. "The crowd looks somewhat unruly. I don't

see too many police. Maybe we should wait until rein-
forcements come."

To his credit, the Congressman opened the door and
got out to a chorus of boos and shouts. He walked ahead
of us like Nero ascending to a high place to see his
burning city. Surprisingly, no one threw a rock or
tomato at that moment, but the jeers grew more intense
as he neared the entrance of the church. Two policemen
stood near the door, nightsticks at the ready, watching
the crowd with alert eyes. It was obvious that the mayor
was late.

"What the fuck was that about?" the Congressman
asked, looking stunned. "What did I do now?"

Sohn and I kept pace behind him. The Congressman
walked into the church, hugged the boy's father, then the
mother, whispering idle promises into her ear. This was
what he knew how to do best, playing the part of the
compassionate lawmaker. We sat in the front row of the
church, watching the brightly robed choir file into their
seats, noticing the pastor frown at his watch. The mayor
and his entourage was more than ten minutes late.

A respectful hush had settled over the mourners while
they filed to the open coffin containing the dead boy.
Some of the mothers in the gathering could be heard
sobbing, their tears full of sorrow and the harsh possi-
bility that any one of their children could have been in
his place in the coffin struck home. Yes, the dead boy
could have been theirs. That was not lost on them.

"Your boy's with God now," the mayor whispered to
the boy's tearful mother, clutching her dark hand as if he
meant every word. The body of the lanky boy was displayed in Baptist fashion, a waxy corpse laid out among
countless banks of funeral wreaths and ribbons.

In keeping with the original arrangement, the minister did not play to the anger of the crowd, choosing instead to recite a text centered around the themes of forgiveness and resurrection. All of the political powers were very happy. Only near the conclusion of his sermon did he mention the word, justice. His trembling voice brought tears to the eyes of those standing in the aisles and in the church lobby.

"I know what it's like to lose your baby like that," I heard one heavy-set woman say to the man with her. "Shot down like a dog. It just tears your heart in two."

The mayor spoke briefly to the mourners about lives pruned before budding, about promise denied, and the need for lessons nurtured by pain and loss. He promised that this young life would not be lost, that justice would be served so that this tragedy would not be repeated. A state representative from the far eastern corner of Harlem called for everyone to pray for the family and the community.

Then the funeral was over after a last stirring hymn from the church choir about the last mile of the way, which only brought more gasps and cries from the family, permitting the others to feel total compassion for the grieving kin. Outside, the crowd said little during the close of the somber ritual when the funeral possession loaded into the caravan for the concluding drive to the gravesite. It was obvious that the single thought of the onlookers was the irreversible splintering of a clan caused by a gunshot.

A gang of reporters, both print and TV, surrounded the politicians coming out of the church, asking questions about the incident, the police, the kid and his death, the upcoming investigation. The mayor and the others took turns before the camera, reciting their prepared statements before disappearing into their limos. People from the neighborhood clustered around the cars in the motorcade, shoving, yelling taunts and slurs at the power brokers despite the well-coordinated efforts of the police to keep them at a distance. In the eyes of these people, the power elite entering the limos was the enemy, the real thugs, the real culprits in this crime.

Despite earlier complaints about a headache, the Congressman spoke to the reporter in a weak voice, careful not to mention anything about the troubling questions regarding campaign finances. I stood with him, noticing that he was sweating more than usual. He had changed shirts before the ceremony but it was sopping wet again. On the way over, he said to his press aide that he felt sick, mumbling something about a fever.

"Sure, there was some booing out there, but for the most part, everyone came to pay tribute to a young life snuffed out too soon," the Congressman said, wiping his brow with a tissue. "The people causing a disturbance were probably paid troublemakers from my opponent's camp. They say I've not spoken up about racism or police brutality. That is not true. Whenever these issues have been in the forefront I've never sidestepped them, but we must be aware that there are other major matters on the national agenda. Everything is not race and racism. We have other things to concern us.

One radio reporter pressed the matter about the shooting. "Can you honestly say there is not a racial component in this tragedy?"

An aide with the Congressman handed him a sheet of paper, which he read, balled up and tossed away. The man who played the role of my stepfather listened for a moment as the crowd of grim faces moved closer around us, almost menacing in their nearness. Their chants rose up in a single scream of rage, a protest for the dead boy now headed for his rendezvous with the soil.

"I believe there are plenty of good policemen and women on the force, so I won't paint them all with a broad brush stroke," the Congressman rasped. "We cannot rush to judgment. We should not act before we have all of the facts. We should be calm until we really know what happened. This matter should be reviewed by the proper authorities. And yes, there might be a few rotten apples among our custodians of the peace but not many. Let's let the law run its course. I assure you if there is foul play here that it will be uncovered."

"What about these people here, their anger?" another reporter asked. "That can't be ignored."

The Congressman waved to someone in the crowd, either real or imaginary, to give him time to fashion a reply. It was an old trick of his. I had seen him do this many times in the past. He finally turned back to the reporter, who was growing impatient with his delaying tactics, and slowly gave his brief response.

"We cannot fight hate or ignorance with more of the same," he glibly said before walking toward the car with two bodyguards on both sides of him.

I looked over his head at the throng lining the street in front of the church, three and four deep, pushing and screaming flesh on either side of the cars leaving a parking lot. It was a tense situation. However, the Congressman seemed to ignore the hostility and to my great surprise, waded into the crush of bodies shaking hands. Either he was brave or stupid. I could never figure him out. One woman passed a small baby to him and he leaned over the police barricade and took the child. The news photographers rang to the heartwarming scene and shot him just as he smiled broadly like a jack-o-lantern and planted a kiss on the child's fat cheek. The baby cooperated by laughing hysterically at the funny face that the old man gave him.

I was right behind him. None of the other politicians had taken the time to mingle with the common folk. A few people cheered him. The Old Master at work. He shook a few more hands and whispered to his security crew to get him the hell out of there.

Chapter 13

MASTERING THE HABIT OF LIVING

Something about the boy's funeral triggered a whole host of thoughts in my mind, old memories. Bad stuff. When I was fifteen, I bugged out in the street and was taken to the psycho hospital out on the island because I couldn't get my anger under control. One of my uncles on my real father's side was in the locked unit at Kings County Hospital out in Brooklyn. Anyway, I had attacked my woodshop teacher with a claw hammer, swinging it wildly at his head as he knelt to pick up some fallen nails. The bastards handcuffed me, strapped me to a cold table with my arms and legs secured spread-eagle. Then and there I learned the world owed me nothing. That it wanted to kill me, kill who I was. That any form of authority was shit, that everything on the earth kills, that the streets kill. A budding homicidal maniac, right? Early in my life, I understood the patterns of madness, knowing murder was but one way of killing one's self by destroying another.

Lady Stevens, my stepmother, complained I was an

out-of-control kid. Completely unruly. She told the politician she had tried everything to reach me but to no avail. Nothing worked with me. Even tough love solutions. Even bribes. But the fact was I was just a nuisance, an annoyance to them. They had no emotional attachment to me, a mutt, a stray dog they mistakenly adopted.

Drunks, druggies, and loonies. I kept to myself. I was a boy of means among the unwashed poor driven mad by their sorry circumstances. A state mental facility for the mentally ill. The complex was a walled community with more than six hundred patients and an army of staff, nurses, social workers, doctors, and police. I was medicated and subdued in a ward for adolescents, down the hall from a ward for the mentally retarded. Each of the pills removed me farther from reality, everything seemed like it was on TV and I was watching it through a soft silvery haze. Another one of the zombies.

For the first week, I welcomed the doctors with silence. They stood outside of the door, just within earshot, discussing my chart, the situation of my dead parents and their grisly end. Their conclusions were the usual ones, centering around a belief that my illness was schizophrenia of either the disorganized or paranoid types. I listened as they talked about disturbances of thinking, of misreadings of reality, of delusions and hallucinations. Flat affect, withdrawn behavior, regressive behavior. What the hell did all that mean?

"I think there might be a bipolar disorder also involved here as well," said one doctor, who had never examined me.

"Yes, it's there," another doctor answered. "The young man was the sole survivor of a family slaughter, a drug crime it seems. His entire family was wiped out, executed. His father, mother, and two younger sisters as well. The reaction to this trauma is typical of what we see in many ghetto youth survivors of major crimes. They never really recover. They usually don't get proper treatment for the emotional damage. Hell, they were never permitted to be fun-loving youngsters before these things happened to them. Never just kids."

"And so just what are you saying here, Henry?" the first doctor asked.

"Well, I'm just saying that those neighborhoods devour these kids and wreck them for life," his mentor replied. "They see death all around them. It's like living in a war zone. They lose their innate socialization skills, become emotionally warped, and get predatory to survive. Young killers in training. I see this kind of thing all the time with young black males like our friend here."

"What is the solution for this?" the younger doctor asked.

The older man laughed. Both men stopped talking as two hospital staffers wheeled a hysterical young black woman strapped down on a gurney past the room. Her screams were bloodcurdling, much like my sister's had been while the gunman raped and tortured them. I placed my hands over my ears, muffling them to a low roar until the woman was out of range. In a place like this, the level of noise, the howls and shrieks of the mad, was deafening. I sometimes thought that the neverending wails would push me over the edge.

Someone walked up and asked one of the doctors to sign something and they quieted. The men paused in their conversation until the intrusion was over, then the older man spoke again.

"Have you looked at him closely?" the junior man

asked. "He's awfully black. Dark-skinned, I mean. I've noticed that a lot of black patients are the darker skinned ones. You think there is a correlation between that fact and their greater numbers in the institutions?"

"I don't know if that is true. Could be just . . . I don't know."

"Just an observation," the younger one said.

"I'm familiar with the ideologies of Shockley, Jenson, Herrnstein, and Eysenck but I don't know if I believe them," the mentor said softly. "A few years back, when I served in the Nixon administration with his top science adviser Dr. Edward David, we had his senior adviser on urban affairs, Edward Banfield, over at the White House to speak at one of the cabinet meetings. Smart fellow, that Banfield. He was an urbanologist over at Harvard back then. He said some pretty impressive things during that session."

"What did Banfield say that caught your attention?"

"Banfield believed blacks in the slums enjoyed their way of life," the older medicine man explained. "He said they didn't care how dirty or inferior their housing appeared nor did they care much about poor schools or libraries. If the facilities were superior, the slum black destroyed them with vandalism or neglect. What other races might find disagreeable about these conditions, the slum black actually found pleasing. A startling theory."

"Do you agree with his theory?"

"I don't know if I buy all of it. However, the black underclass is quite different from the middle class individual of the race. That much I do know."

"How did Nixon respond to Banfield's theory?"

The older doctor laughed again. "You know Nixon, he just sat there grim-faced, taking it all in. Sometimes he was hard to figure. Well, our boy in there is no slum black. He's the adopted son of a black congressman so we've got to give him the full treatment. Get him back on his feet and out of here."

After the doctors finished their chat, the older doctor walked into my room, watched me watching him for a moment, then sat down in a chair near the bed. I wondered if he was going to be like the others. A person's voice can tell you much about him and this man was no different. He was tall, broad shouldered and thick across the chest, with longer than normal legs. His face was similar to the ones on the old Roman coins, all angles and peaks. He introduced himself. Dr. Lauterbach smiled to put me at ease, and touched me gently with the soft tines of his words. He was without a note pad or a chart.

Our eyes locked when the doctor said very softly, "Eddie, I need to understand why you attacked the teacher with a hammer."

I shrugged and looked down at the floor. Time to play the part of the dumb mute.

He kept eye contact with me while he talked. "I notice some of the doctors have written in your chart that you are somewhat uncooperative and very guarded. Why would they come to a conclusion like that?"

"Hell if I know." I kept completely still, careful not to give anything away in my posture or body language.

"Why do you think you assaulted this man who told the police that you were so quiet and likeable in his class? Eddie, he was completely surprised that you would do such a thing."

"What kind of things do you hear in your head?" The doctor supported his head with one finger.

"Bad things, terrible things. Imagine the worst things

possible, the most horrible things you can think up, and ummmm, that still wouldn't do the trick. Sometimes my head hurts too."

"How do you feel now?" the doctor continued, maintaining the calm voice.

I was cautious in the rhythm of my words, placing a flatness in them, something to keep him guessing. "I feel fine, I just want to go home. I was tired so they said I had to come here to get a rest. When can I go home?"

"Not just yet. I know you don't want to be here, but we have work to do before we can let you return to your normal routine. Since this is my first time talking with you, maybe you can talk about the incident that brought you here. Can we start there?"

"What incident? What the hell are you talking about?"

"The incident with the teacher and the hammer." He never got rattled despite my being a total ass, fucking with him. I wanted to get under his skin but he wasn't buying it. Sharp dude.

"Oh that, Mr. Monoso wolfed at me and stepped up to me like he was going to punch me out so I tagged him first," I said quietly. "The fool's big as a mountain and I couldn't take him out with my hands. I picked up something to even the score. A hammer. I wasn't going to kill him with it. I just wanted him off my ass."

"You told one of the other doctors that you felt angry, that something told you to hit him," Dr. Lauterbach said, setting a verbal trap. "You've just repeated that again. Tell me about that."

I was starting to feel irritable. Aggravated. "Oh yeah, the voices again. Angry?"

"Yes, anger. Do you get angry often? Does your temper frequently drive you to strike out against others?"

He examined me with an expression of mixed curiosity and disgust. Beads of sweat appeared on his forehead while he pinched his beak nose nervously. What this white man did not understand was how I felt about feelings, emotions, tenderness and all that. Give me reason and intellect. Facts. Funny coming from someone technically nuts but emotions are bullshit. Emotions tell lies. Emotions deceive. Emotions are not to be trusted. Emotions screw up your head and make you fuck up.

"Sure, I get mad just like anybody else," I replied. "I get pissed off like anybody else. Don't you get mad, Doc?"

The doctor said nothing. He just stared at me as if I slapped him or something. Sheer drama. Shrink theatrics.

"Let me rephrase my question," he started again. "Are there times when you later feel your anger is inappropriate? Anger that is far too extreme for whatever behavior triggered it?"

He might be right, anger over the top. "It's a hard thing to lose your whole family. The grieving period doesn't seem to end. I get mad when the kids at school tease me about my parents getting wasted. That makes me want to hurt somebody. Sometimes when I'm arguing with a person, I might get a bit worked up and want to punch them out. I've gotten better about that lately. Now I just walk away. If I think someone is taking advantage of me or making fun of me, then I set the situation right. Understand?"

"Do you think of your own mortality?" the doctor asked.

"Hell, I think about it," I replied. "I think my own days are numbered. I think I'm next. If my family could get wiped out, then why not me? What is to prevent me from dying?"

"Is that why you are so angry?"

I didn't answer him. I was not the only person walking around with anger and rage. Most of America was suffering like I was. Whenever I walked in the city, I saw the anger in the way people stood, in the way people talked, in the way people smiled at each other. There were very black or white people who didn't feel a constant, simmering anger and rage and they didn't act on it like I did. They let the shit give them heart attacks and strokes. They let the shit fuck up their loved ones. Somebody had to suffer when that rage boiled over.

"Have you ever hurt someone else when you felt like this?" the doctor asked. "Like the gentleman you attacked with the hammer?"

"No, but I've come close to fucking up somebody," I lied. "Nobody likes to have somebody belittling them. I am not a punk."

"Let's go back to something we discussed earlier. Do you ever see things?"

"I know I see myself do stuff but I don't feel it was me," I said. "I do not feel sorrow or remorse for the things I do. I know it's not normal."

"And seeing things, Edward?"

"Sometimes I see stuff that disappears but most of the time I'm cool. Like my mother's face or I smell my sisters' scent even though I know they're dead. And sometimes I hear my parents saying things to me."

He leaned toward me. "Anything else? Do you see anything else other than your mother's face?"

"Yeah, but I don't want to talk about it now. Maybe later."

"That's alright. Don't rush. We have plenty of time

here. Edward, do you feel people want to harm you?
Want to hurt you?"

I sat up in the bed, my limbs obeying reluctantly and
answered him in a hushed voice. "Often. Since my folks
got offed, I think I'm next. I don't trust nobody. I watch
them. Know what I mean?"

None of my words seemed to shake him. He kept a
peaceful look on his face, not one sign of any emotion.
"How can you spot these people who would do you
harm?"

Everything was a threat to my survival. I lived in a
world bent on hurting and maiming me. Like most
blacks with a big target on their backs, I felt stuck as a
person. I knew deep down that no combination of meds
and talk could fix me, cure me. I was broken beyond
repair. Coils and springs smashed to bits like a clock
under a boot heel. There was chatter inside my head. I
was never really medically stable so the voices frequently filled in the blanks for me.

I ignored his question. The doctor took it somewhere
else. "Do you have nightmares or disturbing dreams?"

"I don't sleep well. That's already down there on my
chart."

"There is no free choice in a person's action when
childhood trauma is involved," he was saying but my
mind was off on a tangent.

"What's your name again, Doc?"

"Dr. Lauterbach," he answered cheerily. "Eddie, what
do you think is wrong with you?"

I pointed to my heart with a shaky finger. "Blockage
in here."

"Are you talking about something romantic?" the
shrink asked.

We were talking past one another. "No, heart pain."

Chapter 14

TWISTED

Days and nights of this imprisonment wore on me. I began to scream, hurling threats and curses at everybody. I paced in my room, walking back and forth before the barred window. Twice I almost got away but they overpowered me. Two attendants, angry at my escape effort, came and hit me in the face, busting my nose and mouth. They said another inmate attacked me. I didn't say anything.

I propped myself on the bed, straining against the power of my meds. My arms and legs felt so weak. If I could have seen these faces with the voices condemning me, I would have been able to handle what was said about me. The white attendants called me everything but human, for I was reduced to a beast, brute, and underling. Only they knew what was good for us. We were the product of bad genes, poor codes in the blood that caused us to be criminals, to kill and steal, and to be poor.

The doctors wanted to believe I was a suicidal risk. About the second month of my stay, a female doctor, who resembled Joan Rivers, started having these noon chats with me about making changes in my life to permit me to live easier among other people. I told her to kiss my black ass. Damn females.

"You don't mean that," she said, grinning. She continued talking about me pursuing a normal life, maintaining a loving relationship with a woman, and forming a family of my own.

When she said this stupid shit, I grumbled and rolled my eyes in disgust. I have always known that I would never get married or have a family. I was alone and would always remain that way.

"I bet you think I'm nuts, right, Doc?" I asked her.

"No, I don't think that. I think you're troubled and in need of some assistance in getting your emotional balance back. We want a positive outcome here."

To hell with a positive outcome. I didn't give a shit about what doctors or anybody else thought about me. In moments of extreme clarity, I could hear other people's thoughts and listen to the lies forming at the base of their skulls. It felt as if I was eavesdropping on their souls. I could hold their essence in the palm of my hand, feel its weight, and guess its overall value.

My mind would go off on tangents. It would get away from the world. I remembered there were days when I left my mind and body, abandoned my human form. Nobody fucked with me when I was like that.

What happens to a person when they can no longer feel anything, when they are numb? I was shut down emotionally. What happens when the scabs on the soul are too thick? Maybe I was a textbook case of madness. When the Congressman or my stepmother came around, I pretended to be on the road to recovery. But none of this talking cure shit did me any good. Mainly because I lied too much. I never told the truth. Well, most of the time I told them what they wanted to hear.

Two weeks after the close of the last uneventful session with Dr. Lauterbach, I was in deep despair. Migraines. Violent mood swings. Acute panic attacks. The emptiness returned. The thought of freedom gave me goose bumps. That Friday, I got my cousin Gregory to smuggle three cartons of cigarettes and $500 to me in the hospital. With this contraband, I conned a night guard to look the other way while I slipped off the grounds.

For the next three weeks that summer, I hung out in Central Park, drinking wine and beer, smoking dope with my homeys. There were some professional people, regulars, walking in a herd along the paths with their dogs. Nobody robbed them because they often stopped to talk with us or give us money. Lovers strolled hand in hand through the darkened park, which was closed from one to six A.M.

One afternoon, I heard the angels sing, and waded out into the duck pond, their song so incredibly beautiful. It seemed like heaven was opening up to me. The rays of the sun were so golden, brilliant, and they bathed me in their glow. I felt like I was a saint. I dipped under the surface of the water. When the people on the boats saw this, they paddled over to me, and pulled me to safety. I struggled, screaming that I had been touched by God, but they would not let me go near the water.

I think the doctor knew I was going over the wall. No hospital, especially a nuthouse, could hold me for long.

"Promise me that if you feel edgy or extremely despondent you will call me," Dr. Lauterbach told me just two days before I split from there. "You must promise me that you will do nothing to yourself or to others until we talk. Call me at any time, day or night."

I killed my first woman six days after I escaped from the psych hospital. I was sixteen.

Chapter 15

NICE GIRLS DON'T
LINGER FOR BREAKFAST

On the morning after attending the funeral with the Congressman, I called Grandma Timmons because it had been more than two weeks since we had seen each other. The old woman was suffering from a bad head cold and was unable to tend to her garden. That was getting her down. Activity was what kept her in the game of life. She once said death would be assured if she was forced to retreat to the rocking chair or the sick bed. But talking to her gave me an idea for getting back to Xica. As far as I knew, things had not worked out between her and this other guy so there was hope.

I sent Xica some flowers, nothing special, no tulips or roses, but a home-spun gathering of colorful mums, geraniums, lilacs, and snapdragons. There had been an angry note from her condemning me for taking too long to make up my mind about her.

Xica loved the flowers. When my boy, Harry, took them by her house, she was so emotional that she got all choked up. It caught her by surprise because I had laid low for a long time, no contact at all. No calls, no letters, no nothing. She told Harry to tell me to call that night. Cool. We talked and decided to go to the country, some place she knew in upstate New York. Trees, grass, fresh air, wildlife, and all that.

If I was handling things, we wouldn't have driven to any place out of the city. Too lazy. When I picked Xica up, I suggested going to a bunch of spots in the city, places like the Bronx Zoo, City Island, Coney Island, the Cloisters, or Central Park. We ended up heading upstate in my car on Route 87, going north along the scenic run. That morning, I smoked too much herb, shared a blunt with Zeke after talking to the Congressman on the phone about some junk. He reminded me about his pulling strings when I walked away from the nuthouse. To compensate for this, he wanted me to attend some damn social event at the Plaza with him, a benefit for the Harlem Boy Scouts and the Police Athletic League. Campaign jive.

Nothing would be required of me but to put in an appearance, to look good in formal wear and to conduct small talk with the elite. The talking seal on display.

Did I mention how good Xica looked? Her body was slamming, that chest, that tiny waist, that ass. She had it to spare. Her choice of wardrobe was cool, considering we were headed for the great outdoors, a simple blue blouse and short shorts. Zeke always said she looked like the actress Halle Berry in the face, except she's more brown-skinned, a cutie. I don't see it. Xica was Xica to me. The only thing I didn't dig about her new look was her blonde dye-job, something a bunch of the sisters were doing. This Marilyn Monroe thing that was happening in the Hood. L'il Kim even did the blonde bit. I let it ride, didn't say anything about it.

The ride was pretty good, humming along as we caught the main route not far from Yonkers. Xica was talking about two white folks at her job, her boss and a young girl she caught in a storage room kissing and feeling each other up. Job insurance. She said they didn't even stop when she walked in on them. According to her, they glared at her like what the fuck are you looking at, bitch.

"I walked back on out of there, didn't say shit," Xica said. "But one of them is my boss and the man has been giving me grief since the shit went down. I don't know what his problem is. Next Monday, I'm going to confront him on it, ask what's up."

"Maybe you oughta let the whole thing go, forget about it," I said, watching her suck a cold lozenge with her luscious mouth.

The scenery outside the car window meant little to me, not nearly as much as being with Xica again. Just being in her presence possessed a soothing effect on my raw nerves. Although she had a bad throat and was sucking lozenges, nothing could keep her from running her mouth despite her hoarseness. She told me about stepping with her bare foot on a thin shard of glass night before last, the gash deep and bloody. Two of her gal pals from her crew were pregnant by guys they couldn't stand.

"I wanted you, the silent outlaw," she said. "Everybody thought you were weird but cool. You had a rep and that thing that happened with your folks only added to it. You stayed to yourself. I was curious about you, what made you tick."

I laughed. "I was tripped that you wanted to be with

me. You didn't say anything at first. You just walked up and put a condom in my hand, kissed me on my cheek and walked away. Blew my mind."

"So?" Xica didn't like to beat around the bush.

"I was lonely. And hurting inside."

"Poor baby. That was why I waited until we got out of school to make my move. There was a rumor that you were hospitalized or something for awhile because nobody saw you. Bugged out."

I didn't answer that. I didn't want her to know everything about my life.

A truck horn sounded loudly to my left and the mass of steel rushed past us. Xica glanced at me nervously and I shrugged. Another truck followed the first one by cutting us off, spewing smoke and fumes in its wake.

"Speaking of reps, Xica, you have one for being pretty wild," I said, gripping the steering wheel tightly. "You ever let a dude spank you or tie you up?"

She looked at me, this time with surprise. "Hell no. I like my loving the old-fashioned way, kicking it traditional style. No whips, no chains."

"Why are you laughing?" I noticed her stifle a laugh.

"This touch thing you have. Do you jack off? Pleasure yourself?"

What a thing to ask someone. I swerved to miss a car moving up on my blind side. "No," I lied. "It's a waste of seed. Plus I don't like touching myself."

"It's no sin to pleasure yourself. Everybody does it. There are times when you're horny as shit and nobody's around, so you take care of business with a little self love. Take matters into hand, so to speak.

"Eddie, why are you so against it?"

"Once . . . twice. My Moms did . . . caught me. She

beat me on my hands with a thick belt. Whomped the hell out of me. It hurt like hell."

"And the second time?" Xica was enjoying this. She loved to get the dirt.

"And the second time . . . she held a lit cigarette on my palms. Wouldn't let me put anything on the burns either. Said touching myself wasn't healthy, would make me retarded or some shit. She really freaked out about masturbation. I don't know why."

"Your mother sounds like a trip," Xica said. "Why was she so anti-sex?"

I watched a motorcycle cop in my rear view mirror. "No, she had plenty of boyfriends . . . too many boyfriends. My Moms loved sex."

"Did she cheat a lot on your father?"

I didn't want to talk about this. "Let's switch the subject. I don't want to talk about her anymore. Alright?"

We rode in silence for a time, watching the motorcycle cop shadow a car zigzagging ahead of us. The traffic was slowing down in this stretch because of possible speed traps. I could sense Xica looking at me uncomfortably, causing me to wonder if I should not have been so forthcoming with my secrets. A lot of this private stuff has a way of coming back at you like bad food. People often use what you tell them in a moment of candor against you later for advantage.

"You used to be hooked with Zeke, right?" I asked her.

"Yeah and Raheem too. I kicked it with Raheem before I met you. And that girlie-girlie, but I don't talk about that. But Zeke ain't shit in bed. Good brotha otherwise. But lacking in the loving department. He's got all that meat between his legs and don't know what to do with it."

My eyebrows went up. "How long were you two together?"

"Three months. He's a sorry dude in the sack. No rhythm. Eddie, you were like that too, until I turned you out. I want to know something."

"What?"

"Do you love me, Eddie?"

I smiled. "Yeah, I do."

"Could you hurt me?"

"No, what kind of dumb-ass question is that?"

Xica got real quiet for three beats, thinking over something that she was not sharing with me. "Have you ever thought what it would be like if we got married?"

I smiled again, showing more teeth this time. "Yeah. But why did you ask if I would hurt you?"

Silence wrapped itself around the inside of the car like a thick shroud. Xica said nothing again, only watched me rather suspiciously.

"Come on. Tell me, Xica, what's up? What are you thinking? Why so quiet? What have you been told about me?"

She sighed quickly. "A couple of detectives came by my house three nights ago asking me questions about you. About us. About your habits. About your friends. About your social life. Everything. All kinds of shit. They acted like you were Jack the Ripper. They said they were investigating some killings of some women but you were not a suspect. I told them that wasn't you. I said you were real passive, wouldn't hurt a fly."

I shook my head and kept my eyes on the road.

"You're not involved in anything criminal, are you?"

I frowned convincingly. "No. Nothing that I know about. You know how the white boys are always trying to pin shit on someone black. Black men make the perfect suspects."

"Do you hate women, Eddie?"

It was a nutty question, completely out of left field, but I answered it. "No. I just like my women to be straight-up. Nothing slutty."

"But there were rumors that you were pretty hard on the sistas. Olivia, one of your old flames, said that you were somewhat strange when it came to sex. That you liked the rough stuff."

"Olivia's full of shit. She was a freak. Everybody thought we were the perfect couple. The girl loved her foreplay, loved to tease. Everything but penetration. No positions. Anything oral was cool with her and that included being tied up. One night, I got tired of that foolishness so I walked out of her apartment and left her strung up to her bed. Who needs that?"

Xica laughed. "You're crazy, Eddie. Anybody ever tell you that?"

"Everybody tells me I'm crazy but I could care less," I replied. "Who gives a shit about what the world thinks about me or my ideas. I live for today, now."

"Baby, you don't take care of yourself enough," Xica said.

"Sometimes I feel like my life is passing me by, like I'm just a spectator in my life. I know I won't live to get old. I know I won't see thirty. I know that."

Xica made a face. "A lot of you black guys say that. Why are you so fatalistic? I hate it when I hear you say that. Raheem used to say that all the time."

I shifted my legs. "And it came true for him. Raheem got shot over a damn coat at a party. Was in a coma for a month and died. He knew what he was talking about. You can feel it when your time is up or getting close."

A fly buzzed in through the window and landed on my arm. She swatted at it and missed. I stared at the wooded hillside, thought whether the Garden of Eden existed, whether there was a place where serenity could be found, where God was ever compassionate. The car shuddered as we turned off the main highway down a rocky access road leading into the forest. It was a park of some kind. I had no idea where we were. We drove on past the small group of cars and campers along the road farther into the bush. Xica was unnaturally silent, glancing at me as if she expected the worst. I could feel her fear.

I wish we had brought backpacks, supplies, and hiking boots so we could wander off along some mystical grassy slope, climb high ridges, and ascend the hills above the wildlife. Go into parts of the forest where nobody had ever walked. Discover lush green valleys crisscrossed with creeks and lakes. Maybe we could catch and broil some trout or bass for dinner. Sleep the night away in a tent and awake to bathe in the chilly lake water, then pour out a cup of steaming hot coffee from a thermos. Walk the morning hours off with a hike along the unmarked trails. The city boy roughing it.

"Eddie, you scare me," Xica said sullenly. "I don't think I really know you at all. You're so mysterious at times."

The road led to a larger one that took a bend near an old country store where its frail, leathery owner warned us about driving around in the wilderness without a map. I assured him that we were on a one-day trip, nothing serious. He told us in somber tones how his grandson and his girlfriend were killed during the March snows when their car skidded off the road, crashed through a railing, and plunged through the lake ice. He spooked Xica with this grim Edgar Allan Poe story but not me. It was not winter but early summer. There was no snow or ice.

"Maybe we should turn around and go back to the city," Xica suggested. "This is like one of those movies where the big guy in the ski mask stalks the college kids and kills them one by one. That old man gave me the willies."

"What an imagination!" I teased her. "Let's just hang out and have a good time."

She settled down and we bought a few things in the store: lunch meat, Ritz crackers, cheddar cheese, potato chips, two apples, two plums, a slice of watermelon, a large bottle of ginger ale, a Butterfinger candy bar, a six-pack of Bud, and a bag of roasted peanuts. I waved to the old man when we pulled off but Xica wouldn't look at him. Bad luck or something.

An hour later, we stopped the car alongside the road and saw a small lake a few feet away. Seeing the peacefulness of the spot recharged Xica and her gloomy mood passed. I enjoyed the smell of the wildflowers and the tall grass. The terrors of the city and the killings seemed so far away. We gathered up our food and a blanket from the car, walked down the sloped road to the trail leading to the lake.

I pivoted and limped toward Xica like one of the zombies from *Night Of The Living Dead*. "I'm c-o-m-i-n-g to get you, Xica," I said in a creepy Vincent Price voice.

"Stop it, Eddie, you're scaring me," she screeched.

"What's up with you?" I protested. "You act like I'm the bogeyman or some monster. Don't believe everything you hear."

We stood beside a rock pile, listening to the birds chat overhead. This glorious sunlit world. The perfect counterpoint to the tension between us. I set the bags of food and drink down, ignoring her erratic moods, and started stripping off my clothes. The shimmer of the lake looked inviting, refreshing, especially in the rising noon heat. Xica unfurled the blanket, sat down with her legs folded under her Indian style, and watched me run bare-assed to the water.

I stepped gingerly over the moss-covered stones and dove into the lake. My arms took me effortlessly out into the middle of it, dipping down into the strong current, then popping up to get a glance at her on shore. She was on her feet, walking upstream, toward a group of large granite rocks. Her back was to me. She appeared to study her reflection in the ever-widening ripples. I arched my body and went back into the depths, down, down, down. The water was not as warm as I expected. As I opened my eyes underwater, I saw Xica's beautiful form submerged, moving in effortless strokes toward me. The mythical power of water. She looked at me with her accusing eyes, her condemning eyes that quickly turned into two knives of powerful crimson light. The color of fresh blood. The rays penetrated me, sliced me open like a split melon. I felt like I was shrinking. My head was acting up. Then her well-contoured body moved away from me in a flash, her muscled legs churning mightily. Instantly, everything around me was transformed; the images became so crisp. Fish swimming past my head were suddenly arrayed in different colors, some dark blue, some bright yellow, some spotted, some striped, and some even transparent. Their spines and other bones were visible. I spun around in the water amid spirals of bubbles. I grabbed one of the fish, a yellow one, and my hand got real cold, felt almost frozen. My entire body began to vibrate as if I was shocked with a strong electric current. For a terrifying moment, I found myself upside down, totally dazed. I couldn't see the bottom of the lake despite the clarity of the water.

I emptied my head of all thought. Again there was the voice at my ear. *Look out for the bitch. She is responsible for this.* I fought down an overwhelming sense of panic. After a few seconds, I relaxed, gathered my strength and shot to the surface like a performing dolphin at Sea World. I bobbed in the water, refocusing my eyes. There in the distance, I could see Xica, her image superimposed in black against the bright green of the trees.

Later, when we were finally naked on the tender grass, skin to skin, she put her mouth to my moist cheek and whispered softly: "Eddie, make love to me, make love to me like this is the last time you'll see me." I didn't bother to absorb this. I was still reeling from the fact that her clothes were bone dry, that she said she had not gone into the water. And what about the fish? I didn't tell any of what I had seen. Yet there were tears in her soft brown eyes. She wiped at them but wouldn't tell me why they were running so eagerly down her face. Her tears angered me for some reason. But I had no power to kill her. To reap her soul.

Chapter 16

INCHES FROM
THE BONEYARD

My first thought the following morning was to find the Deacon, to go by there and let him know that I was thinking about him. He had been on my mind since my visit to Grandma Timmons's place a few weeks ago. I tried to figure out why there was such reluctance on my part to see him. Then it hit me. Going to his apartment was like going to church, complete with stacks and stacks of Bibles, holy texts of all kinds, tier upon tier of burning religious candles. He was a God freak. In between the rows of Christian and Islamic books on the various incarnations of the Divine, there was barely room for anyone to sit or sleep. There were two rooms in his place but I saw no bed or refrigerator. Just tons of Holy clutter.

He wasn't in when I first went there so I walked to the bodega on the corner and bought a tasty Cuban sandwich and a Corona beer. My seat on the bench across from his apartment building assured me of spotting the old-timer as soon as he arrived home. It was a hot and humid day. The sweat rolled down my neck along the seam of my spine, wetting the entire back of my shirt. I couldn't wait too much longer for him.

As I was about to catch the train back uptown, I spied him struggling with two large boxes. A neighbor's black chow chow sniffed eagerly at his ankle, which made me somewhat nervous. I trotted across the street, greeted him with a smile, and lifted the boxes from his hands. He patted my shoulder tenderly, a show of affection, overkill for him. The streets were empty with everyone moving in slow motion from the oppressive heat. About ninety-six in the shade, with the humidity adding another seven degrees for good measure. Nobody in his right mind would be out and about in weather like this. A lonely ice cream truck trolled down the block, its bell ringing solemnly, not one hungry youngster in sight.

"My boy Eddie, how have you been?" Deacon asked, trudging up the stairs. Each step appeared extremely labored, the march of an old, worn-out man.

"I'm cool, deluxe in fact." I trailed him with the boxes.

"How's that ornery Grandma of yours?" he asked, turning the key in the first of five locks on his apartment door.

Security was serious business to the Deacon. A crackhead had robbed him eight months ago, held him captive in his own home for days, until he tired of the surroundings and moved on to another ritzy place crosstown where he and his sidekick got busted. The Deacon refused to testify at the kid's trial, said he wanted no trouble.

My eyes blinked when I saw how empty the apartment was, no Bibles, no crosses, no candles, nothing.

Blew my mind. Desolate. I set the boxes down on the floor near the sofa and the small night table holding an ancient box radio, the old wooden Philco, waiting for the Deacon to switch on some lights. He did and motioned for me to sit down.

"Where's all of your religious stuff?" I asked in total surprise. "I don't recognize the place without it."

"It's a long story, son," he replied, pushing one of the boxes along the floor. "Things can happen to you in life that will derail you if you let it. I've had a rough year."

"Grandma told me that your woman, Betty, died." I picked up the other box and put it down in the kitchen area, four feet of reclaimed space near a sink and a new mini-refrigerator, which had been concealed behind some boxes. A new addition was the microwave oven sitting on the tiled counter below the shelves containing countless cans of tuna, salmon, mackerel, beans, peas, and creamed corn. Four boxes of Jiffy corn muffin mix, one of grits, another of oatmeal, and three packets of cherry Kool-Aid.

He reached behind the cans of vegetables and retrieved a tall bottle of bourbon. Without asking me if I wanted any, the former holy man brought out two glasses and filled them halfway. We toasted better days and kinder landlords. The drink was sheer rotgut. A legion of goosebumps immediately rose up along my cheekbones upon my second swallow and my vision dimmed somewhat. I was a punk when it came to downing cheap spirits.

"Got a girlfriend?" he asked, holding the glass like royalty.

"Part time." It was supposed to be a joke but he didn't laugh. I didn't tell him that I went to the roof of Zeke's building after our trip to the lake, twelve floors up, and thought about taking flight. Ending it. But I didn't. Instead, I went down to the park and bought a joint.

"That's bad. Man wasn't meant to be alone. We don't keep too well without a woman's touch in our lives somewhere. Lord knows, my life ain't been the same without Betty. You kinda take a woman for granted, like you both have all of the time in the world. So when she gets sick and dies on you, it's a shock that you never really get over. Know what I mean, Eddie?"

"Sure I do." Truth was that I didn't know shit about real love. Lust maybe. But not real, deep love.

The Deacon took an alkie's gulp of the burning liquid. "I never thought I would see her suffer like she did. No, life ain't fair. All the prayers in the world sometimes can't do squat to change things. The die is cast and that's that. I remember when Betty got the cancer diagnosis, the death sentence, the damned stomach-turning chemotherapy, our last vacation to Tampa, her times at home in the old house in the hospital bed we kept in the study, the final hours, and the funeral. I remember it all, every damn bit of it."

Grief is a bitch. I could see he was still in pain from her loss. If I expected a light, easy visit, all bets were off now. He was in the bottle now and the hurt was boiling up to the surface.

"Got a cigarette?" he asked. Another surprise. He never smoked. Lectured me all the time on the dangers of the killer weed.

I fished in my shirt pocket. No, fresh out. He got to his feet and slowly shuffled to the nightstand where he pulled out a drawer containing a carton of Camels. Saying that life had been kicking his ass lately was an understatement. You could see it in his body language, the way he carried himself, still tall but stooped.

There was something frail in his movements. A slight tremble in his wrinkled, gnarled hands. Even his once-strong, deep baritone voice seemed drained of its power and vitality.

"Ever think about joining the service?" he asked. "A black man can do himself proud these days in the army or navy. Couldn't do that back in my day. You could go to school and learn a trade while you're in there. Computers, electronics, something like that."

"I don't follow orders too tough," I answered.

"What about going to college?"

"Maybe some day. I'm still young. I've got time, plenty of time." I sipped the bourbon, its searing heat igniting my windpipe and stomach.

"You got to get ready for old age," Deacon said matter-of-factly. "Got to get ready for the time when you get sick and feeble. Can't count on nobody when that happens. Look at me. My kids are nowhere to be found. No calls or letters. Look at what happened to Betty. She was bedridden for the last six months, skinny as a matchstick, in constant pain. Endured three bone narrow operations, then the damn IV feedings at the end. Oh, it was horrible. And one of the kids only came to see her once."

"Didn't she have some family here in the city?"

He turned the glass up and drained the last of the bourbon, then poured some more. "That's what pissed me off, the way her family ran for the hills. We all knew she didn't have long because the doctors told me she wouldn't leave the hospital. The cancer was that advanced. It was just eating her up. I asked her family point-blank if they were going to chip in to support her in her last few months. They backed off. A lot of people

can't deal with bad news well. They tune out everything
that doesn't have a smile attached to it."

"So nobody helped out?" I gulped a little of the drink
down to keep pace.

"A good friend flew in twice from Seattle but most of
the time I was it," he said sadly. "Betty deserved better.
When she was in the hospital, I stayed in the room with
her, sleeping in a chair for days and weeks. I stayed with
her because that's what real love is. I was there in the
dreadful midnight hours when she was afraid to close
her eyes for fear of not waking up. I listened to her talk
for hours about her fears, dreams, and feelings. Everything. She talked sometimes like she was trying to get
everything out before her heart gave out. I didn't ignore
her like the rest of her people, who pretended as if nothing important was happening. They were content to let
her die alone. The greatest sin a loved one or a family
member can do is to let someone they love die alone.
Nobody should die alone."

"That's a heavy situation to go through for someone
not helping," I said, intentionally not thinking of the
lives I had ended. Somehow Betty's death seemed more
real to me, maybe because of the Deacon and his feeling for her. I knew her and she was a great lady. Faithful
to the Deacon to the end. The others that I had killed
meant little or nothing to me because there was no connection.

"Everybody left her but me," he said proudly.

"Did you love her?" I watched his face over the glass.

"Lord yes, I knew this woman for over forty years and
loved her for more than thirty years but never told of my
feelings until the day she died," Deacon said. "One late
night, we sat in the hospital, waiting to get a bedpan
dumped, she touched my hand and asked if I had

brought some liquor she asked for. I had refused her request for a time because I didn't know how those pills she was taking would react to the liquor. I didn't know if they would mix."

"You guys got drunk in the room." I laughed.

"Sure did, she was a church woman and had never tasted good bonded liquor, never drank in her life, so I got her some. We sat there and got tore down, as my nephew likes to say. She'd laugh and drink some more, laugh some and drink some. That bottle went fast. Afterwards, we sat there and watched the snow fall out- side. It was a beautiful moment. I'll never forget it."

"Did you tell her you loved her?" I asked.

"A pain hit her bad and she held out her hand and stroked my cheek," he said, his voice low and struggling to retain its potency. "Her pretty little fingers squeezed my hand as jolt after jolt of suffering coursed through her body. Although she was one sick woman, she looked fine as Lena Horne in her middle years. My impulse was to snatch her up from that death bed, hold her close in my arms, confess my love, and kiss her. But that was not what happened."

"Did you tell her or not?"

"When my wife died, I never thought I would ever love another woman like that," he said, looking off at some dis- tant corner of the room. "I whispered to her that I loved her. She acted as if I never said it. Maybe she knew, maybe she always knew how much I cared for her."

"Did she ever tell you she loved you?"

"No, not in so many words. Betty was scared and bitter near the end. She felt that God had forsaken her. I told her no. God may test us but He won't abandon us. I believe that."

I tried to keep from smirking. "What happened to all

your religious stuff then if you believe that? Did you have a crisis of faith?"

"Crisis of faith? Where you hear that said?"

"Grandma Timmons calls it that. Those times when we doubt God's will. I have them a lot. It seems like life is always kicking my butt."

"Yes, I had my crisis when some of her family suddenly appeared out of nowhere at the hospital at the end," Deacon went on. "They had been busy searching through her things trying to find out how much money and property she had in her name. Her husband, surprisingly, wasn't a part of it. The vultures came to the hospital once in a group, only once, and that was to sign a form to order doctors not to bring her back if her heart stopped. It was a form to let her die. I don't think they even went up on the floor where her room was."

"People can be cold-blooded," I said. "You should give me the addresses and let me visit them."

"Don't be a fool," he said. "You wouldn't do anything but get your crazy self in trouble. Betty was upset when a nurse slipped up and told her what they had done. She kept clinging to life after that, suffering pain I wouldn't wish on nobody. I prayed for her to die. The night she passed, I told her: 'You don't have to stay around here. You've done your work. Go to God, baby, go on.'"

"Do you think we come back to earth as someone else?" I asked.

"Reincarnation. I don't believe we do."

"But you believe in God and Heaven, don't you?"

He took another long swig of the bourbon and laughed sourly. I could tell he was blasted. It was like his soul was aflame and he was using the alcohol to put out the fire. He needed a lot of it to do the job.

"There just has to be God or we're all fucked," he

muttered. "Excuse my French. But I think you get my drift."

That shut me up for awhile. I stared at my glass and drank as much as I could get down. Bourbon straight is serious drinking.

"What are you doing with your life, Eddie?" he asked finally.

"Yeah, I'm making my mark," I smiled. "I'm keeping busy."

"Doing what?" He was shaking the bottle, almost empty.

"Looking for work. Staying out of the Congressman's way. He's all over the place like a virus."

"Eddie, he's a power-mad colored boy and there's nothing worse. A bad nigger. I'd stay out of his way. I'm old. I've seen his kind before. He should be proud of you. Instead of holding you back, he should be lifting you up."

He held the whiskey bottle up and looked at it. Empty. I saw his hand go into his pants pocket and come out with nothing.

"Flat broke," Deacon slurred. "Another three days until my pension check arrives. That little piece of change don't stretch worth a damn here in New York."

I went into my wallet, opening it to check my folding money. Dead presidents on paper. The old-timer reached over and took the wallet from me, checking out a small photo of my butchered parents. It was my only picture of them together, taken on an Easter Sunday at Coney Island. The rickety roller coaster ride was in the background.

"Your mama wasn't a bad looking woman," the former holy man said, taking two fives from the wallet. "Never did like your father. Reminded me of a mongoose or a ferret in the face. I'll give you back the ten when I get my check. Thank you kindly."

Before I stashed the wallet, I glanced a last time at my folks there at the beach. All hugged up, with not a care in the world. Grinning like lovebirds. The picture doesn't show the dark bruise under my Mom's right eye or her split lip where he punched her out the night before. She had come home, wiped out on pills and booze, smelling like a truck driver. He lost it and whupped her up. The trip to Coney Island was his way of saying he was sorry, that he would never strike her again. Which was a big lie.

"Want some red Kool-Aid?" the Deacon asked me but I was ready to leave. I was starting to feel nuts. I wanted to reap.

"No, thank you," I said, shaking his hand. He didn't look well. His skin was a sad washed-out color and there was room in his pants for another person. Very thin.

He stood there in his apartment of bare walls and thanked me for coming to see him. I could tell it meant a lot to him. Being the Southern gentleman that he was, he apologized for going down Memory Lane with the Betty business and her death. He leaned away from me, already feeling the loneliness that would swallow him up as soon as I left. Old and alone.

"Are you alright?" I asked, seeing him sag from the inside out.

"Yes, Eddie." He stood tall as if he was a soldier on inspection.

Right then I found myself doing something that I never do with anyone. I hugged him, held him against me for a minute. He didn't resist. I didn't look him in the face after that. With the deed done, I quickly turned, let myself out, never looking back.

Chapter 17

COUNTERPRODUCTIVE

The detectives hauled me in to the precinct two days later. They came to my job and escorted me out to an unmarked car, one walking on each side of me. The ride there was uneventful, with nobody saying anything. They were polite enough not to handcuff me, but I was left sitting outside the interrogation room for hours. I think that was another scheme to try and wear me down. With my eyes closed, I imagined I was somewhere else, anywhere but in a police station. That didn't stop me from listening to what was going on in the office next to me. As Pops said, pay attention.

Two officers were talking to a homicide detective about my murders, filling him in on new developments and leads. The tall uniformed cop told the suit that two nutcases had confessed to the killings over the weekend, but nobody took them seriously. Both confessions had been recorded, dissected, and neither really checked out. All of them concluded that the killer was still out there.

"Charley, who are we waiting for?" one cop, a stocky guy, asked.

"Bradley, he wants to talk to this kid we got outside," the detective replied. "He went with Sarge out to Rikers on some business and should have been back by now. What did the ME say about the last broad, the one they found over by the Henry Hudson?"

The other cop, almost chubby, read from a paper in his hand. "She was worked over with a knife, lacerations of varying depths, real clean cuts but not too deep. Plus she has three blunt force wounds on the head, depressed skull fractures. Bruises on the arms, shoulders, and legs. Signs of a real struggle. No sign of forced vaginal or anal entry."

"Any incriminating forensic evidence?" the detective asked.

"None at all," Chubby answered. "No hair or no blood evidence. No semen, no fibers, no prints. Nada."

"This prick may be a psycho but he's a pro," the detective said. "He knows what he's doing. No clues. Nothing left behind to implicate him. I can't figure out how he gets these chicks to go with him. If I was a dame and there was some nut out there killing women, the last thing I'd do is go off with some guy I knew nothing about."

"But you know a good line of gab," Chubby said. "Maybe this maniac's a real smooth talker. Who knows. What's with this black kid again outside?"

The detective replied that Bradley thought I knew something about the Harlem killings, that I was a possible suspect. I waited for more than an hour before this Bradley dude showed up, walking in like he was a black John Wayne, all full of himself. He called me into his office. The other detective and Chubby sat in with him as he questioned me. None of the others seemed to know the real deal except Bradley.

"You're Edward Stevens, right?" Bradley said. "I hope

you don't mind if we have these guys join us for our little chat. Thanks for coming in on such short notice."

"Did I have a choice? Your guys strong-armed me from my job. Snatched me up like some criminal. So what's this all about?"

"What were you doing last Friday night?" Detective Bradley started with the questions, his voice firm but still friendly. "Can you account for your movements that evening?"

"I was out walking, getting some air."

"Did anyone see you during your walk?"

"Nobody but you cops. I paid them no mind."

"My men lost sight of you for several hours. Where did you go? Don't bullshit us."

I made sure that my voice was very calm before I answered. "I took a walk through Central Park, just chilling out. I got tired of being cooped up in the house so I went out. Is there something wrong with that?"

"Did you go anywhere after your walk?"

"I beg your pardon. I didn't get the question."

"Where did you go after that, your walk in the park? Don't play dumb. Don't lie to us."

My throat went dry. I swallowed and locked stares with the detective. "I don't remember."

"We know you didn't return to your apartment before two in the morning. We had a car stationed outside your building. The lights in your apartment went on about two A.M. Where were you?"

I shrugged. "I don't recall."

The detective leaned closer and narrowed his eyes. "Mr. Stevens, we believe you're somehow involved in the series of murders of young women in this area. You're our prime suspect."

I smiled sheepishly. "I don't know where you get that

from. What evidence do you have linking me to these killings? I haven't killed anybody. What do you want me to do, lie about my actions? I don't recall where I went. And that's that."

"Do you often walk in the park?" Bradley asked.

"Once or twice a week. Whenever the mood strikes me. I like trees and grass. I like the wildlife."

"Do you have a girlfriend? Someone you date."

"Why should that matter to you? Why ask me when you already know that I do. Your guys have already talked to her, asking her a bunch of dumb-ass questions, putting stupid ideas in her head. Why don't you leave me and my friends alone?"

"What's her name again?" He ignored my plea.

"I don't recall." I replied and smiled.

He switched up on me, took a friendlier approach. "Oh. You want a cigarette, a soft drink or something?"

I frowned. "No, thanks. I'm cool."

"Do you own a gun?" he asked after a few seconds. It was quite obvious that I wasn't going to break down and confess. Nor was I going to say anything that would trip me up.

"No, I don't own a gun. Why would I need one?"

His look changed to a very intense one, very accusatory. "Young man, why are you so belligerent, so angry? Are you one of those hardcore black boys who feel the world has done him wrong? Huh, you can tell me. You're among friends here."

His buddies laughed and waited for me to reply. When I didn't, he looked at them and they stopped grinning. I was cold as ice. I gave them nothing.

"Sure. Does your father know you're a killer, that you butcher women? What would he say if he found out?"

"Go to hell." I shifted in my seat and gave them a look

that said I was bored with this stupid grilling. These punk-ass questions.

"Watch your mouth. Have you ever thought what this will do to him when you're arrested for what you've done? And you will be arrested. We will get you for these killings. It's just a matter of time."

I said nothing, just sat there, watching them watch me.

"Eddie, can I call you Eddie?" The detective lit a cigarette and waited until I nodded. "Eddie, we know all about your real father, big shot slum dope dealer, and your mother, his partner in crime. A real Bonnie and Clyde team. They crossed somebody, maybe one of their suppliers, and got whacked. And your little sisters too. We know all about that."

"Your point?"

"Eddie, did you know I knew your father? Even arrested him once. A common thug. A real piece of shit. You remind me of him. It doesn't matter who adopted you. You're still scum, just like your old man."

"Is that all?"

"Well, the apple doesn't fall far from the fucking tree," Chubby chimed in.

I laughed. "Another asshole adds his two cents. Who gives a shit what you think, Porky?"

The detective, who was sitting to my left and hadn't said anything, slapped me real quick and hard across the face. I didn't flinch. I mumbled, police brutality, under my breath. I tried to act tough but what he said about Pops hurt. Hurt me deep inside.

"Damn you bastards." I looked away at the wall, my eyes starting to fill with tears.

"Eddie, you know we'll get you," this Bradley dude said,

talking to me like a pal. "You're not so damn smart. You'll slip up and then we'll lock your ass up for life."

"Can I leave now?" I stood and wiped away a tear with the heel of my hand.

Bradley and the other cops talked for a moment among themselves until my interrogator nodded and stood as well. He walked with me to the door, patted me on the shoulder, and repeated what he'd said about me slipping up and getting caught. I glared at him. Asshole. Then he did something real strange. He shook my hand. Whassup with that? I wiped my contaminated hand against my pants, letting him know that I was no fool. As I turned to walk out, I saw two detectives, the same guys from the weekend, getting into a car. My police shadow. With all of their eyes on me, I walked away, swinging my arms and whistling the theme song of the TV show, "Moesha."

Once at home, I looked out my windows and the bastards were still camped there. I was totally pissed. Considering that I had not slept for four straight days, I was incredibly cool at the police station but it took everything out of me. I struggled against the voices urging me to go to the streets to kill, to reap another wicked soul.

I sat in front of the TV for the next few days. I got fired from my job. My boss said he didn't want any troublemakers working for him. I didn't eat anything for all that time, no bath, no shut-eye, no nothing. I watched some detective discuss the discovery of the bodies in a small geographic area on the news, said there have been no eyewitnesses to the killings, so they lacked a physical description of the madman. His word, madman.

According to him, patrols have been beefed up throughout the black community with the sole purpose of identifying and apprehending the killer. He admitted there had been a delay in concentrating the full resources of the police department on the case although black women were disappearing regularly and being murdered. He added that the killer was cunning but a dogged investigation would nab him.

"This fiend, this monster, will be caught and punished to the full extent of the law," the cop said in answer to claims that police were still dragging their feet on the case because the victims were black.

With that statement, I switched off the set. I was extremely restless, pent up, and the impulse was on me. Despite the police shadow, I got out through an alley and drove past the main thoroughfare in midtown Manhattan where the hookers gathered, stopping cars with a flash of tit and thigh, offering their services at discount rates. The street was full of them, hot flesh for rent. I tried to see if any of them fit my requirements for the next victim. If any of them possessed the glow, the amber light, then and only then could I move, pouncing like an owl out of the skies on a rabbit.

So now I was sitting in a late night diner on Eleventh Avenue, waiting for some food and watching the night whores through the window. The waitress, a saucy Polish number, returned with my order of a jumbo cheeseburger, fries, cole slaw, and a Coke. It was after eleven at night and I shouldn't be eating this late. Everything was piled dangerously on one plate. I smiled at her before she turned to walk away, then splashed a clump of ketchup on the fries. There were about five people in the place. Between chews, I glanced out the windows at the feminine shadows marching up and down on the pavement.

The waitress, a blonde with a nice build, stopped at

my table again and asked if there was anything else I wanted. I smiled and she stiffened. I wanted to yell at her, hell yes, but you wouldn't give it to me, Miss Vanilla. Instead, I shook my head.

Feeling pretty shitty, I speared a few fries and went over in my head how I was a loser with the girls. A baby step from being queer. Every dude in my Hood had a baby or two and I had nothing to tally on my list. Too damned respectable. The Black American male at his lowest. They teased me about it all the time. Got to start making headway with the women. No Xica. No sex. Probably that was why I had zits so bad, my cheeks covered with them. If I had a good piece of ass, they would go away. I just know they would. I chomped on the burger, thinking how damned my life was, and finished the last of the fries. Distracted now by the drama outside, I washed it all down with the Coke and burped.

"Love your braids," the waitress said, leaning over the table. She was scribbling out the check.

"Dreads." I dug my hair. It was cool. Rasta-style.

"Yeah . . . they're nice . . . or rather different. I see a lot of young black guys have them now. I didn't like them at first but they grow on you." She collected my plate and eating utensils, her soft blue eyes locked on my hair.

One of the things that had been worrying me lately was that I had been spacing out in my head anywhere at any time. I could be driving on the Hudson or the FDR and suddenly these pictures, images would just flood into my mind. Crazy things. My eyes would be open but you see shit happening that you know is not real. I've been reading up on this stuff. Could be just another reason why I should be back in the loony bin. Seeing things that don't exist. Anyway, I sat there at the diner counter, staring off into a corner of the place and saw myself waking up in a dark room but my body was still stretched out on the bed. The sight of this stunned me at first yet my curiosity compelled me to touch this other self. My sleeping self. I passed my hand right through the sleeping form. Cut right through it like a hot knife through butter. As I pulled my hand out, I got this strange sensation as though my fingers were jammed into dry, hot sand. Same texture. A waking dream of some sort.

"Are you okay?" the waitress asked, her face much too close to mine. "You're just staring into space. I was going to shake you but I thought better of it. You're not sick, are you?"

"No, I'm good," I answered, coming out of the trance. "I was thinking about something and forgot where I was."

She laughed, showing a dimple. "Wish I could forget where I was. Don't get off until four."

After I paid off the check, I walked on the avenue, the noise of the sex trade and the raunchy smells around me, and was immediately surprised by the number of cars driving by. It seemed every man in the city was out tonight, trying to get some. Joe Trick with weekend money to spend. Eleventh Avenue was packed with cars, horny guys, teenybopper onlookers, sailors, Japanese tourists, stop-and-shop girls, and macaroni pimps. I looked across the street to where I had my car and sighed when I saw it was still there.

I was so caught up in everything that I didn't see the knock-out Latin girl who walked up behind me. A hot salsa queen with an overripe body, juicy lips and hips, and a blonde dye-job like vintage Madonna from her Material Girl phase. All of this Latina beauty stuffed

into a tiny white dress. I looked closer, the body was
sheer heaven. She looked like she could cripple a man
in bed. My hormones were subdividing and splitting
wildly as I watched her strut back and forth, parading
for the men in the cars. God, I wanted her.

It was only a matter of time before she noticed me.
"Hey sweetheart, you wanna go out?" The Latina, who
smelled of some exotic perfume, smiled a gap-toothed
smile at me.

My big moment had come and I was speechless. I
didn't know what to say. Words fled from my head. I
didn't make it a habit of speaking to whores, usually
I just killed them. She caught me off-guard so I stam-
mered while I watched the swell of her plump breasts
rise and fall in the lamplight. She wore the tightest
white dress I'd ever seen. You could see the bulge of her
sex through the fabric. I wondered if she had on any
panties underneath. Close up, her face looked hard and
tough. She had been around awhile. A vet.

"Well . . . I . . . I." Damn, there was no tongue in my
mouth.

She looked at me and laughed. "Come on, make up
your mind, lover. I won't bite you. I'm disease free. And
I promise you the time of your life."

I decided to play it slick. Like the man of the world I
was. "I . . . I . . . I don't know. I'm just cooling out."

Whores have the attention spans of gnats. A car honked
at her and she bent over to give its balding driver a better
view of her sensational ass. Two youngbloods, walking past,
whistled in appreciation. The Latina turned back to me. "It's
the heat, brings them all out. They're riding around all night
with their dicks in their hands. Want to spend that hot nine-
to-five cash on some new *chucha*. So baby, what are you

going to do? I can't wait around all night for you to make up your mind."

Never spend money on whores. Never buy pussy. My mottos. The thought of spending any part of the sixty bucks in my pants pocket for this slightly used piece of ass turned my stomach at first. Yes, but when was the last time I really got laid, a dynamite fuck? Don't forget a rubber, diseases.

"I don't know if you're worth it," I said, fronting.

"How old are you?" she asked, squinting up her eyes.

"Old enough to fuck," I snapped.

I was pissed that age was suddenly in the picture. Couldn't do anything in this life without worrying about how old somebody was. Do you have proper ID? Are you legal age? But I could fight and die for this country. Right? I couldn't wait for my next birthday, the big two-one, so I could do whatever the fuck I wanted. Wonder what it felt like to be thirty or forty. Must be a trip. Nobody would be able to tell me shit then.

The Latina snickered and unbuttoned the top of her dress to show me more breast. "You don't like me? You don't like what you see? I'm sure we can find something to do that would be fun for both of us."

About then, I looked over her shoulder at the woman who was stepping out of a shining vintage Jaguar, a bronze goddess. When did whores get this pretty? My eyes almost bugged out. She was beyond lovely. More than those supermodels Iman and Tyra Banks combined. Or Naomi Campbell. Or even my fave, Halle Berry. This woman was perfection dipped in a nut brown chocolate. What the hell was she doing out here, selling herself?

The Latina noticed what I was looking at and backed away. No competition. She was mad as hell. "If you want that slut, you're welcome to her, fuck you," she yelled at me. She stormed off toward the Lincoln Tunnel to get some of the incoming New Jersey trade. Honking cars, traffic tie-ups, screeches, rants, and bad air from the exhausts. The Avenue was getting crazier as the night wore on. But this one woman, this marvelous image of flesh . . . oh man! I watched her wiggle her ass as she walked down the block. I followed her at a distance, watching, wishing, hoping. What in the hell would I say to a woman like that?

She crossed the street, walking against traffic, and the cars seemed to part magically to let her pass.

Determined not to let her get away, I ran across the street, keeping her in sight, narrowly being missed by distracted drivers. I must get this woman before anyone else does. She is mine. Once at the car, I fumbled with my keys, my hands unsteady with anticipation, and they almost fell into an open sewer grating. I finally made it after two nervous tries, started the car, and did a quick U-turn to get to her.

Gunning the engine, I whipped the car around, barely missing two cabs and a whore flashing her naked body under a long coat at a man in a pickup truck. Another car full of rowdies, wannabe gangstas, tried to get to my woman first but I cut them off. As I was winding down the window on the passenger side to shout at her, a thin, wiry brother, with his long hair in jheri curls, walked through the chorus line of pretty whores to the woman of my dreams. The hair style totally dated. He was dressed in an expensive gray suit, Italian, possibly Armani, very well tailored. He whispered something in her ear, yanked her by the arm, then slapped her so hard that she went down on all fours. The other girls backed away, like a herd of antelope passively watching

the killing of one of their own by a hungry lion. They
wanted no part of this trouble.

You could hear the menace in the pimp's voice:
"Bitch, more work, less chatter. I want a full trap
tonight. No excuses. I want a full share. And remember
this, bitch, you turn rabbit on me and I'll fuck you up so
bad that your mama won't know your sorry ass. You
work for nobody but me. Got it, slut?"

The woman mumbled something from her sprawl on
the pavement. But Iceberg Slim was not finished. He
leaned down and slapped her again, backhand, her face
snapping around in a blur. She shrieked but didn't cry.

He stomped her once for good measure before strut-
ting off. What happened next made no sense. I could
have been killed, shot or some shit, but I wasn't thinking. Before I knew it, I opened the car door and jumped
out. The other girls, shocked but not surprised by the
ass-whipping, were already gathered around their fallen
sister. I pushed my way through them, knelt beside her
and whispered to her that everything would be alright.

The sound of footsteps on the cement stopped before
my face. It was the pimp. "Get the fuck away from her.
Unless you got cash money to hire her out." The girls
scattered like startled crows at the sound of a loud gunshot. I stood up and hit him in the face before he could
catch a breath. He swung at me, a wild right, which I
slid under and pounded him in the belly. The pimp
reached for a pocket in his jacket, fumbling for something, but I caught him under the jaw with an uppercut
and he went down on his side. I kicked him in the nuts
twice. He balled up and retched at the curb. I kicked
him again, in the face this time. To mark it, to bruise it.
He moaned and flipped over.

One of the girls screamed for me to stop beating him.

The pimp lay there in a lump groaning, one entire side of his face puffed up and bleeding. My hand slipped inside his jacket and removed the gun, tossing it to the street where one of the young hood rats quickly retrieved it. I stood over the pimp. He lifted his battered head, groggy, his hands pressed between his legs, comforting his aching crotch. In his eyes, I could see him wondering who the hell I was and why I had whipped his ass.

I walked back to the beauty and dropped to one knee beside her again. Once she was standing, I got a tissue from my shirt pocket and dabbed at a line of blood dripping from her nose. Sir Galahad. She smiled sweetly at me as I asked her if she was alright again. The other girls cheered and clapped. Hail the conquering hero. One hollered that I was a real man, a true black man.

The beauty whispered breathlessly that her girlfriends liked me and I could get anything I wanted. Her features seemed foreign like she was part Egyptian or Arab or something. She kept rubbing her face where the pimp hit her. Her face was framed with a riot of wild black hair to match her fierce eyes. Her curves were slamming. Pear curves. Great skin coloring, the richness of brown toffee or caramel.

"What's your name, oh sweet prince?" she asked, a cute smile.

"Marco," I answered, telling the first of several lies I would tell that evening.

"You don't look like a Marco." She gave me that look, the bedroom look.

"But I am," I replied, walking to my car. I didn't want to kill her anymore. The world would be a better place with her in it. She had potential. Maybe she would walk away from selling herself. I couldn't see myself choking the life from someone so lovely, despite the strong urge to harvest stirring within me. To kill. God was with her this night. I took a bow to more applause and shouts from the girls, got in my ride and went on about my business into the quiet night.

Chapter 18

HYMNS OF DARKNESS

I was curled up on the floor in an apartment of a woman I had just killed. It was late, around two in the morning. Her blood was all over me. The TV was on, with a re-run of Oprah asking some man why he refused to end his harassment of his ex-wife, who was now married to someone else. In the bluish-white glow of the screen, the body of the woman seemed as if she was still alive, her eyes were open and her face very pale. For an instant, just an instant, I wondered what her life must have been like before I stepped into it. It was a passing thought but it made me think of other things while I lay there on the wood floor amid the sweet blood smell.

For months, I've tried to understand why I do the things I do. I don't hate women, I truly believe that. In most of my relationships with them, I've spent much of my time trying to prove to them that I'm worthy of their love. I bend over backwards for them, buying them things, taking them places, spending money like you wouldn't believe. But they play me. Play me like a chump. They hurt me, torment me, humiliate me, and punish me. And still I remain. Usually I stay and take it all without complaining.

Somewhere along the way this blood began, the killings. Even I don't know the why of it. But I can't switch it off.

I decide their fate, the women. I am the judge and jury. For once, I have control. Sometimes I pass women on dark streets, in deserted subway tunnels, at quiet bus stops in the middle of the night, women alone in situations where I could easily overpower and kill them without much resistance. But I do not. The prey escapes for another day. Wonder if God gives me points for these moments of mercy? Hell, I don't understand the entire process of thinking that allows me to do this. Look, the women aren't real to me, in a sense. They're types, images, symbols, much like the sexy photos of them in the magazines, but never really human. I wonder how many men feel like I do.

While killing one of them, I look into their eyes and see the fear and dread, yet it doesn't register for some reason. At that moment, nothing matters anyway. The anger and rage I feel overrules everything else. The bitch must die. Something goes off in my head and the knife sinks into flesh or the hands tighten around the throat until the eyes roll back in the head and the life is gone.

If they plead for help or beg, I tune them out. I refuse to let them become flesh and blood. *Human*. If that happens, I cannot finish what I've set out to do. I cannot kill. No guilt, no remorse. I never torture them. I don't cut off body parts and save them as souvenirs. In fact, I try to make it quick, professional, efficient. I'm not Ted Bundy or Jeffrey Dahmer or John Gacy. I'm not that crazy.

The goal is to kill without getting caught, without going to jail. Some things I never do. One rule is that I never ride around with a body in my car. The cops stop black men all the time for no reason. Can't chance that. With this kind of thing, you make sure that the body can be left where the killing took place unless the situation does not allow that. No danger of screwing up.

You are nervous and excited before a kill. Often you have to calm yourself so you don't make mistakes. Being too eager is bad business. You've got to think of everything and leave nothing that will lead them back to you. When it is done, there is a very pleasing sense of calm, of detachment that is almost sexual in how it penetrates your body.

I stood up and walked over to where she was sprawled on the sofa. The knife was there as well, near her lifeless left arm. She didn't mind me unbuttoning her blouse so I could sneak a look at her breasts and hers were very large, capable of filling both hands. I didn't touch them, just looked and imagined how many men had been with her before me and what they might have done with her. I won't do anything sexual with this one, maybe just put two fingers in her down there to see what she feels like. But maybe not.

For the most part, I want to be held, to be told they love me, even if there is a knife at their throat. Most women will say anything to save their lives. Most of them say it very sincerely with real tears in their eyes. It touches my heart. Then I kill them.

"Do you love me, baby?" I asked the dead female on the sofa and then imagined her answer. There was still some warmth and tenderness in her lifeless eyes. Nobody could hear her reply but me. It was yes.

Chapter 19

FOR YOUR OWN GOOD

One of the real torments of my life was never getting a chance to talk to the Congressman alone, without the advisors, aides, spokesmen, and bodyguards present. There was always someone in the room with him. My other disappointment was never having the opportunity to interrogate his third wife, Margaret Taylor-Stevens, good ole stepmom, about who he really was. The man was a puzzle. He worked hard to remain a mystery to me and to most people who lived and worked around him.

His passion was politics. His hobby was keeping his family in an uproar. Events lacked any real meaning unless a tension existed and the potential for a blowup, cruel words exchanged. Of the pair, Margaret, who left a career as a fashion model to marry the baby kisser, really intrigued me more than he did. She proved to be a deep thinker, charming, generous with compliments, and pleasant.

Courtesy limited my visits to their new country home on the Hudson, their first major step toward retirement and life after Washington. The place was stunning, a pompous style statement: a Mediterranean villa fronting on the river, high ceilings, arched doorways, three baths, six bedrooms, eat-in kitchen, two working fireplaces, wrap-around porch, pool, and tennis court. A couple of steps from the house were four acres of open woodland, giving the location an outdoorsy feel that the couple enjoyed.

I always wondered if the property was purchased with campaign money, party favors, and gifts from the faithful. Politicians are crooked and he was no exception.

Life was full of surprises. Margaret, without warning, turned up on my doorstep late one Friday afternoon. I had no idea how she found me. As usual, she was dressed simply but with great taste. I took note of her dark blue pinstriped coatdress, sleeveless, buttons down the front. Light fabric. One of her Dior originals. The sandals on her feet gave her just enough of a casual look to put me at ease. She held a wrapped dozen of cut red roses under one arm and her purse under the other, stepping in before me.

A glance at her face revealed she wanted to talk about something that had bothered her for some time.

"How are you today?" I asked, coming back into the cramped living space of the tiny studio apartment with a vase. I was house-sitting for a friend, a trumpeter, who was touring with Latin percussionist Ray Barretto in Europe. He would be gone for another five weeks.

My stepmother, Marg, was so beautiful. She had a circle face, with wide-set brown eyes and a sensual mouth, and a gymnast's lithe body. I felt sorry for her, the fate of a pol's wife, his faithful companion during the thick and thin of a rigorous campaign. The Congressman seemed under siege on many fronts, ground-sea-air, like the frozen Nazi army meeting the mad offensive of ragtag Russian troops. The only indication of her hard times was the abundance of dark rings and puffiness under her lovely eyes and the lack of spark in her body movements.

"When I was little, I played with my dolls and imagined what it was going to be like to have children, to be a wife and mother," Marg said, sitting down slowly on the black leather couch that pulled out into a bed. She paused, reached into her purse for a cigarette, and lit it in one fluid motion. I loved to watch her move, like a graceful ballerina.

In this light, her face appeared a bit haggard, her eyes sat deep in the hollows of the sockets. Something was worrying her. I was surprised at how quickly she made herself at home with an ease that comes from having money and supreme self-confidence. I could tell this was not a casual visit.

"A mother?" I said to her as I went back to get two glasses of iced tea. It was still summer and the heat, with the humidity, fried everything in its path.

"I wanted lots of children, lots, and then I didn't have any," Marg said, sipping the cold liquid. "Couldn't have any, something was wrong with my uterus. When I thought about being a mother, I knew it would be wonderful to have a baby who would love me unconditionally, who would adore me in a way a husband never could. I lived for the moment when my baby would say: 'I love you, Mommy'."

How female, her regrets. I could hear the low hum of the air conditioner underneath the gentle rhythms of her words. The media onslaught was kicking her ass, wearing her down with each new revelation about her man's money woes, botched career, opposition within his own party, and love life.

"None of that happened, the diaper changing, the wiping up of spilled juice, the holding them after scary dreams," she said solemnly, letting the smoke issue from both nostrils like a mythical dragon. "But then you came into our lives and nothing was the same."

"Did you like me?" I asked. "I could never tell."

"Eddie, you were so shy, so quiet when you came to live with us. You made us a family. I spent a lot of time with you but Dad was always busy with his political life. I resented that Washington crap because it kept him away from us."

I hated to hear her call the Congressman "Dad," her pet name for the shyster. Somehow the nickname gave their relationship this shady edge, this hint of kink, this sinister chord of pseudo-incest. I told her that once but she still used it when she spoke of him.

"I tried to be flexible, schedule my activities around the needs of a young boy on the verge of puberty, and set up quality family time for all of us, but Dad was always busy," she said.

I bummed a cigarette from her, which she handed over reluctantly. She said I should stop smoking while my lungs were still pure. Whatever that meant. From Mrs. Chimney herself. I can't remember a time when I saw her without a cigarette in her hand or mouth. A true nicotine addict.

"The Congressman's too moody, too uptight, too hyper," I said. "I usually kept my distance if he seemed strange."

"Why didn't you treat him like he was your father?" she asked. "He wanted that so badly. He really did."

I protested immediately. "Because the punk wasn't

my father. My father's dead. Also, he never acted as if wanted anything to do with me."

"When you ran away at fourteen, he was so worried about you," she said, noticing the countless sheets of music on a stand in a corner of the room. The zillion plants. "It hurt him deeply."

She smiled and lit another cigarette. Nerves. "I kept waiting for you to call or come home. But you didn't. You were convinced that you were an adult, a grown-up able to make your own decisions. Living in that abandoned building with those people. Dad said you were trying to sort things out in your head and needed space. He wouldn't let me lift a finger to help you."

"Yeah, when I got busted, he wanted me sent away, tried as an adult. Like a hardcore thug. They were going to let me go but he kept insisting that I get sent to Spofford in the Bronx. Said it would teach me a lesson. Said I needed tough love."

"I know, I know," she said quietly. "I'm so sorry about that."

In my head, I was trying to figure out what was really going on with her, with them. It wasn't the campaign finance ruckus, the illegal soft money, because it would take more than that to bring the Congressman down. Problems like that are handled quickly and effortlessly with promises and handshakes in a backroom somewhere and they disappear like a puff of steam. No, this was something else. The crisis was rooted in another region of their life, something personal, straining a part of their marriage where the public could finally see the damage.

"I know Dad fools around, has his little affairs, but this scandalous business in the Washington papers is unnecessary," Marg finally explained, her voice dropping in volume to a raspy whisper. "His handlers say I must label them as unfounded and outrageous allegations. I must say that this woman and her lawyers are pursuing this matter for financial and political gains because my husband is vulnerable in this election year."

"Sorta like this girl popping up with this phony Daddy claim against Bill Cosby just after his son was killed. Timing," I chuckled. "Political blackmail. Everything's timing."

"It might not be blackmail," she said. "It might be true."

Silence. She picked at a thread unraveling on her dress, not really preoccupied. I watched her closely, this aging cutie, as she stabbed the cigarette out in the ashtray at her elbow.

"Do you know the woman?" I asked.

"No, Eddie, thankfully I don't." Her face tightened with anger.

"Doesn't he know how much this kind of thing hurts you?"

"Sure, but that doesn't stop him. He doesn't think before he does these dumb things. He forgets he has enemies, enemies who would go to great lengths to bring him to ruin."

"And the tabloids love this scandal mess. Sells copies."

She laughed sourly. "People will say and do anything when money is involved. Some of the details of this supposed affair are being leaked to the press by the very people who work for him. He knows this, yet he doesn't let it stop him from chasing skirts."

"What an idiot!" I sighed. "He only thinks of himself."

"One of these parasites says he drove my husband to the woman's apartment and waited outside until the horrid business was finished. His advisers want him to go before the press, much like Clinton did in 1992, and deny the whole thing. I would stand next to him like the devoted wife, like Hillary did, and show my support. Remember Clinton sitting there before the cameras, looking repentant, not really denying sleeping with other women. What did he say? Do you recall?"

I scratched my head. "I don't remember."

There were bitter tears in her beautiful brown eyes. "This woman, whoever she is, is saying they had a thing that lasted fifteen years on and off. She was seeing him even before you came to live with us, back when I miscarried that first time. *Hard Copy* has been calling me for two days offering me obscene sums of money to get me to betray him. But I won't."

"Why is this woman doing this?"

"A guy who does security work for Dad says she told one of her slutty friends that she was going to bring him to his knees, bring the uppity nigger down. How could he be so stupid?"

"Is the woman a hottie? Is she cute at least?"

"A what?"

"A hottie. Hot, pretty, cute. You think this woman played him? Ran a game on him?"

She inhaled some smoke. "I don't know. I've never seen a picture of her but I'm sure she must have something going for her. I know his taste. He does not waste his time on women who look average or common."

I felt sorry for her. "So what happens next?"

"Dad says he won't acknowledge her lies publicly, says he'll ignore her and she'll go away, which is crazy. She wants either money or a Guess Jeans commercial. I told him that's a mistake. Look what happened to Gary Hart, Wilbur Mills, and Bob Packwood. This is a fire that must be put out as quickly as possible. You don't ignore something like this."

We smoked silently for a time. She looked around the room some more, taking in the large number of CDs on twin vertical racks across from her and the cage with the gray parakeet in it. Feeding the feathered bastard was my sworn duty and a part of my fee. Her eyes stopped on the large poster of Tito Puente, the master Latin musician hammering away on the congas with a big-breasted Hispanic girl dancing lustily in a trance before him, her skirt rising high above her shapely brown thighs.

She swallowed more of her tea, closed her eyes and talked in spurts. "I explained last night to Dad that he is putting himself out on a limb. He has alienated himself from his fellow Democrats with his constant support of the Republican agenda, from his hard anti-pro-choice rhetoric to his attacks on affirmative action. The people in the Black Caucus won't have anything to do with him. He's isolating himself."

"I don't talk to him about anything having to do with race or politics," I said wryly. "He's the whitest black man I know."

"He won't listen to me," she moaned. "I told him the Republicans want to turn the clock back on black people, to rebuild the old social barriers that held us in place for so long. He says the Republicans are honest at least about their intentions and don't give a damn about what anybody thinks."

"Right. The Grand Old Party of Lincoln. They hate niggers."

"Please Eddie, I hate that foul word. Use another one to describe us, alright? We deserve better. He doesn't realize it but he's playing into the hands of his enemies. So I really ticked him by quoting Honest Abe."

She asked me if I could turn up the air a notch, the

heat was getting to her. I did and the room soon cooled somewhat.

She closed her eyes and recalled the words. "Lincoln said: 'The legitimate object of government is to do for the community of people whatever they need to have done, but cannot do at all, or cannot do so well in their separate and individual capacities.' When I recited these words, he poured himself a drink of scotch and walked away. God, he hates to be wrong."

"You got that right," I exclaimed.

Another sip. "You know what he values above everything else in the world?"

"No, I don't."

"A letter from former Republican senator Ed Brooke, mailed to him just before he ran for Congress that first time in 1986. He handles that letter like it is the blessed Magna Carta or the Holy Grail. It's wrapped in plastic. I see him reading it at least twice a month."

"Is he nuts! What does the letter say? Do you know?"

She shook her head, her hair moving ever so slightly. "No, he's never let me touch it. I've no idea what it says."

Marg winked at me and chuckled wickedly. "I'll tell you something no one knows about Dad. Mr. Skirt Chaser. This was one for the books. Don't ever tell him that I told you this. When he was around your age, a young buck, he was involved in a four-car crash in Boston, which left one man crippled. The police, listen to this, found Dad and some woman, both drunk and naked from the waist down, in the wreckage."

"What happened?"

"Somehow a leg or knee hit the gear shift while they were having sex in the front seat and the car went flying out into traffic on a busy intersection." She laughed. "It smashed into two other cars and another car crashed into them. His father, Mr. Big Shot himself, went up there, spread some cash around and got the whole business swept under the rug."

I covered my mouth with my hand and howled with laughter. "That's wild. The Congressman is really off the hook, totally out. If you look at him, you'd never think he'd do something nutty like that."

"Yes, looks are deceiving. I guess there is a part of me loves that he's a rascal. The ultimate bad boy."

Both of us laughed. My eyes drifted to the vase of red roses, their colorful radiance warming the room, illuminated in fading afternoon sunlight. I thought of the meals served in our large dining room, the lightly starched tablecloths, gleaming silverware, spotless china, at the place on the Hudson, and the vase of red roses. Always red roses.

She commented that she smelled the aroma of baked goods fresh from the oven, and I informed her that there was an Italian bakery on the first floor, which sent the sometimes annoying fragrance of cooling breads and pastry throughout the building.

"Eddie, do you think I was a good mother?" she asked, looking me directly in the eyes. "Tell the truth."

I hated questions like this. "You weren't a bad Mom. Sometimes I thought you tried too hard, worked too hard at it. It didn't seem natural for you in a way. Nurturing a kid looked like a chore for you."

"I just did what I saw my mother do." She became quiet, then continued. "Adopting you saved our marriage, saved me in a sense, because we were drifting apart before you came along. Yes, children can be an adhesive for a family in most cases."

"He didn't act like that," I said. He reminded me of my real Moms.

"I remember when we went out to the agency to get you," she recalled. "We walked through these mammoth, windowless rooms, and all of them were filled to capacity with children, needy and abandoned children, most of them black or Spanish. The place smelled of a strong pine cleaner, an odor that clung to my clothes afterwards. As the children saw us coming through with our escort, they ran to us, grabbing us, touching our clothes, our hands, our faces. That moved me to tears. Dad gave me a look. All of them pleaded for us to take them home, but not you. No, you were this lanky, thin boy with the most haunting eyes, just sitting in a corner by yourself drawing stick figures on a sheet of paper."

"So what did you do?" I had heard this story time and time again.

"I came over to you and hugged you and you stiffened like I was going to hit you," she said.

"I guess I was still in shock from the murders," I said, trying to keep the bloody pictures from entering my mind. My dead family strewn throughout the house, butchered and full of blood.

"Well, the agency got you ready to leave, horrible clothes, shirt sleeves too long and high water pants, and we walked you out," she recalled. "The press and cameras were there in mass, in full force, and you kept your head down and stayed close to me. That publicity was Dad's doing. We brought you home and you didn't speak for months, didn't want to be held or pampered. Didn't trust us one bit. Sometimes I hate to say this, I wondered back then if we made a mistake in taking you out of that place. You were such a strange little spirit."

Marg loved the past whereas I had no use for it. The

past was the reason for the deformity of my soul, the nesting place of my demons and the cause for my bloody obsession. Fuck the past. Fuck the present too.

"What are you going to do about this other woman business?" I asked with a shaky voice.

She suddenly stood and walked to a window looking down on Amsterdam, a Korean grocery store, a hardware store, and a laundromat. "I gave him an ultimatum. Stop sleeping around or I walk. I don't like abuse."

In that instant, I felt her tears although she was turned away from me. An urge to go over and hold her came and went like a swift exhale of air. She stood still, sobbing, trying to hold back the waves of pain and grief as any cultured woman would. Public displays of emotion are taboo among the upper crust.

"The rotten bastard, the dirty rotten bastard," she muttered under her breath.

I leaned back in my chair, wanting another cigarette in the worst way. "What does he say about all of this?"

"Dad tried to deny it at first, but he has a history of doing this shit, excuse my language," she replied, still at the window with her back to me. "When the photos of him with these various tramps turned up in the tabloids and even in legitimate newspapers, he denied it all. He told me that the photos were doctored, the stories fabricated, the intent malicious. Later during our vacation in Capri, he says his view of love was European, which meant you can sleep with whoever want as long as you remain faithful to home and hearth. Flings were just that. Think continental, he says."

The Congressman was a bastard and I had known this from the very first time I saw him. Him and his Adam Clayton Powell rap. He wasn't fit to wipe his idol's toilet seat. Power corrupts.

"There was a period when I almost lost my mind," she continued. "He moved into an apartment down in Chelsea with one of the mayor's press secretaries, a tall redheaded bitch with silicone tits, facelift, the works. One night I was tired of him not being with me. I was so lonely. You were gone, the house was empty, my friends were on the Island, so I called the number of his love nest. He answered the phone, recognized my voice, cursed me out, and hung up. We didn't talk for months."

"You should have left his ass then, right then."

"No, I couldn't," she murmured. "I tried. But I made him pay for what he had done. We made up only after three months of long stemmed roses, endless wining and dining, a priceless Harry Winston diamond brooch, and a simply gorgeous Halston gown. He begged and pleaded to come back. It was relentless. He would not give up so I took him back."

"Why can't you leave the bastard?" She was so mad that I could get away with some name-calling. I hated the fool.

"I don't know if I can. You become accustomed to a certain way of life, the parties, the power, the perks. It would be hard for me to adjust to a regular life, an existence without him. We've lived through a lot of things together, important things, and despite all of this hurrah, we're still best friends. Sometimes we talk so candidly, so openly, that I think it can't get any better than this."

I leaned forward, looking at the abundant curves barely concealed by her dress. "Like we're doing now."

"Yes, like we're doing now," she said, then paused. "Eddie, for a long time, I was frightened of you. There was a part of you that I could never reach, a part of you that you let no one see or know. A dark side."

"I know why you say that," I replied. "I think I know. But what are you talking about exactly? Is that day in the bathroom . . . when I was fourteen?"

"I don't remember," she said, her trembling voice giving her away.

"Yes, you do. I saw you in the bathroom . . . naked."

Marg turned from the window to face me, her face a severe mask. "Now I remember . . . the day in the bathroom. I didn't like the way you looked at me. You should have seen your eyes, so piercing, so full of lust. Like a young wolf watching prey. It was scary. You just stood there, staring and staring. It gave me the creeps."

"And you slapped me," I said. "Hard across the face."

"I'm sorry but you had stepped over the line. I didn't like that look, so predatory."

Predatory. She would never know how much I lusted after her, my hormones running amok. That image of her standing near the sink, dripping wet, her body all curves. The total bomb. I relieved myself sexually many a night using her image, holding a stolen T-shirt of hers, complete with sweat and perfume, to my nose. Often I thought I would wear her out if I got the chance.

"See, you're giving me that same look," she laughed. "What's on your mind, boy? Let's go for a walk and get some air. I have to get home to the Central Park apartment before too long. We're entertaining the Liberian ambassador and his entourage tonight."

We walked along Amsterdam, going south past the projects, mixing in with the crowd. A bus passed at the corner of the 145th Street, spewing black smoke, as it jockeyed for position in the thick traffic. The pavement made a hollow sound under our feet. I kept thinking of that day in the bathroom, her body, the dark triangle of curly black hair between her soft brown thighs. My stepmother. My stepmother.

She touched my arm gently, smiled and stepped out into the street. "Eddie, I've got to go. If I'm not there to supervise the preparations, Gabriella will mess it up for sure. Come and see us sometime. Don't be a stranger."

"What are you going to do about the Congressman?"

"Stick by him. He said the other night that he'll make this woman problem go away, one way or another. I don't know what that means but I hope he doesn't dig an even deeper hole for himself. Still, I'm not the kind of woman who runs when things get tough."

"If he dumps you?" I asked.

"He won't. He needs me too much for his political career."

Then Marg asked me to give her a hug, which I did. While I pondered why she had come uptown to see me, I tried to search her face for an answer but there was none there. Maybe she just wanted to talk. I held her tight, body to body, and looked over her shoulder at cars moving on the street. She smelled so nice. That day in the bathroom. The beads of water on her marvelous brown body. We stayed that way for a long moment, then we parted. She smiled queerly, one eyebrow rising in a curious expression. A gypsy cab pulled up, jerking to a stop, and then she was gone. I looked down at myself and noticed I was aroused. Damn. Busted.

Chapter 20

PUSH DOWN AND TURN

A postcard from Xica was in the mailbox several days after I saw the Deacon, three sentences in red ink on the flipside of the two splendid black dancers, a male and a female, in artful embrace from the Alvin Ailey Dance Troupe.

Enjoyed our day together. Worried about your head and the way it punishes you. Our love is shaky but it can survive this madness.

Fondly, X

I read the damned thing over twice before tearing it up. Love can screw with your mind. Xica figured I was in a rut and couldn't change. That is the problem with us as a race. We don't believe in change. Change is good. What black people have forgotten is that nothing remains constant. Life runs hot and cold.

Often I thought of Xica. I even followed her sometimes. I watched her at her gym as she sat in a yoga position reading a book on karma or child-rearing or one of her women's magazines. The first stirrings of desire were always there, undiluted, pure. I visualized her under her clothes, her fantastic breasts, her great legs, the small scar in the curve of her back, the curly tuft of black pubic hair between her legs. Lust, a key ingredient of love, was still there, where the sexual part of the love was yet burning bright. That part was dead between us.

But Xica would hurt me if given half a chance. That was just her way. Lust was still standing. Lust was happening because I was denied pleasure with her for a long time. Without Xica to satisfy me, my mind played tricks with me, my mind rearranged reality. I walked in the streets like a zombie drunk with wanting the touch of soft flesh.

It was a terrifying hunger. Sometime I walked behind a woman wearing a thin summer dress on a hot day. Bare legs. The lines of her panties visible through the sheer cloth. The press of the fragile dress suddenly against the swell of her butt. The perfume of her feminine sweat. Wonderful.

I love Xica. Maybe I won't love again. Maybe after this is over, I will never feel anything like this. But I don't trust Xica. Often I don't like who she is. Often I do not understand how she can treat me so. But I never doubt I love her. Whenever I got closer to unraveling the riddle of her, she eluded me, always one step ahead of me. Often it was hell to love her. What a bitch! It feels like we break up every other week, fight, bicker, and then we're back together again.

But then if I didn't have Xica in my life, I would have to settle for someone less intriguing and stimulating. Xica was never boring. Maybe Xica had never loved me but I wanted her anyway. Stupid, huh? Still, I won't let her mess me over. I won't let her play me like a fool. A chump. She told me everything was cool with us then the next thing I know it's real frosty. Just like a female.

Later, Zeke told me he saw Xica with a new man, another one after the Spanish guy, a white man. A man taller and bigger than me. A white man with a red battered face and big hands. Zeke warned me that Xica was bored with the sameness of our sex life, with the routine and wanted to stretch out and try new things. That was what she told him.

Regardless of how much I told myself that I didn't need her, I found myself calling and calling her. Begging her to take me back. But now the tables have turned. She said she had moved on. She said she gave me a chance to get back with her and I blew it. So I turned punk and pleaded with her for another chance. Later, I would think back to how I begged her like a fool to take me back after she broke my heart with someone else. I was a chump and knew it.

See, it was the damning self-talk that fucked me up. The black man talk that says he wasn't shit. Unworthy. My mind spoke to me in a soothing cadence, calming like a parent's baby talk, with the most threatening words: *You worthless nigger . . . you know nobody wants your ass . . . why don't you do all of us a favor and kill yourself . . . if you died who would miss your ugly ass? . . . Nobody loves a loser and that's what you are . . . you're just taking space on earth . . .* The accusing chatter went on and on, sometimes for days. I sat there on the bed covering my ears, trying to shut out the torrent of self-hating thoughts I think so often. I know I am sane. I know I am sane. I know I am sane.

I waited for the words to return but they did not. My legs folded under me twice on the way to the bathroom, as weak as a puppy's legs. I lay on the tiled floor, shivering again, teeth chattering. It was then I knew I had lost my mind. No doctor could cure this.

Finally I got up, gathered my power to venture outside. It was the call from the musician that did it, he was coming on Friday. Probably the reason I went to the concert of African drummers was out of a need to break out of a pattern of going nowhere. The days and nights resembled one another, cookie-cutter similarity, rendered dull by their sameness. I walked into a small church across the street from Washington Square Park down in Greenwich Village, plopped on a pew in the back of the holy place. It was the first time I saw Xica since our outing.

A small white man with a startled expression on his face introduced the troupe of African drummers, all coming from someplace in Gambia, to the crowd of tourists and world music fanatics. Six very dark men in remarkably colored native garb talked among themselves in soft voices as they stood in front of the long wooden drums. Once the music began with its energetic rhythms, I was quickly transported to another life, a tropical world of heat and sensuality, a mental space far from my self-imposed monkish existence.

Two Gambian women danced wildly to the mysterious beats and accents of the percussion, authentic traditional movement of erotic dips, bends and twirls that went beyond anything I'd ever seen on Soul Train or at any house party. I was totally hypnotized by them. The men beat the drums so fiercely that two assistants stepped forward between numbers to mop the sweat from the musicians' glistening foreheads. I imagined that this was the closest I would ever get to the ancestral villages of Senegal or Gambia.

"I'd like to thank everyone for coming out in this horrible heat to experience such wonderful music," the small white host said to the audience which was already standing and exiting through the large doors. "Remember that the music of the Mandinka, which you heard tonight, has been performed in West Africa predating recorded history. It is a living, organic music that is constantly changing with new variations appearing continually. We also would like to thank master drummer Mamadou Ky of Gambia, for bringing his Mandinka drum troupe of the National Ballet of Senegal to our humble church for tonight's marvelous event. Good night and get home safely."

As I stood near the door on my way out, Xica came down the aisle, walking with two girlfriends, all dressed in pseudo-African clothing. A brother, a refugee from Wall Street, tried to hit on her, leaning over between the two sisters to whisper something in her ear that was annoying. The church was emptying out in the darkness. She turned from the distraction, laughed with the girls, then flashed a purely exquisite smile, all teeth. Odd, puzzling, but inviting. What did it mean? I was too stunned to say anything so I watched her walk elegantly out into the heat.

Another three weeks passed before I saw her again, not a minute too soon because I was obsessing on having let her get away. The next time we ran into each other was at an exhibition of war photographer Susan Meiselas, her work in El Salvador and Nicaragua, at a gallery in midtown. It still seemed like the dog days of summer but the sun's heat was beginning to wane. She was alone and walking very fast, pushing her way through the mob. I thought she saw me at first, because she turned and looked in my direction for a moment before disappearing into the crowd.

Somehow she vanished in that room because I zig-zagged through the people several times, looking for her to no avail. I gave up and decided to take in the rows of color photographs of life amid revolution. I knew Meiselas's photographs from different magazines the Congressman kept in his neighborhood office, which I occasionally visited whenever I needed to put the touch on him for cash. The El Salvador photos were gripping to say the least, each one a testament to Meiselas's courage and the heroism of the people caught on film. Two white handprints marking the door of a man slain by the death squads. A bored private security guard with an automatic weapon outside the home of a rich family. Bloodstains marking the spot where a student was killed while handing out anti-government leaflets. A row of coffins containing dead students forming a somber line in a town square. Soldiers digging up the bodies of three slain American nuns buried in an unmarked grave. Totally real.

On the other side, I walked before the war photos taken in Nicaragua, stopping before the image of two bloodied children taken from a house hit by a 1,000-pound bomb. Someone's hand can be seen touching the chest of one of the shorties, comforting him. The card under the terrifying shot said both kids died shortly after the picture was snapped. For some reason, I was com-pletely overwhelmed by the photo, the slaughter of the innocents sacrificed by war. Wasted life. This was during a time when I did not view death as I did later. A cure for the corrupt and tainted. A method to prune out emotionally diseased women.

Xica walked up to me while I was talking to a man

about the traditional Indian dance masks worn by the rebels to conceal their identities during combat. Or rather he was explaining to me why the rebels chose to wear the disguises.

"At the African drum concert a few weeks ago, the Mandinka drummers . . . ," I said quietly. "I wanted to talk to you but you seemed to be busy with these other clowns. Especially with that business guy that tried to hit on you."

"They don't bother me," she said. "They're a nuisance."

"Why did you smile at me?" I asked. "You just smiled mysteriously and vanished. Why did you do that?"

"You didn't answer my card," she replied. "We need to talk."

"My head is not up to it." I was getting mad again.

"Well, when will your head be up for it?"

"Soon. Maybe we'll have a coffee or something and chat." I didn't want to be eager. After all, I was the wronged party.

She smiled again, that same oblique smile. "I don't drink coffee, but a tea or hot chocolate would be great."

See, I understood Xica was just being polite. She loved screwing with my head. The truth of the matter was that she wouldn't answer my calls or notes. Is this how we were supposed to end? Did she hate me so much? What did I do to deserve this kind of treatment? Was I supposed to crawl back to her begging for another chance?

If there was any doubt as to the unpredictability of women, it occurred eight days after the photo gallery incident and Xica called me out of the blue, saying she was no longer mad at me. We really needed to talk about things, about us, about our future. No games. No lies. A straight-up, nitty-gritty tête-à-tête. She said she had been thinking of me a lot and felt the need to set the record straight before too much time passed. I asked when this royal audience would be granted and she answered in a few days. Wisely, I didn't press the issue and let her call the shots.

Later, I received a command to meet her at a jazz club in the Village, a place called Visiones, down the street from the higher-priced Blue Note. As a club, it was more into the college crowd, the bohemian element, the spill-over Soho refugees seeking some cool sounds on a hot night. When I arrived, Xica was already there at the bat wearing a low-cut dress that could break up any happy home, drawing a small herd of horny males to her. She was tossing back drinks, straight scotch, in a way that I'd not seen before.

"Don't you agree, Mr. Stevens?" she asked me as I walked up.

"About what, your Highness?" I played along with her game before ordering a beer, a chilled Heineken.

The crowd in the joint was the usual for a weekend night: a pair of NYU sweeties taking a break from the books; some Navy types on a short liberty; a handful of jazz buffs slumming because they were unable to get into the ever-crowded Knitting Factory; three old codgers looking for young coed nookie; a couple of tables with Japanese tourists; and the ring of drunks and randy bar-flies on the make. I don't come down here much. This was only my second time to the club, but Xica hit all of the nightspots, jazz or otherwise. The Luna Lounge. African dance nights at the Marc Ballroom. Clit Club. Jackie 60. The Tunnel. Club Broadway. The Cooler. Anything, any time, anywhere.

She was totally getting messed up on the drinks. The conversations around us blended into one high-pitched roar like a jet engine, making it damn difficult to talk. You couldn't hear anything said. A couple at a far table began arguing about some financial misdemeanors, money spent on recreation rather than bills, and the consequences. The club's management tolerated the swirl of white noise because the band was still setting up and the cash register was working overtime.

"There was no one else," Xica was saying, waving her glass in the air. "Thelonious Sphere Monk. When you say his name, there's nothing else to say."

I thought of the many times she had gone off into this Monk routine, her jazz patron saint of the odd note, the twisted clusters of jagged melodies. Every room in her apartment was blessed with a photo of Monk: Monk backstage at the Village Vanguard chatting with Baroness Nica; Monk with Trane on the bandstand at the Five Spot; Monk performing in a Chinese beanie alongside Charlie Rouse in Paris; Monk kissing his baby son; Monk in a beret outside Minton's; and Monk laughing with Bird and Dizzy. Her place was a damn shrine to the man.

"How did you get turned on to Monk?" one of her admirers asked. The other white boys leaned closer to hear her answer.

"My father was into jazz when I was coming up," she said. "He had everything Monk had ever put out, either solo or otherwise. Every time the man played anywhere near New York, my father was there, sitting as close to the stage as possible so he could see the musician's feet. He had this thing about the way Monk moved his feet when he played. Monk would also dance as he played and my father really dug that. Monk would rock and sway or spin in a circle while someone soloed in the band. When Monk died in 1982, my father went to the tribute they gave for him at St. Peter's Church on Lexington Avenue, joining the other mourners. He told me the story of it over and over, with the same kind of joy that he'd put in the tale of how he met my mother at Macy's. It was magical and I never forgot it."

Another member of her court asked if her father ever met Monk in person for a one-on-one encounter, face-to-face. She sighed, took a long sip of her drink and recalled how her father ran into the musician in his old San Juan Hill neighborhood back in the old days before it was carved up block by block for the monstrosity of Lincoln Center. A lot of poor black and Hispanic people lost their homes so that white folks could listen to opera and that dry-ass classical music. Supposedly her old man walked up and greeted Monk warmly. I'd heard the story several times during my long, frustrating courtship of Xica. Monk, hatless but with shades, was going to a nearby grocery store, walking slowly, but he did not ignore her father.

"I love your music, Mr. Monk, there's nothing like it," her father said. "I'm a big fan."

"Thank you, thank you. I'm glad to hear you say that you dig it." Monk kept walking, keeping time to that special beat in his head.

"I saw you at the Five Spot every night you were there," her father said. "Coltrane and you put on quite a show back then. What are you doing these days?"

"Living, for the most part," Monk answered, suddenly changing direction. Her father was left, standing at the intersection, watching the cranky musician shuffling through the crowd on the other side of the street. Faked out by Monk.

Xica finished her Monk story, gulped the remainder of her drink, and bent down to look into her purse, permitting the restless horde to peer down the dress at her cleavage. The boys loved that. I was getting angrier by the second, feeling the barbs of jealousy pierce my cool front, and the need to act out was becoming stronger. The boys laughed nervously at her show of flesh and she murmured lewdly, teasing one of them, putting her pretty face close to his.

"Oh I love Monk, he makes me so hot," she moaned sensually. "Do you fellas love Monk too?"

They nodded their heads like the good little sheep that they were, each so eager to please, each praying that he would be the chosen to see Her Highness home to the royal bed. I did not want to create any problems, but I resented the woman I loved playing the role of a bitch to a packed house. She was obviously getting her kicks by tormenting these white boys, the horny Joe College types who would love a piece of hot chocolate.

"I think my man here is getting upset," she said, adding that catty Eartha Kitt thing to her voice. "Are you upset, sweetheart?"

"No, I'm not upset. But I think, Xica, that you've had enough to drink. Otherwise, you're going to be sick and you don't need that. Come on, don't drink anymore."

"Oh dear, Daddy's mad at Baby," she reached out and patted my thigh softly. "Don't be mad. We're just out to have . . . to have a good time. I worked hard all week and tonight I want some fun. Eddie, you're becoming a bore. You mope around all the time. You never smile anymore and everything is so serious with you. You need to lighten up. Chill the hell out."

"Talking to you is like talking to a brick wall," I snapped, getting up. "I'll talk to you tomorrow. Don't hurt yourself."

I felt utterly betrayed. Now, of all times, when I

needed her, she was unavailable to me. I hated her for it, at the same time I still longed for her with a passion that was as strong as my growing hate for her. I was her boy toy, a thing she played with and tossed away without the slightest afterthought. Tonight, I felt the sensation of being detached from her, apart from her power, her evil ability to twist my emotions to her will.

Still, on the train headed uptown, she dominated my mind, held her grip upon my thoughts and would not let go. Later, I found myself standing outside her apartment in the cold of night, thinking of her there with the white boys in the bar, thinking of her betrayal, thinking of her dead.

She arrived several hours later, struggling to get out of the cab, staggering like a wounded soldier toward the front door of her building. Unsteady from drink, she fished around in her purse for her key, pulled it out and dropped it twice upon the ground. I had to laugh. Not because the scene was funny, but because it occurred to me then how easy it would be for me to take her lousy life, to kill her as I had done the others. Another dead bitch. Snap her neck like a twig. Stab her twice in the chest. Put a plastic cleaners' bag over her head and twist it about her throat. All of this came to me, this jumble of warped thoughts, while I picked up her key and used it to open the door. Stunned by my sudden appearance out of the darkness, she stared with wonder at me as I slipped an arm around her and helped her to navigate the stairs. Her legs did not want to cooperate but we made it to her door and into her apartment. I flicked on the light and laid her across the bed.

"You're mad at me because of what happened at the bar, right?" Xica mumbled from her sprawl on the bed.

". . . just having fun . . . fun . . . fun . . . meant nothing by it . . . let's kiss and make up."

I ignored her. "Want some aspirin?"

"No, I want to talk. We need to talk. We never talk anymore. Eddie, I'm growing emotionally. I want to try new things, learn new things, not just do the same shit over and over. You don't want to grow. You're content to stay in the same damn rut you've been in as long as I've known you. You live in your head. That's where you live and that's what is fucking killing you."

"Oh really now?" I replied sarcastically. She only cursed when she was drunk. And pissed off.

"Eddie, you killed what we had," she said, pushing herself against the bed's headboard. "What we once had was hot and passionate but now it's gone sour and cold. You've become like the rest of the men who come on to me with a lot of promises and don't deliver shit. They wouldn't know a loving relationship if it bit them on the ass."

"How much did you have to drink after I left?" I asked, sitting on a stool across from her.

"Don't do this, Eddie. Hear me out. I'm not that drunk that I don't know what I'm saying. It's men like you that make women hate the word, love. At first, you act like you're so emotionally open, then you end up giving nothing of yourself. Ask you to put up or shut up, and you run like a scared little boy. All of you guys do that. Why, Eddie? Huh?"

"I don't know what the hell you're talking about," I said. "Are you on your period or something?"

"That's exactly what I'm talking about," she shot back. "You'll do anything to not have to deal with yourself. You do the same thing with your life. Run, run, run. One day, Eddie, you'll have to stop running and all the stuff you've been ducking and dodging will catch up with you. And it won't be pretty."

I shook my head and looked at two Monk photos over her head: one of Monk at the piano as a French freedom fighter with a machine gun slung over his shoulder and a bound Nazi behind him; and the other one—the famous black-and-white W. Eugene Smith shot of Monk puffing a cigarette. Monk at low ebb. Make no mistake about it. I didn't understand anything she was saying, the words or their purpose. She was trying to make me mad; she wanted me to kill her. Why else would she be saying these things? Bitch, bitch, bitch. Why couldn't she just let things be as they were? Why didn't women just let things alone? Always shaking things up. Always putting shit in the game.

"It was wonderful being in love with you at first, but now I don't know how I feel about you, Eddie," she said out of nowhere. "You don't let me in. I try to love you and you fight me. What am I supposed to do with that?"

"Stop bitching so much. Let's have fun like we used to."

She rubbed her bloodshot eyes and tried to sit up straight. "It's not that simple. It takes all of my strength to stay away from you. I can't take your bull anymore. I can't take your sex hang-ups. I've got to cut you loose."

"So you want to dump me, huh? Who's the new nigger? The new stud waiting in the wings. Huh?"

Her gaze went to the ceiling and stayed there for awhile. When she spoke again, it was with the type of voice reserved for retarded kids, hard-of-hearing old folks, and puppies. And this only made me madder, more determined to hurt her in some way, to shut her up.

"There is no one else," she said in that patronizing voice. "If I do fall in love again, it will be with someone who loves me more than I love him. That way I won't get hurt as much. No man is ever going to put his boot on my neck again, ever."

"I've never treated you bad, Xica, never," I said. "You must be thinking of some of these guys you're kicking it with. I've been real cool with you."

Suddenly she shouted at me. "No . . . no . . . no, Eddie, you ain't cool. You hide out all the damn time. Either you're playing the hermit and don't want to do shit with me or you disappear and nobody knows where you are for days at a time. What's up with that?"

"I got business to tend to, so I go off and do my thing. But I always come back to you, right?"

"I'm not going to end up like my mother did," she said sadly, now looking directly at me, fire in both eyes.

"What are you talking about now, woman?"

"Not like my mother," she repeated in shorthand. "Guys like you, Eddie, are what makes me think marriage is overrated. I want a partner, a soulmate, an equal, not a damn child. You remind me of my father. My mother served him hand and foot, ironed his socks, washed his stinking underwear, even cut up his meat on his plate. My mother did all that and raised all five of us, spent her life in bondage. He handled the money, gave her a small allowance for food and stuff, and church. When my father died, she didn't know how to write a check. She was lost without him."

"And what does that have to do with me?" I asked, confused to hell with her tirade. She was ranting like that white boy Dennis Miller on TV, just running off at the mouth and not making any sense.

"For me to keep wanting a man, he's got to treat me

good all the time, not just at bedside, otherwise I walk. Eddie, you were romantic and exciting when we first met. Then you changed. And so have I. It's not that great. It's no longer enough. I don't feel emotionally satisfied. You don't understand that."

"You just want to get rid of me, don't you?"

"Yes, I do."

"Fuck you." I wasn't going to listen to much more of this. It was giving me a headache, stupid bitch shit, more anti-man garbage. All females do is talk. Talk bullshit.

"Imagine how better things would be if you opened up and talked to me when we had problems between us," she said calmly. "The way it is now, I do all the work. It's like pulling teeth. If I bring up anything heavy, you withdraw, mope, brood, and don't say anything so nothing gets solved. That drives me crazy."

"Well, that's not true. Some of this is just your opinion."

"Eddie, I'm sick of you shutting me out and shutting down. I can't handle that anymore. Maybe you're just stunted emotionally and don't know any better."

I leered at her. Stunted, my ass. The longer I lived, the more I realized men knew so very little about women or their needs.

But she wasn't finished with me. "One other thing, Eddie, is how I feel with you now. You oppress me. With other people I'm outgoing and fun-loving, but when you come around, I get all quiet and go inside myself because of what you might say. You are always flirting or showing off if I try to have fun."

"What about your sexy routine with the boys tonight?"

"Fun, just having fun, just feeling wild and free," she

replied. "I used to feel that way all the time. Don't you ever feel that way, Eddie?"

"No, never." I mumbled it.

"What's wrong with you, Eddie? You've been weird for months now. Nothing I do seems to have any effect on you. I can't take this, baby. I can't take it anymore. Talk to me please."

I felt so alone then, like she wasn't even there. "X, maybe I can't love anymore. Maybe everything inside me is dead."

She talked too much. Even drunk. She didn't hear what I was trying to tell her. When or if the cops caught me or killed me, I could imagine her telling them or reporters that he just didn't seem like the kind of guy who would kill women. Not my Eddie. Not my stupid, simple little Eddie. He didn't say much but he wasn't a killer. Bullshit. Bitch never knew who I was. Or am. Most people do that, fix up an image of a person in their heads and never once go beyond that. Then boom, surprise. The person does some off-the-wall thing, kills somebody or rapes a young girl, and instantly everybody is scratching their heads in shock.

The ingredients for the horrible crime were always there, waiting to be stirred, waiting to come together in some fucked-up formula so the whole thing could mix, fester, and explode.

Suddenly I felt tired, drained, and curled up on the couch, smelling her perfume, her woman smell, my sweat, and the aroma of her favorite incense, Egyptian musk, that scent which saturated everything in her apartment. She kept on talking, yakking and yakking. Her chatter sounded so far away as if it was in another room or on the street below. Sleep took me in its lovely arms, held me tight and I did not resist.

Chapter 21

REGARDLESS OF
HOW WELL WE PERFORM

A week after the Xica run-in, I promised myself that
I would be on my best behavior, no more killings, no
more late night running around. No more, no more anything. Still a promise is just that, a promise, and what
the will attempted to impose can easily become over-
ruled by demons. This much I knew.

One night I heard footsteps in the apartment or maybe it
was outside the door or rather in the hallway. I believed it
sounded like a man's step, heavy and menacing, and my
heart stopped and I couldn't get my breath. Panic seized me
in a way I had never known before. I searched the apartment and there was no one or nothing there, and when I
yanked the door open, it was the same thing. Nothing.
Nobody.

Finally the woman in the apartment across the hall
looked out. She seemed startled by my presence,
the fact that there was someone up and about this time
of the night. The look on my face prompted her to force

a smile, somewhat reassuring her but not calming or comforting. I didn't want to talk to her but she was determined to strike up a conversation, so I humored her.

"Did you see anyone in the hall?" I asked in a shaky voice.

"No, nobody, just you," she said as she was about to close the door.

I didn't sleep at all that night, for I kept hearing things, footsteps and voices. Sounds. Morning could not arrive soon enough.

Two nights later, another strange thing happened. I came into the apartment from shopping, both hands full, and an odd, chilling breeze blew over my face. On the couch in the living room sat two women, or something resembling women, full female forms, blue in color, covered in stab wounds. Their stench almost made me puke. I don't know how much time I spent staring at them. I could not move or take my stare from them. Hallucinations. Tricks of the mind.

"You know what you are doing is wrong, you know that," one of them said in a voice devoid of life. The voice of the dead.

The other stretched out, waving her arms. "Why did you kill us? We didn't deserve this, to have our lives snatched so cruelly. No one deserves this. Why kill someone you don't even know? Why?"

While the women spoke, I felt something beyond fear and terror. They looked at me very hard as if trying to memorize my essence, and the expressions in their destroyed faces saddened like they pitied me, a fellow human being gone awry. I covered my eyes when I took to seeing things that were not there and it was beginning to worry me. Trembling like a man who had just witnessed his own death, I yelled once, much as a small child would do if suddenly startled, and ran out of the apartment. I didn't stop running until I reached the safety of an all-night diner three blocks away.

When I returned home, I searched for anything that reminded me of what I had lost. The only thing left from those early times was this note on manila paper, which I carried around everywhere, my lucky amulet, my totem, wrinkled and smudged from too much handling.

> *Eddie:*
> *You fill me, you complete me, you connect me to emotions and places which you only master. I feel blessed every time you enter me. Your words and your thoughts are unlike anything I've ever experienced. The ways you warm and comfort me continually stun and surprise me. You are a miracle chiseled from tears and sorrow. You are such a treasure, Eddie. This love we share feels like nothing else in the entire world. I'm here for you, please know that. All you need to do is ask and it's yours. Whatever.*
> *Love, X*

My hands, the same hands which reaped life, could not hold a coffee cup or a glass of water. Trembling like a lush's hands. I imagined Xica with someone else, another man, or woman, whatever. I started to think of ways to hurt her, to maim her, to kill her. In the past when I read in the papers of some dumb bastard stalking a woman, standing outside her home, following her to work, driving behind her bus as she goes to work, lurking in the bushes while she held hands with her new man, I laughed and considered the man a fool.

Now, I understand because I've done all of these things with Xica. I didn't want to let it go. I didn't want to let her go. I didn't want to lose her to someone else. She'd already started to go out with other guys, just dating as she calls it, nothing serious. Still, I didn't know how long I'd be able to behave.

Much of my time was spent trying to keep cruel thoughts from assaulting my head and then there were voices that returned, too powerful for pills or magic talk to calm. One thing, a visit from the Congressman, did create a welcome diversion in the downward spiral. I could tell he didn't like the address or neighborhood because he kept asking me if there was a coffee shop nearby. He'd do anything to get his tired Brooks Brothers-wearing Uncle Tom ass out of the Hood, away from the underclass, the heathen masses he swore to protect and serve. The bastard took his hand and swatted at a few grains of dust and lint on the couch before he sat down.

"Edward, you should come out and join me in Brooklyn." The Congressman sat on the edge of the sofa, ever vigilant of a roach or an ant. "I'm doing a follow-up to a recent visit out there by Jesse Jackson, the liberals' mascot. I plan to really burn their ears up with some straight-forward talk about minority crime. The Reverend said one thing that I agreed with, for the students to work with the police by informing on drug dealers and thugs with guns."

"What's the school?" I asked, noting that his handlers were now dyeing his black hair in grey streaks near his temples to make him appear more distinguished. More like a statesman. He still worked out every day, at his private gym, so his body was taut and trim. A black man trying to hold back the ravages of time.

"We're going to Thomas Jefferson High School in East New York," he replied proudly. "Tough neighborhood. They kill each other in that community with more regularity than in Harlem. It's not as bad as it used to be. A larger police presence is starting to turn the situation around in that God-forsaken place. Thank the mayor for that, whatever else you might think of him."

I didn't respond to that lob and asked him if he wanted a cold soda. He waved me off and stared at an article I'd snipped out of the newspaper with the bold headline: SICK KID BEATEN TO DEATH, supported by a smaller one—Mom's Beau Went Berserk At Mess: Cops. The story was a sad one, a three-year-old boy was pounded to death by Mama's boyfriend with his fists because he was sick from a stomach virus that gave him diarrhea, making him shit in his pants. The abuser messed him up real bad then told his hospital crew that the kid fell off his bike when his condition became serious and his heart just stopped. He rushed the boy to the hospital but it was too late. He bled to death inside, drowned on his own blood.

"Why did you cut this story out?" the Congressman asked, one eyebrow elevated. "This is a fairly nasty business, the killing."

"I save stories like that, child abuse and murders, got a whole scrapbook of them," I said. "About 320 of them. It's like a hobby. You know, moms killing their kids or dads fucking them up."

"Why? Why collect this sordid garbage? You spend too much time dwelling on the dark side of life."

His face contorted when he said that to me, the arrogant expression he reserved for inferiors and mental midgets. In the past, I would have felt like shit if he had spoken or looked at me this way but now I knew him for the bastard that he really was. There were times when he was at the place up on the Hudson sitting with his homeboys, sipping brandy and smoking cigars, exchanging tales of power. The flip side of this was the "sincere" mask he could put on at the drop of a hat, the look Mother Theresa used for the sick and dying or Barbara Bush reserved for the illiterate. It was all an act on his part. He didn't give a damn about anyone but his damn self.

I guess the look in my eyes was fierce because he stopped mid-movement, stunned by its intensity, and sat back in his seat, hands folded in his lap. I loved playing crazy with him.

"I hear that you and Margaret saw each other not too long ago?" I heard something in his voice when he asked the question. Fear maybe. Fear of the woman accusing him of sex crimes or fear of the woman who as his wife knew the most about him or fear of the Congressional committee snooping around in his money matters for any hint of financial impropriety. I knew the bastard couldn't be afraid of me. I didn't matter that much to him.

"Yes, we did." I was bored as hell.

"What did you two talk about?" He was worried about her, about whether she would stick with him through the bad times. The man treated her like shit, like a stage prop before this recent dark period, but now he expected full loyalty from her and his questions to me were to check up on her. He was here to pick my mind.

"We talked, nothing special. Just chitchat."

"I don't believe that. Margaret doesn't chitchat. What did you two discuss? Anything about the matter with the woman and her ridiculous accusations . . . or the campaign funds?"

I shook my head, hating that he was now talking to me as if I was some dunce. He had never shown any real affection toward me, father to son. Never a hug or even a pat on the cheek. Still, there was a connection in my heart to him, this man who had taken me in when there was nowhere for me to go. It had never entered his mind that the deep wound in my soul could have partially healed with a tender touch or a kind word.

The Congressman scowled at me, his eyes burning with disgust. "Why do you act like you're a damn odd-ball? You're not as stupid as you act. What you need to do is get up off your ass and find a job, do something with your life and stop wallowing in what happened to you. People have a lot worse happen to them and they keep going. Look at those miserable souls in Croatia or Rwanda. They have something to cry over, not you."

I could feel beads of sweat pop out on my forehead although the room was cool. The Congressman was like the rest. He had no idea what was occurring inside me, what the tragedy of losing my family had done to my ability to live and love. He never saw how troubled I was. Like everyone else, he believed I would grow out of it, that some sessions of talk or some good loving would erase the bruises inside me. The real deal was that I was being swallowed by the rage in my soul, which I had held in check for so long, which now threatened to overwhelm my life. Nobody, including him, gave a damn about me or what I felt.

"Do you hear what I'm saying to you?" he roared.

I nodded my head, the obedient puppy submitting to his master's voice.

He was really pissed. "You know what is wrong with you? You spend too much time in front of that television. That damn thing is not going to pay your bills or make a career for you. Either you take action with your life or I will!"

I remained quiet, battered by the blunt force of his words.

"Edward, you cannot say that you have not had good role models in Margaret and myself," the Congressman said. "You've lived the kind of life that anyone, any child, would want to emulate. That ghetto bullshit is behind you. You have nothing in common with that jungle element, nothing. And what is this mess with the police? Questioning me about your actions and friends. What have you got yourself into now?"

"Nothing." I could not look him in the face.

His voice shamed and condemned me. It told me the things he could never say. I would never do anything that he would have approved of, not one fucking thing. I was no better than those niggers up in the projects, the welfare underclass he so deeply despised. No doubt he knew about the killings but I could not tell if he connected me with them.

"Do you have any plans to better yourself?" he asked.

"Yes."

"What the hell are they? I want to hear them."

I realized that nothing I could say would please him. "I'm still working on them. I'm young yet so I have time."

"Not as much as you think. This life passes quickly and before you know it, you'll be forty and fifty and standing on a street corner wondering where it all went. America is not a place for dreamers, especially for young black men. You can't dream, you've got to act. Do something with your life. Hear me."

Again I nodded, this time I reluctantly brought my eyes to his. "Do you want something from the kitchen?"

"No, sit your ass down. Listen to me for once." He

got up and walked over to the barred window to look down at the cars parked on the street below.

Like a true politician, the Congressman launched into this long tirade about life's obstacles, pitfalls, and setbacks. You had to admire this dude. He could teach me a lot as an elder about slipping a move, peeping an ambush, dodging that unexpected blow that comes out of nowhere. He had nine lives and more. Like the man in the White House, he thrived on crises, mishaps and disasters. Make the shit work for you, kid.

After he finished his song-and-dance, I piped up with the very thing he had been avoiding—the other woman. He had a rep for being a ladies man. Through him, I understood what the deal was: that plenty of those who were powerful lived this way, the unquestioned life, the sweet cars and the even sweeter honeys, everything at your feet. Someone called it the "the arrogance of power." Check that out, meaning nobody can tell you shit. Your word was Law.

"About this honey claiming to be your other woman, your side stash," I said. "She's got some heavy stuff on you, saying things that are catching folks' ears. It's like this . . . I don't believe you would jeopardize your marriage and home. I saw her and she ain't a beauty queen. No way. I see something I want, I go after it. Too much is expected with love, too much sacrifice and I want no part of it."

"Pardon me." He acted as if I caught him off-guard.

"Why didn't you protect yourself from this whore?" I was mad at him being careless. His recklessness reminded me of Moms and her fucking up costing the lives of her family.

"There's nothing wrong with love," he said softly, like he knew love personally, up-close. "Yes, it's true that it's hard to sustain that love in the world in which we live, the magic fades, but the marriage need not fade. You do new things together, weave yourselves deeper into the fabric of one another's days and that's how the relationship stays fresh."

"And that's why you screwed around, right? To keep it fresh?"

"No, not at all." He knew there was lust and not love with this woman.

"You were thinking with your dick, right?"

"More vulgar language and the conversation's over, got it?" His voice carried two fists that threatened to knock me on my ass if I got out of hand.

"You know I was little when I was first adopted by you," I said, choosing my words carefully. I didn't want anything misunderstood. "You never made me feel safe or wanted. I was a thing, a cause, a charity case. I was a living piece of publicity."

Some stuff always stayed with you. You couldn't shake it. No matter how hard you tried. He knew my adoption was equal to a margin of victory in votes.

His face tightened up. He got closer to the window where he could see his silver Porsche below on the street. "What? We gave you every goddamn thing."

"I needed you to love me, to listen to me, to spend some time with me. But you never did. You were never home."

He fidgeted with his hands. "How can you possibly know what it means to be a parent? Being a parent means bringing home the bacon, keeping a roof over your child's head, covering the bills every month. You have no idea what this kind of responsibility is about. Don't talk about things you don't know about."

I got near him, off to the side of him. He didn't like

me standing so near him. I was taller than him. He worked out but he was old. I could take him. It made him nervous and he said so.

"You were a tyrant," I shouted at him suddenly, the beginnings of tears in my eyes. "Everything was by your rules, your orders, your commands. I want this, I want that. You never listened to anybody but yourself. That was totally wack."

"I protected you and gave you my name," he sneered. "What more did you want?"

"Some love." It came out before I even thought about what I was going to say. I blurted it out. Words with nails in them.

He turned to me, narrowed his eyes, and slapped the hell out of me. I went down on my knees. He got me good. I thought about offing his ass, busting a cap in his lame ass. Hit me? Slapped me like a bitch and then left the apartment. The last thing he said was: "If you're going with me, get your butt in gear. I'll wait downstairs for five minutes, then I'm gone."

I was still on the floor, clearing my head, refocusing. Couldn't believe it. Slapped me like a bitch, walked like royalty, and slammed the door. That Prince Charles action. My face stung, burned like a female had run her fingernails along it. So he got me. But I felt cool because I got him first. I drew first blood.

Chapter 22

LAMBS AND WOLVES

For much of my teen years, I'd watched the Congressman play the role of the high and mighty, always speaking on what was right and wrong, but without any real involvement in the lives of the people he served. He was apart from them. They were voters and little else. He didn't recognize them as human beings or consider their struggles in a society that treated them as shadows. His phony concern for their pain only surfaced at election time. The rest of the time he didn't acknowledge their existence.

Man, I didn't want to go to any more of his campaign stops. However, he assured me that I had no choice but to accompany him to the high school. Before I left the apartment, I snorted some blow and popped a few reds to get in the proper frame of mind. Blurred. I was raging inside, everything on tilt, and there was nothing I could do about it.

On the way to the school appearance, the Congressman blabbed on and on to his underlings in the limo about how he had worked to place his political allies in key state positions. His lackeys. One of the gofers mentioned that large checks had arrived from one of his conservative think tank pals with GOP ties, a new friend gained from an appearance in Wisconsin where he had attacked the issue of an increase in the minimum wage, slurring those who coddle the poor. The Good Negro. No one talked more about the merits of The Contract With America than my stepfather, who saw Pat Buchanan as the best candidate put forward by the Republicans in the election of 1992, better than Dole or Alexander or the rich man Forbes. In the next election, he was pulling for the son of former President Bush, especially after the current man in the White House got caught with his pants down.

"Pat Buchanan spoke for the little guy and the big boys on the Beltway didn't like that," the Congressman said. "He was a fly in the ointment. Everyone wanted him to shut up and go away."

"Part of his problem was that he wasn't plugged in," said Corbin Broder, one of the old man's many white advisors, looking up from his clipboard. "Buchanan positioned himself too far to the right or he might have had a shot."

"Speaking of plugged in, do you know the joke about what Goldwater told the all-powerful LBJ during the 1964 campaign?" Jay Larkman, his chief Congressional legal mind, asked. When everybody shook their heads, he completed the yuk-yuk. "Goldwater said Johnson was so charged that all you had to do was plug him in and the whole city of Washington lit up."

Everyone busted up like a bunch of nutty chimps on laughing gas, while I sat there and looked out the window. The Congressman laughed the longest and loudest. Politics, politics, politics. Boring as shit. Larkman interrupted the chuckles with the notion about The President sounding more Republican than his opponent in the last campaign, but always going back to his old New Deal routine. Lower taxes, smaller government, states rights. Whitewater, Vince Foster, The Vice President siphoning funds from Buddhist monks, the erratic stock market, Greenspan, the uses for the Christian right, Monica, and questions about Kemp's sexuality. Four slimy lizards chatting in a big black car.

"The President will survive all of this womanizing business because the ladies love a bad boy," Broder chimed in. "You don't need character when you got charisma."

"Unlike you, Congressman, we've got to put the fires out, both with this campaign finances matter and the woman," Larkman said. "We have no time to lose on these things."

Brendel, the old man's chief strategist, cleared his throat and quietly said both situations were being handled. Which meant someone would take the rap for the funny money deal, going only two minutes to jail for a white collar crime, and in the other matter, the tattletale woman would be paid off or get run down by a drunk driver. Or killed during a botched robbery by a crackhead. Everyone looked in my direction to see if I was paying attention. I kept my eyes glued to the glass.

I could have an accident too, squashed like a bug under a brogan. It was quiet as a wake in the car for the remaining twenty-five minutes to Brooklyn and the school in the deepest part of the borough.

Although this school was outside of his jurisdiction, the Congressman felt he could get some good media coverage from this gig, while doing a favor for the pol from the district who was laid up with the flu. He probably promised his crony that he would crayon within the lines and not say anything to stir up the locals. During the last time the Congressman ventured over to these parts, a weeping woman told him that the only time she went out was in the middle of the day and that there was no guarantee that she would not be hit by a stray bullet in a drug shootout.

He hugged her close with moist eyes and promised her with a firm voice that "the carnage," his word, would end. Their picture was splashed on the front pages of the newspapers, both local and national, along with an account of his tour, and the following day and hours were spent on the telephone soothing the ruffled ego of the Congressman representing the district. That was four years ago. This was the first visit to East New York, a neighborhood that traditionally led the city in murders every year, since that time.

Inside the limo, Broder noticed that a cut above my left eye had suddenly started to bleed, a thick red trail flowing down my cheek. He handed a tissue to me, saying it was getting on my clothes. With an annoyed look on his face, the Congressman commented that I couldn't go into the auditorium looking like a beat-up boxer, leaking blood all over the place. I frowned.

"What happened to you, kid?" the bodyguard asked, leaning forward to get a better look at the damage.

"He popped me before we left and that's what happened," I said, pointing at the Big Man himself. He probably cut my face with his oversize ring. The truth was that I had noticed the cut before, but it was deep enough to cover my cheek with a crimson wetness. Asshole.

"You boys play rough," Broder teased, but no one laughed.

The Congressman was miffed that any domestic

quarrel was hogging any of his prep time and with a wave of his well-manicured hand, he switched subjects to his appearance at the school, asking which members of the media would be there, what possible photo ops existed, and which two or three points in his speech needed polishing. While the men talked business, nothing else was said during the ride to Brooklyn about the cut or the incident. I was mad as hell.

It was muggy inside the school. We walked in a group through a side door like victorious soldiers going to accept the surrender of a rival army, trailed by the press. No metal detector. The Congressman shook a few hands, hugged several ladies along the way, smiling his shit-eating grin the entire time. He whispered in my ear that I should wait in the principal's office, remaining out of sight while the event was in progress. My services would not be needed inside the hall.

A woman in a tight-fitting dress sat behind a desk in the principal's office. She was nothing to rave over, but her body held its own share of curves. Serviceable. She watched me come in with a blank look.

"How are you?" she asked. "Are you with the Congressman's party?"

"Yes, I'm his son. I'm to wait here until the program is over. He doesn't want me in there."

She smiled, keeping her gaze on me while I stood there, holding the bloody tissue to the wound above my eye. The flow had not stopped. I figured if I maintained pressure on it that it would cease bleeding, but it didn't. The woman opened a drawer in her desk, searching for something among the papers stored inside. Her hand retrieved a first-aid kit, possibly with Band-Aid or gauze.

"We should dress that cut," she said, getting to her feet. "It looks pretty nasty. How did you do that?"

"An accident." I stood still as she cleaned the wound, dabbed some mercurochrome on it, then applied a Band-Aid.

While she came close, I checked her out. Her jet-black hair was trimmed short just under her ears, framing her heart-shaped face. There was no lipstick on her thick lips. I imagined she was the kind of woman who lived alone, possibly with a few cats, and spent her evenings in her own company with a glass of white wine. A spinster. She wasn't that tall, maybe five-six or so, but solidly built, wide hips and full breasts. When she noticed me giving her the once-over, x-raying the essentials, she smiled faintly and continued her nurse routine. I guessed that she was used to men checking her body out.

"What's your name?" she asked.

"Eddie. What's yours?"

"Julie. Julie Crouch. Why don't you find a seat? You can listen to your father's speech over the P.A., without having to go to the auditorium. The principal uses it for her morning announcements and for emergencies. It'll come through pretty clear."

I took a seat on a bench facing her desk, dreading every damn minute of my wait. She was reading a copy of *Essence* magazine, the men's issue with Michael Jordan on the cover, smiling smugly as if he didn't have a care in the world. And he didn't. The man had a pretty wife, cute kids, slick home, and more money than he could spend in one lifetime.

"Do you like working in this neighborhood?" I asked her, trying to break up the monotony. "East New York is pretty tough."

"It used to be bad around here," she said quietly. "But it's much better now after the police started raiding the crack houses. You'd see people walking down the street smoking the stuff before the police got serious. Some of the dealers even walked right into the school during lunchtime trying to get the students to buy that mess. It's much safer now."

"Well, that's good."

"I'm a big fan of your father," she said, looking at me. "It's people like him that make a difference in our lives. Most politicians don't care about the little guy but your father is not like that. He strikes me as the kind of person who is always thinking of others and seldom thinks of himself. We black people can be really proud of him and what he has done for us."

Talk like this turned my stomach because I knew him for the bastard he really was. The Congressman only cared about Number One: Himself. If anyone wanted to know how self-serving the bastard was all you had to do was watch him on TV, jawing with Larry King, flirting with that toothy blondie on *Good Morning America*, laughing with the ever-perky Katie Couric on *The Today Show*, or chatting up B-ball with Jay Leno on *The Tonight Show*. And the handkerchief-head didn't even like basketball. He was always on. His guard was never down. You never see the real person.

What bull! And the folks up in Harlem saw right through his ass recently at this tribute to Betty Shabazz, who died after her grandbaby burned her up, so this phony Uncle Tom takes the podium and started yakking some jive about the black community being "a bunch of crybabies wallowing in the rigid ideology of victimology," about how we love self-pity, about how we spend more money on useless things, then criticize the White man for making us poor, about how he was tired of dumb-ass conspiracy talk with the government being involved in everything bad that ever happened to blacks. His words, not mine.

He finished up with something like the real deal is that we Americans, blacks too, are better off than we ever have been and should thank God every night for living in such a blessed country. Now I happen to know that he was wearing a bulletproof vest so maybe he figured he could just say any damn thing without suffering the consequences. No way. Man, the crowd booed, taunted, and cursed him until the pastor pleaded with them to show him some respect. They called him turncoat, race traitor, Oreo, and Uncle Tom.

"I thought this event was to celebrate the generous spirit of the widow of Malcolm X, instead it was totally politicized," the Congressman replied to the cameras and reporters.

Upon leaving with the white mayor beside him, he waved to the congregation as though they were cheering him. Damn hypocrite. He later told me in the car that we blacks have short memories, that they would vote for him in the fall like they always did.

"They're about to start the program," the Crouch woman said, smiling and putting down her magazine. "You know, I heard your father speak at the groundbreaking ceremony for a new AIDS facility in Harlem down the street from my aunt's house. He was so compassionate, so caring that day. His words will always stay with me."

"Stepfather, stepfather," I repeated, touching the Band-Aid on my face. "He's my stepfather. He adopted me. My real father's dead."

"Whatever," she mumbled and turned her chair in the direction of the loudspeaker mounted on the wall in the corner of the room.

Some noises and static came from the speaker first then the bullshit began to flow nonstop, much of what he was saying seeming not to be directed to the kids but to the press who had been prepped for his speech beforehand. In fact, copies of his speech had been passed to the media before we arrived so those folks with early deadlines could file their stories. The Congressman didn't miss a trick.

"Someone might ask me why I haven chosen this occasion to speak on the issue of black-on-black crime," the Congressman started solemnly with a rasp in his voice. "I'll tell you why. I must talk about it because some experts say that our young people like you are a ticking teen crime bomb, that you've done untold damage to our communities and if we don't do something about your violent nature, you'll do us in. They say homicide is the leading cause of death among our youth. One FBI estimate says over 8,000 young black men are killed every year and mostly by each other. Something is wrong. But nobody wants to talk about it or deal with it. My liberal friends at the NAACP and the Civil Rights Coalition would rather I keep my mouth shut, keep our dirty linen in the closet. I say no. I cannot remain silent while an entire generation of our young people is wiped out."

The Crouch woman applauded loudly, showing every capped tooth in her mouth, and turned to me, nodding as if to say, what a man. I sat there on the bench, laughing myself silly inside, knowing what a con artist the man was. Even when he was saying all the right things, there was a big payoff in it somewhere for him. He was a true politician in every sense of the word, with a deep love for the good life and power. Neither of those precious things would be taken from him without a fight.

"They're calling our young men and women super-predators, many of them youngsters like yourselves either pre-teen or in your teens, robbers, rapists, murderers, gangsters, who have no sense of right or wrong," the Congressman continued, building up steam. "They say you carry guns, use dope, join gangs, terrorize neighborhoods, with no idea of morality. They say you don't know what restraint is, they say you want what you want when you want it. They say you are incapable of love or commitment to anything other than yourselves. In other words, you are animals. Is that what you are?"

The shouted response of NO! from the kids made the speaker reverberate from its loudness. I could just see him up there gloating, egging them on, waving his arms like a game show host. And now for the Double Jeopardy question. But he didn't stop there. He wanted them screaming and yelling for him until the needle went right off the meter.

"They say the number of gun homicides by juveniles has tripled since 1983 and that you are the ones responsible," he said mockingly. "They say you don't care if innocent children are caught in your crossfire, you don't care if you kill for jackets and sneakers, that you kill for just the thrill of it. It's your nature. Let me tell you this."

A pause from him. "I agree with some of what they are saying because there are some people among us who don't care about the rest of us. They'd kill us in the blink of an eye over our cars, money, and jewelry. They prey on us. They have turned our communities into jungles, hunting grounds. I feel nothing for them and their kind. When I say this, people say I'm too conservative, a closet Republican, and a traitor to my race. How can you say you love our race if you turn a blind eye to what these people are doing to our own kind? Where are our so-called leaders on this issue? Why aren't they speaking out on this? I love us, our people, so I speak out."

The clapping was erratic, in waves, because he had thrown them a curve. The teachers and parents gathered there were confused by his sudden change in direction. What was he saying? He didn't like crime and criminals but was he also saying our kids are bad too? I loved it. The Congressman, like all good politicians, could be all over the place on issues and the gullible public wouldn't know the difference.

"How can you do to this to your own kind, young black brother?" he asked in an almost pleading voice. "How can you do this to your community which has loved and nourished you? Why must we fear and loathe you when you are our future?"

The applause was more solid, more sustained this time. He had them where he wanted them now, had them by the throat and was not about to let go.

"I am not a liberal, never have been," he said proudly. "I believe in an eye for an eye. I believe if you commit a crime, then you suffer the consequence. I don't believe in mercy or compassion when someone has been raped or killed. Forty percent of the arrests for violent crimes are thrown out of court or not prosecuted at all. Eighty percent of the thugs convicted don't do hard time. That's wrong. I say lock them up and throw away the key."

The place was in bedlam now. They were cheering as if the home team had scored the winning points in the final round of a championship game. He was milking for it for all it was worth.

"They say the crime is down, that our communities are safer," he added. "That is a lie. We still can't go out at night in some neighborhoods. The thugs still rule. We must get tougher. I voted for the Crime Bill in Congress, supported mandatory sentencing and the three-strikes law, more money for police and prisions. If a young person rapes and kills like an adult, I say sentence him like an adult. Forget rehabilitation. Lock him up and throw away the key."

The people cheered wildly but I wondered if they were really listening to what he was saying. He talked as though he wanted concentration camps built for young black brothers and sisters, lock them up and forget about them. They're a lost cause anyway so why waste our time on them.

"Let's cut back on parole and probation," he continued. "Let's turn our backs on these repeat offenders. A quick arrest, a bold prosecution, and longer imprisonment, that's what we want. There is no room for mercy here. They have not shown us any. For those who live by the law and play by the rules, we promise to protect you and your loved ones and your property. We will not fail you. I will not fail you."

By this time, the Crouch woman was clapping as if she had lost her mind, jumping up and down. I could only shake my head. I remember something my real father once said: "The best lies have a teaspoonful of truth in them." The Congressman, from any viewpoint, was a king of liars, a master. With a man like this, I knew if I was ever caught for the shit I had done, he would be the first one cheering for them to fry me. Burn his no-count black ass.

When the ruckus died down, the Congressman tied a ribbon on his speech for the potential viewers of the six-o-clock news. "Our culture is at war with families, decency and morality," he said, adding that bass thing to his words. "Everything seems designed to trip up our youth, to ruin their lives. The only cure for what is wrong with our communities can be found in our homes, in our families. It's time for parents to start acting like adults. Take time with your children. Teach them values. Read to them, love them, nurture them. It's time for you young people to act responsibly, to know that your actions have consequences. Stay away from drugs, away from thugs, away from sex. Do the right thing."

The fact that this crowd was eating this shit up made me want to puke. I couldn't take it anymore. He was lying to them. He didn't give a damn about poor people. How many politicians do? It was just talk, that's all. Things must get worse before anybody does anything. Blacks had to riot before the white man gave the right to vote. However, the Congressman always liked to say that black men were in a stupor, with no vision or purpose. Unlike him, right? A lot of black men feel that whites don't want them around and even black women have no need for them either. They aren't needed in the family. Why do I need a worthless nigger underfoot in the house when I got a job and can take care of myself? I can do bad by myself. Society loves this shit. But this is where I come into play. I'm the by-product of all this madness. Me and young people like me. I am the lesson. I am the price to be paid.

I got up, enough was enough. I could wait in the car until they came out.

"Your father's a powerful speaker." The Crouch woman sighed. "We need more like him. They will turn things around for us in no time."

"Stepfather," I corrected her. "I'm going to wait in the

car for them. Can I borrow your magazine until they're finished in there?"

"Sure. Borrow it, but give it back before you leave. Okay?"

I nodded and took her copy of *Essence* with me to the car. The wait was a long one, twenty-five minutes more, and I was almost at the back of the magazine when they came out, all smiles.

"You were great in there, Congressman," Broder said as soon as they entered the car. "The TV guys got some good stuff for the evening news, strong bites. We did good today, that's for sure."

The Congressman looked at me with a question on his face. "What are you doing out here?"

"I was bored so I came out here to wait."

As I was getting out of the car to return the magazine, I could hear him asking Broder if he should have used the stat that black men have a higher mortality rate in Harlem than the men do in Bangladesh. Broder shook his head and replied that was dated information, almost ten years old. Larkman agreed. Inside the school, the Crouch woman smiled when I gave her the *Essence* back, but what she didn't know was that I had copied her address from the front cover sticker. I had plans for her.

Chapter 23

SOMETHING NEVER BEFORE MADE PUBLIC

It happens every time I spend time with him, the insults, the shaming, the pain. I was totally crazed after the Congressman dropped me off, on his way to another political function downtown. I failed him again. What good was I? The voices swirled in my head, the throbbing, and the urge was there—lurking. I hated the world. I hated the Congressman and all his lies. I felt so alone, all alone. There was a song I heard on the radio: "I'm not sick but I ain't well. I'm not sick but I ain't well. I'm not sick but I ain't well." I knew all about that.

Everything was bugged, on tilt again. There was no hiding place from how I was feeling. I walked along Broadway, looking outwardly like anybody else, watching the females coming out of beauty salons, check-cashing places, bodegas, number joints, and bakeries. Watching for the death glow. Waiting for one of them to ask me to kill her. I felt evil, I felt wicked. I felt out of control. I'm not sick but I ain't well.

On the subway the other day, I was reading the book Zeke's old lady gave me, Carson McCullers's *The Ballad Of The Sad Café*. Slick writing. But something she wrote stuck with me: "But the hearts of small children are delicate organs. A cruel beginning in this world can twist them into curious shapes. The heart of a small child can shrink so that forever afterward it is hard and pitted as the seed of a peach." Those few lines touched something in me, so I wrote them down. They came back to me while I watched a young woman wink at the man at the newsstand and put a little something extra in her walk as she strode away.

Who can predict what anybody will do? Who can predict behavior?

I walked out among them, waiting for one to catch my eye. There are those who will tell you that they can spot anyone who is dangerously antisocial or deviant. Society is surprised every day, another bad apple pops up and kills six or ten people or his wife or kids. Or her husband or her grandmother. All it takes is a certain kind of stress, getting kicked around as a brat, totally abused, and then add the color thing on top of that. And presto, some weakness in you gives and the water spills uncontrolled over the dam. Then somebody gets dead. I'm not sick but I ain't well.

For some reason, I thought back to a story I read in the paper the other night involving this young eight-year-old Chicago boy who shot a girl classmate. Fired her ass up. I clipped it out. He shot her in the spine with a semi-automatic and when the cops questioned him, the boy asked them: "Is this going to take long? I've got some place to go tonight." Too cold.

Kill and go to work. Kill and have some lunch. Kill and go to church. Kill and act like nothing happened. It has all gotten worse with me in the last year or so, completely crazed, walking the streets, driving around. Mind aflame. The handle of the knife in my jacket feeling so good against me, so good to the touch. So calming. A need surfaces and becomes behavior, a thought becomes deed. Unruly hormones. I know this shit has got to stop, someone needs to tell me why I do what I do. This warped revenge. The seed act.

Sometimes I sat to write it down, to write it out, to purge it from inside me. What I felt, I would put it on paper. The shrink told me to do it. Said it would help, said it would calm me. Calm the voices inside.

> At the start there is not much left
> only worthless words and a ripped heart
> my tomorrow pretends that way
> when doubt erupts
> every minute illuminates
> sure I remember injury
> pain as proof of living
> fat frying and wormy flesh
> no charms or hope remaining
> the solitary text of the outsider
> what I learned before I was consumed
> wholly from the times when I was not touched

Did you know that my mother could slap your face, then kiss you on the lips as if nothing had happened? She'd clutch you close to her and smother you with kisses. Totally mess up your mind.

I heard voices even then, when I was little, my toys talked to me, said wicked things, my stuffed alligator talked to me, my Casper doll talked to me, but they couldn't help me get normal in any way. The voices repeated the things my folks said, that I was stupid, that I was a no-count, a lump of salt, not worthy of the breath God gave me, that nobody would ever love somebody like me.

The codes of conduct have shifted. There have always been neighborhoods where you could look at somebody wrong or say the wrong thing and get shot. As a shorty, you expected your Moms and Pops to protect you from evil, even out in the streets. But that's jive. Their specialty was to punch your little nigger ass around and make you hard. Either as entertainment or as Survival Skills 101, they'd say. The Hood is full of punch-drunk niggers with all of the love and tenderness knocked out of them. That was where my voices came from, the ones I heard all the time, low and constant, louder and clearer. Buzzing away in my head like a handful of angry wasps.

Check this out. A TV newscaster interviewed this one young dude, fourteen and locked down in Spofford, a jail for juvie perps in training. He told the white man: It's a bitch to be young and black, without love and dreams, no legit way to get paid, and able to buy a gun anywhere on the streets.

When I got home from roaming the streets, I wrote a few things down, drank some hot chocolate and tried to chill. But I couldn't. I couldn't sit down. I couldn't calm myself. There was another unmarked car parked in front of the building. It had been out there all night. I thought they caught the dude. But the cops watched me on and off, along with a few others they suspected of committing the murders. I was back on the suspect list. It didn't mean a damn thing, because there was a way out if I wanted to leave, out over the roofs.

This restlessness went on for two days. Couldn't take it any longer so I slipped out that next afternoon and took a bus uptown, up past Washington Heights to the Inwood neighborhood where the Crouch woman lived. A wolf stalking unknowing prey. I still had her address from the magazine and waited down the street from where she lived, watching and waiting. Hours passed. Then she got home, still dressed in her work clothes, the office uniform. There was another hottie with her but Ms. Crouch peeled off to walk to her house. I stood back under the trees, hidden by the overhang of their branches.

I was patient. Looking up at the old pre-war building, I saw a light come on in one of the front rooms, and her shadow moving back and forth behind the shade. It was early evening now and the sun was not entirely gone. In ten minutes, the Crouch woman stepped out of the building, dressed in jogging clothes, with a yellow headband around her forehead. Headband or no, I could see her aura, the death glow, and she was marked. Marked to die.

She slowly removed her house keys from her pants and locked the door, shook the knob a couple times to make sure it was secure. I ignored the people on the sidewalk around me while I pulled out my leather gloves. My dreads were pulled back from my face in a ponytail, tied with several flesh-colored rubber bands. I was in all black, black T-shirt and jeans, black boots, and a black watch cap folded in the pocket of my black jacket. A hunting knife, which was a childhood gift from an uncle, was strapped in a scabbard on my leg.

I followed her at a safe distance, careful not to lose

her in the evening rush hour crowd. In the old days, when I first started on this quest, I had no plan, no nothing. I would just grab my victim in a deserted place, beat her down, and plunder her soul.

Now I was much more skilled in my purpose. Nothing was helter-skelter. I took more time, was careful not to leave anything that could lead back to me. She acted as if she almost knew I was stalking her because her walking picked up pace. I was right behind her. At the next corner, she went into a small grocery store, inspecting fruit, looking at the front page of the *New York Times*, then stopping to grab a small bottle of water. The owner of the place, an old Dominican man, was somebody she knew, for they laughed and joked for a time. I didn't let myself think of her as anything other than prey, something that must be killed.

For the next few minutes, I shadowed her from across the street on Broadway, while she moved briskly to the maze of paths and paved roads on the grounds near the Cloisters museum. She began a serious trot once she reached the dimly lit road running on the edge of the medieval building on the hill overlooking the Hudson River. Reminded me of King Arthur and His Knights of the Round Table and junk like that. Camelot. My eyes took in other gray figures in the deepening darkness: two gay guys with a poodle, another jogger doing stretching exercises, and a young couple leaning against a tree, kissing. I must keep my focus, I told myself over and over. Focus. Focus. The Crouch woman must not get away.

I could not see her ahead of me but I could hear her breathing, the low panting of someone who did this running thing regularly and was in good shape. I was moving swiftly, silently behind her like a cheetah or a leopard zooming in on lunch. Also, her Walkman over her ears prevented her from detecting me. That was a plus. I slid the watch cap over my face. There was no sound for an instant and then she was right there, in front of me. I snatched her from behind, spun her around, and almost knocked her ass out with one punch but she was strong. She staggered away from me, dazed, unable to scream. Before I move in on her, I glanced in all directions, the path was deserted; she was mine. We wrestled some, with her trying to knee me in the nuts but I turned my legs away so she couldn't get a good shot. The pressure of her wiggling body against mine made me hard, excited, pressing against her ass, my hand clamped over her mouth.

She couldn't scream. I could see tears glistening on her cheeks, she knew what was next, she knew who and what I was.

Do this shit the right way. Most people do not give up their souls willingly, without a struggle. Crazy with fear, she hit at me with both fists on my chest and arms, swinging them as females do. No power behind the blows at all. Suddenly I slung her to the ground again, and hit her again and again and again as hard as I could in the face. The bitch passed out for a second but came out of it. I brought out the knife, her eyes went right to it, anxious and afraid. She saw the blade gleam in midair and screamed as it buried itself to the hilt under her right shoulder. My punches softened her up a bit so her screams echoed faintly in the small space around us then died quickly. No one could hear her. No one could save her.

In a bold last effort, she kicked and battled fiercely but I plunged the knife into her with short, rapid thrusts. Very fast at first, then slower as the blood began to flow. The blade went in and out cleanly, slicing flesh, bone and organs with each stab. One of her hands clutched at me, trying to pull up my watch cap, to see what manner of human being would rob her of her most precious possession. Surprisingly, she palmed the knife with a hand in a sudden move, its sharp edge gashing open her fingers straight across. She punched me in the face with the other. Her blows flew into my head with alarming speed, catching me completely off-guard. Shocked the hell out of me. I could have sworn I heard her growl.

She tried to get up but I slammed her down on her back with a hand gripping her throat, cutting off the air. Die, bitch, die. Thinking only to stop her resistance, I put my knee in her chest, lifted the knife to finish the job. What a brave fighter! I had to give her that. Nobody had ever fought me like this. A mousy principal's assistant at that! The frantic woman attempted to block the blade again with her butchered hands and twice it penetrated one of her palms yet she did not scream. She was focusing on living, on surviving me. Realizing she was weakening from loss of blood, she put everything she had left in one last valiant stand to save her life. As I went to stab her again, she turned underneath me, angling her body on its side, giving me a smaller target. Somehow her elbow slammed solidly against my forehead and I saw a white light and stars and before I knew it, she was gone, out of my grasp, scurrying into the pitch black, into the bushes.

I was on all fours, listening for any sound. Nothing! Fuck! In an instant, I thought I must be covered with blood after fighting with the woman, so I got up, tucked the knife away and walked along the path toward the lamplight. Not a minute to waste. I quickly stripped off my jacket and got myself together. Pulled off my watch cap and put it in my pocket. I felt some panic but I told myself to be cool. I must find her, finish the job. One stab through the heart. She was weak, she couldn't get far.

I walked quickly through the bushes to the level grassy area on the far side of the museum, then I saw her. She stumbled out of the woods to my left, only a few feet away, her hands holding the many wounds in her chest. Stumbled out into the parking lot. Oh shit! I couldn't get her without being seen. I can't get her! I'm fucked! This would ruin everything. I could see her staggering between parked cars, in view for a moment, then out of sight in the shadows.

She crawled out from a car. As I was about to pounce, she collapsed and fell forward on the pavement. Blood covered her face and body.

A voice behind me shouted: "You! What are you doing to that woman?"

I looked in the direction of the sound and saw a group of men running toward me. People came out of nowhere. I backed away and lost myself in the darkness. They surrounded the victim, yelling for an ambulance and the police. Somebody said there was a man with her. I was wise enough to ease down into the hedges, through them down to the street below to the main avenue. I tried to blend in with the others. Although the sound of police sirens could be heard in the distance, I walked slowly and calmly to Broadway, hailed a gypsy cab, which I took to a corner two blocks from where I was staying.

Once inside the apartment, I paced back and forth, my mind racing. I fucked up, I fucked up badly. I told myself nobody saw my face, that I had nothing to worry about. But I had been sloppy in the kill and now the woman could possibly tell the cops something that would lead them to me. And what about the guys? My back was to them so that was cool.

I went to the window and looked out. There, two cars back, the unmarked police ride. Still on the case. I decided to wash my hands for awhile, that would relax me some.

Chapter 24

THE CHROME VOICE

While my bloody jacket soaked in the sink, I listened to the old fashioned rent party in progress next door, the place overflowing with revelers talking, laughing, and dancing. It must have been an older crowd because the music was blues stuff like Clarence Carter, Etta James, Ray Charles, Otis Redding, Irma Thomas, and Al Green. Tunes that the younger hip-hop generation didn't care about much. My arms were tired. My body still felt in battle mode, sweat poured down my forehead and neck. Soon I'd have to move again, split, cut out of this dump.

I lay on the bed, feeling fully charged up, energized after the fear passed. The thought of keeping my appointment with the shrink tomorrow brought me back to earth because I wondered whether the Kraut would be able to see the aftereffects of the kill in my actions. I might give myself away. Killing always left me feeling odd, exhilarated but completely spent in an almost sexual way. Worn out like after a good fuck.

Whenever I closed my eyes, I saw the Crouch woman struggling underneath me, her eyes wide with fear.

None of the pills in my bag did me any good anymore because my head still throbbed like hell. All of the time. Even now. I saw the Crouch woman struggling underneath me, her body twisting and turning, her punches landing and teasing me into a sexual frenzy much like a warm tongue on the tender part of the inner thigh. But she got away. Instead of dwelling on my fuck-up, I popped two extra-strength Tylenol capsules into my mouth, grimaced at the taste, and held my face under the tap in the bathroom sink.

The cold water, flavored with a little rust from the pipes, slid gently down my throat, comforting me with a memory of the old house back in Brooklyn. The rusty-red water from the pipes there.

There was an entire box of other pills that I could take. Head pills. They didn't do me any damn good. I twisted the top off the plastic vials of Xanax, medication to ease my blues away, but I tried Tofranil, Zoloft, Paxil, and Prozac. What good were they? I was still out on the street killing people. I flushed them down the toilet and smiled at myself in the cracked mirror above the sink. The person didn't look a bit like me. A fucking ghoul.

Thinking of my shrink, I always felt that she saw herself as my mother in a way, using her concern to worm her tentacles into my buried emotions and dark secrets. But I was only going to give her so much of me.

Man, if she gave me a chance, I'd bust it out. Tear her up with the truth. This article I read said a lot of patients who did the mumbo with their shrink bugged out worse and had to be hospitalized. Another bunch of them, fourteen percent, tried to off themselves. Tried to kill themselves, for real. Who is nuts? It's one person's word against the other. Still, the patients wouldn't be worth a damn. Who would believe them? The shrink would say that the parent hallucinated, exaggerated, or misunderstood what went down. If you're a head case, you have no rights.

The phone rang a few times but I didn't answer it. My stuff was packed. Made up my mind just that fast. I was moving again. House-sitting is tiring. Everything is tiring. I rolled a blunt, smoked it, and watched a tape of the *X-Files*, with the sound off, a spooky episode where space roaches were killing people.

A window was open and I heard a flute playing a bird-like riff in the night air. Sweet. Maybe a glass of hot milk might help me. I poured some into a pan, one of the few still clean, and put it on the stove with trembling hands. The phone rang once more and I ignored it. Eddie ain't home. The rent party was still going strong. I smoked one cigarette after another, staring out the window in the dark at the unmarked cop car until I heard the milk boiling. Three sips of it turned my stomach so I fell onto the bed, still sweating from the stress, and pulled the covers over my head.

On the way to the shrink's office the following day, I walked slowly, almost skipping as a little kid would do, so the cop on my tail would not lose sight of me. I bunny-hopped down the subway steps. Here comes Peter Cottontail, hopping down the bunny trail. It was better to be cooperative in a case like this. He got on the downtown Number One train just two people behind me, careful not to press too close, never looking me in the face. But I knew who he was. And he knew I knew.

I sat next to three young Columbia coeds, laughing and giggling about some toothy buffed white boy on

Baywatch, the beach TV show with steroids and silicone. My mind went into my fifty-minute hour on the couch and all the junk she would ask me. Wonder why she never gave me her cell phone number or pager? What was up with that?

I arrived early and sat in the outer office, leafing through a magazine. None of this therapy shit ever did me any good. What was the purpose of me coming here? I still didn't feel like a whole human being.

Finally, my session started and I dropped the bomb. Frau Schmidt was in one of her longer dresses, no leg or thigh, and today she was not alone. A thin balding guy sat with her, some chump she introduced as a colleague. Ugly dude. He looked like that stiff who played Andy Griffith's deputy on that Mayberry show. Barney Fife. Looked just like the man. He didn't say anything the whole time the session went on, only nodded and smiled in the way people do when something really bad has happened to them. Traumatized, right?

"Why do you feel that leaving therapy would be a wise move for you now?" she asked. Barney leaned over more so he could hear what I said.

"We go over the same shit and I don't see any movement in my life," I answered. "Nothing's changed for me. I feel the same as I did when I came here all those months ago."

She thought about my reply, almost frowning because I decided to do this on a day when we had company. It was like you acting out when your Moms had people over for dinner and embarrassing her. Barney whispered something to her and she scowled at him. I couldn't make out what was said.

"You're not as depressed or distressed as you were

back then, are you, Edward?" she asked. "A honest answer, okay?"

I smiled and looked at her. "I don't really know. I don't feel any different. I really don't."

"Are you taking your meds?" She was trying to make a point.

I lied. "Sometimes." That caused her to lecture me on the need to follow the drug regimen so the symptoms of my illness would be lessened. Full recovery was just a pill away.

She waved Barney down when he tried to say something during her lecture and lit a cigarette, a first for her. I could see him already measuring me up for some locked psych room over at Bellevue, lock the bastard up and throw away the key. He perked up a bit when I told my shrink about suffering nightmares and panic attacks in the past few days, and being totally unable to sleep.

"I need to sleep," I said, adding a dullness to my voice. "I have many bad habits and maybe not getting any z's is one of them."

"Habits can be broken and changed," she began in that Mother Superior tone of hers, ever righteous. "Changing a habit does not mean that you have to give something up. It just means that you create new patterns, more positive patterns in you life."

I was curious about this. "There are things that I do that I feel that I have no control over. Impulse things. Things that control me, rather than me controlling them."

Frau Schmidt loved when I discovered something for myself. "Like your anger and rage. This is the reason we've devoted so much of our time together to looking back at your childhood and examining your time with you biological parents because I feel the root of your problems lies in that period."

I laughed bitterly. "Probably so. Lately, I've wondered why nobody ever came to rescue me or my sisters when shit was going so bad at home back then. It's like the kids now in the homes with their parents abusing them and nobody gives a shit or thinks enough to save them. People only talk up after they're dead or so fucked up and then the whole thing becomes a big deal in the papers."

A wry smile came to her face. "Talk about that some more."

"My folks were junkies. Did you know that all of us were born with drugs in our system?"

She was stunned for a second. "No, I didn't. Go back to your feelings around that time."

I steeled myself and spoke. "I felt crazy back then, completely nuts, so full of pain and rage that I took a hot iron and placed it on my bare leg. It made a sizzling sound as the metal made contact with my skin. I never made a sound. Never cried out. My Moms came in, yanked the iron off and started knocking me around. She was so angry at me. Not long after that, I started having seizures; I'd get dizzy and pass out. Or get this strange sensation in the front of my head and go into a fit of twitching."

"Did you receive medical treatment for that? Were your convulsions ever properly diagnosed?"

"Not really. The seizures just stopped by themselves. Do you know that my mind never rests? It never shuts off."

She ignored that. "Did your parents ever take you to a doctor?"

I began chain-smoking cigarettes at that point, and

blue plumes of smoke toward the ceiling. "No. Both of my parents used drugs, got high, so they didn't trust doctors. Once my Aunt Seal wanted to take me to a doctor because sometimes after my father whipped my ass, I'd sit there in my chair and bang my head against the wall. Daddy told her he'd fuck her up if she didn't keep her nose out of our business."

"Were you afraid of your parents, Eddie?"

"Hell yeah. You know, sometimes it's probably better to have no parents than parents like the ones I had. I'd be less fucked up today if I'd been an orphan."

"Why do you say that?"

"Because nothing works. The pills are shit. Xanax, Thorazine, Clorazil, Amoxapine, Trazodine, Tofranil, Inderal, Klonopin, and Prozac. They don't work. I'm still fucked up."

There was no expression on her face. "Eddie, it's a matter of finding the right meds. We want to help you function in the world. That's our goal. And I agree that the pills don't offer us any illumination as to what is at the bottom of your problem. I agree with you there, but then that's why we're here."

We stared at each other in silence.

"Sometimes everything's cool, so clear, so focused," I began softly. "I can hold a job and act like other folks, then something happens and everything goes haywire. I'd start yelling at my co-workers, trying to pick a fight so I can kick somebody's ass, because the voices in my head are telling me that they're making fun of me. I can't tell you how many jobs I lost because of getting into fights."

"Was there any history of mental illness with either of your biological parents?" asked the Mayberry dude.

I shot him a dirty look. "My real mother was depressed

sometimes, wouldn't leave the bed. She'd just stayed high all day and watch the soaps and sell the shit to the junkies that came around. She'd do dumb shit, fuck around with the men that came to buy, come to the door with no clothes on. Shit like that. Hell, she could have had a breakdown and nobody would have known."

The corners of Barney's mouth dropped into a disapproving frown. "Do you do illegal drugs?"

"I don't know you so I don't have to answer that. Let me put it like this, chump. I don't do drugs as much as I could."

Barney was on a roll, although I could tell his partner didn't like him butting in. "Do you think your parents loved you?"

"Not really. We were a nuisance to them. My father wasn't that verbal. He showed his love for you by shouting or with a slap or a curse. Sometimes he bought us toys. My mother was mainly in a zombie state unless there was some nigger around that she was trying to impress. She was closer to the girls, my sisters, than to me. Whenever I needed anybody, nobody was there for me. I was ignored for the most part."

"And?" Barney wanted more.

"Shit," I continued. "My real father didn't like being touched, no hugging, no kissing. I never even shook his hand. I never knew anything about his past, where he came from, and the same was true about my mother. They didn't talk about shit like that. It was like I was a test-tube baby."

"Edward, because your mother had lovers, did you feel like you had to fight for her affection?" Barney asked, probing.

"I don't know what you're asking," I said. "Ask something else."

"Eddie, you often refer to women as bitches or hos, why?" my shrink asked. "Do you know why you do that?"

"Most of the brothers I know call them that. Maybe because they're fast, sexually aggressive, with no ties to one guy. They can't be trusted. They'll fuck anything. Check out the young bitches and you'll see what I mean. If a gangsta had cheddar, they're all over him, freaking and shit."

"Cheddar?" Barney asked.

"Money, cash, dinero," I set him straight.

"Would you consider your mother a bitch?" Barney asked and I didn't dig it. I was getting up from my chair and my shrink told Mr. Fife that that was uncalled for and the white bastard apologized. I was getting ready to get in his ass. Whip his honky ass.

"Do you ever have fantasies of violence?" asked Barney, not letting up.

"Most bloods do, most people do. We live in violent times."

This line of questioning made me feel uncomfortable like those times when I would wash my hands over and over, feeling as if I was dirty or something and I couldn't get the stain out. The filth out of my black skin. I felt as if I stank really foul and everybody on the street could smell me. I would wash my armpits and private parts until they were raw. That nigger odor.

"Did you ever feel violent toward your parents? Toward your mother in particular?" Barney was on to something, he thought.

I didn't answer. Sure I felt violent toward them because they treated me and my sisters like shit. They abused us. We moved around so much that I was never in one place long enough to make any friends. I learned from them never to expect anything from anybody. Everybody will fuck you over if they had the chance, not just whiteys but niggers. Mostly niggers. Your own kind. That's what the old man called them: niggers. The Congressman called them that too when he had a couple of drinks in him. Sure I once thought about pouring gas on my parents while they were asleep and tossing a match on them. I didn't do it though.

"Was there ever any sexually inappropriate behavior in your home?" Barney asked.

"You mean, did I fuck my Moms or did my Pops bust me out? Hell no. Nothing like that. Yeah, I wanted them to love me but not like that. I wanted them to love me like the parents on TV loved their kids."

I thought about what he asked about my mother. Did I want to kill her? Was that the reason I was killing these females out in the streets? Who knows? Moms did everything she could to make me hate her. I came home from school and she was high on her knees giving head to this one friend of Pops. She saw me, got up and slapped the shit out of me. I wanted to kill her then. Kill the bitch. They killed her before I could do it. I developed a deep hatred for her and her kind, bitches, sluts, whores. Pops with his dumb ass knew she was fucking anything in pants for years, since I was small, and it was breaking him down. So he started making mistakes, errors in judgment, spending cash money, the Benjamins had belonged to his suppliers, coming up short. All because his mind was on her and her Jezebel act. She ruined him, ripped out his heart, and got everybody killed, him and my sisters.

She had no regard for him or any man, that stiff meat was her obsession, and the beast attached to it was incidental. I often heard her and the nigger of the moment thrashing away in her locked bedroom while Pops was out. I warned the girls not to say anything because the result would be pretty bad for us. Why couldn't she be a normal woman, a normal Moms? But she wasn't any different from many of the bitches with kids today. The papers are always full of some kids being beaten to death, thrown off a roof, or starved to death. The females, the Moms ain't shit and the kids end up fucked up. They pass the illness on to another generation. Much of what is wrong with the Hood can be traced back to these bitches, getting high, sexing everybody, and not taking care of business. But nobody wants to talk about this shit. Everybody dogs the brothers, easy targets, but nobody deals with these females. A mother is the anchor of the home and family.

"How did you feel about your mother, Edward?" Barney asked.

"We was cool," I replied, thinking of how she once told me I was evil, the Devil's curse on her. I didn't tell the shrink the truth, the whole truth about what the deal was between Moms and me. After I broke a glass, she once struck me with a skillet and left a large cut on my face. She made me tell the child welfare worker that I fell. They wanted to charge her with endangering the welfare of a child and take my ass away. They should have.

"How do you think you have dealt with their tragic deaths?" he came back at me again.

I could never tell them about the unexplained injuries that all of us, me and my sisters, went to school with, the bruises and welts on our faces, arms, and butts. Cigarette burns on our arms and legs. Burns on our bodies from scalding water. When shit was bad for them, our parents, it was worse for us. This society, this world, hates kids. Read the newspapers for one week and see what I mean.

"I'm cool about it, I got over it pretty quick. Wasn't no biggie." I lied. It still messed with me.

"Are you telling us that you have mastered your pain and rage, Edward?" Barney asked in a snide voice. The Chrome voice. Lifeless.

"I don't know." Again I lied.

I watched my shrink's face for her inner stuff, nothing showed, then I switched over to Barney, whose eyelid was twitching nervously. I'm sure that bastard wanted to give me a shot of that shit they used in the movies to make people talk, so he could make me tell everything and leave nothing out.

"Do you hate women, Edward?" Barney asked. "How do you feel about women in general? Do you hate them? Or are you ambivalent about them like so many men?"

I answered idiotically. "You're fucking with me. I don't need all of this. I just want you to help me with all this junk in my head. You have a detailed history on me and you ain't doing shit. I'm dying inside."

"Answer the question, Edward." Barney still persisted.

"I don't know." Fuck them, I thought.

They said nothing to me, just whispered back and forth between themselves. And that was messing with me big time.

Maybe I was supposed to figure everything out for myself. Not count on them. How could a white shrink or a white person know what it was like to be black? To live in our skins day in and day out? Those manuals of theirs didn't cover all of the junk we faced because they were written by whites for whites.

A few sessions ago, I asked my shrink if she could interpret a dream I had. My favorite aunt was feeding me cookies, large pecan-and-raisin ones, the taste of them in my mouth made me feel like she was rocking me in her arms, rocking me to sleep. I felt truly loved. Warm inside. Suddenly, she produced a huge pair of scissors, grabbed my limbs and clipped them off as you would the stem of a thorny rose. It hurt like hell. I woke up crying and screaming. The sound of my voice startled me and I looked around the room for any sign of my aunt or the cookies. Confusing, right? She told me she couldn't answer the puzzle of the dream then, that I should wait until next time, but she never did solve it.

"It sounds like your mother was your primary influence," Barney said. "We all know that little boys don't learn how to be men or fathers by watching Mom. But boys do learn how to relate to women from Mom. If that connection is not sound, there can be trouble later. Also, we are not born with low self-esteem or bitterness, but learn these things from our parents who are often fighting the same problems themselves. Children learn about love, sexual roles, and many other things by watching the interaction between the man and woman in their homes."

"What does that mean for the young dudes who are being raised by single Moms in the Hood?" I asked and his blue eyes flared. "Will they all be fucked up? They'll all be punks or bums, right?"

"No, but let's stick to what we were talking about," Barney replied, shaking his head. "Understand this, the first woman in a man's life is his mother. That relationship is an important one since it impacts on every other one he has with women throughout his life."

"What does that have to do with me?" I asked.

"What you don't understand is that you are not free of your biological parents although they have been dead for years," Barney said, making a note on the yellow pad in his lap. "Their deaths have not brought you freedom or a normal life. In a sense, you are still under their spell."

"And this is a male thing? Only the men get this, right?"

"No, women face it too," my shrink said. "Ask many daughters and they will tell you that they did not feel free until their mother's death. And maybe not even then. All of us ask ourselves: What would my mother have thought?"

"But not every woman who pushes out a kid is a mother, a real mother," I said. "Check that out."

"You've had two fathers," Barney said. "Both seemed to have disappointed you to some degree. How have these disappointments shaped you? Influenced your behavior?"

"I don't know. That's something for you to figure out. I'm not the professional here. That's why you get paid."

"What about your current girlfriend? Edward, what do you think of her?"

"I think Xica is promiscuous, oversexed," I replied, my words coming from my anger for her. "She likes to screw around."

"Why do you say this?" Barney again.

"I just know. A hunch. I know her. I know females."

"Then why do you want her as your girl?" He was pressing again and my shrink sat there, pouting.

"Because I've always been attracted to women who could hurt me," I said truthfully. "The bad girls, the wicked ones."

My shrink cut into the chatter. "Wicked? Do you hope to reform them? To redeem them? To fix them?"

"I don't know," I said.

"Maybe you just want to punish yourself, Edward," Barney said.

"I get no joy from them. I don't believe in marriage because I don't think a man can totally satisfy a woman. She'll always stray."

"That's pretty cynical." Barney smirked.

"Doc, I can't remember seeing one marriage that worked and was for real. Can you? Either the man or the female was coming up short."

Barney sat back in his chair and smiled a salesman's bogus smile. "I know many couples who have very satisfying, loving marriages. You can't judge the world by your own limited experiences. They exist. They're all around you."

I shrugged. Just then Mrs. Lau, the receptionist, knocked and came into the room. She whispered something to my shrink, who then whispered to Barney. Barney nodded and watched the two women leave. In a few minutes, my shrink came back and talked quietly to Barney and the pair exited. While they were gone, I got up and searched her desk, noted a big book labeled *Diagnostic and Statistics of Mental Disorders IV*, and looked beyond that to a packet of notes with my name on them. Once they were folded and safely in my pocket, I walked to the door, listened, then ran down the hall to the street. When I got home, there was a message on the answering machine at the apartment where I was staying, my shrink asking me in a furious voice to call her at the office. The Chrome voice again.

Chapter 25

SOULSVILLE

At two in the morning, I stood staring at the shattered mirror again, watching the face of a stranger in its fragmented glass. I did not know this man who looked back at me. My head was now shaven, gleaming with a few bloody razor cuts on the top of its dome. The demon himself. *How sad it is that this part of your life is only open to you, the secrets you only share with yourself, the private hurts, the twisted fantasies, the abnormal urges*. The public self, the private self. There was no way to break down the barriers inside myself, nobody will help me. A young black man lost.

What is a normal self? I stared at the mirror, not noticing the tears coursing down my brown cheeks. *I am dead inside*. I lay across the bed, still holding the mirror which I yanked from the wall, walking with bare feet across the broken shards of glass on the floor. Of course, I did not feel the deep cuts on the soles of my feet, bloody prints, on my way to the large drafting table in the corner of the room.

Sitting at the table, I tore off a sheet of blank paper

from a pad and started writing what was in my head.
The pen trembled in my hand as it wiggled across the
page.

You are trapped in hue
you are helpless
you are trapped by the sores in your mind
you are being beaten and enjoying it less and less
you are cornered
you are starved for attention
you are a mugger in this story
in this version you cannot change places with
   anyone
you are broken and want to take turns
you are not what this world had in mind.

The water was boiling, the kettle's whistle sounded
with an annoying squeal. I glanced at the remains of my
hair, the nappy curl, and the long thick dreads that now
looked like small lifeless snakes. The new Michael
Jordan. The Yul Brenner android from the weird sci-fi
flick. Dazed, I stumbled to the kitchen where I prepared
myself a cup of black coffee, the blacker the better.

Back at the desk, I opened the folder with my shrink's
notes about me, the patient, leafing through the pages
quickly, scanning for the good stuff. Looking for what
she really thought about me. Not her jive office act.
There were so many terms I didn't know or recognize,
the jargon of the mind docs, *etiology, temporal lobe,*
perinatal injury, developmental fixation and schizo-
typal. But other items fell right into my net: *anxiety*
beneath the protective armor, shame, denial, projection,
occasional incoherence, delusions, hallucinations, pos-
sible mental syndrome, rule out infection, possible

lesion of temporoparietal lobe, multi-voice auditory episodes, racing thoughts, tangentiality, progressive psychomotor agitation, prone to rage and violent impulses, close supervision and monitoring in case of need for intervention or institutionalization in a locked unit.

Suddenly, I had read enough of her lies. What happened with somebody like me was the doctors decide early on that you are crazy, label you such-and-such, and that tag sticks with you for the rest of your life. Even if it was wrong. I started ripping up the pages, tearing them to shreds and crumpling them into balls, eventually filling the metal wastebasket with them. The matches in my hand appeared out of nowhere, that sound of lighting them and the whoosh of the orange-and-yellow flame, the fire spread across the filthy lies on paper.

The record of Edward Stevens was consumed by fire and nibbled to harmless ashes. I sat there and watched as my mental health dramatically improved by the second.

The phone rang. I listened to the answering machine click over, the robot voice appeared, welcoming all callers, and the taping began. It was Xica. She wanted to see me. She just wanted to talk. I yanked the receiver up and told her late afternoon would be cool. I felt better immediately.

Soon, I moved back to the bed, nodded out and didn't snap out of it until I heard her knock, Xica's light rapping at the door. It was unreal. Xica stood there and I took a shaky step toward her, wrapping my long arms around her waist. She sighed, putting her face against mine. Her mouth, hot and soft, closed on my own, seeking comfort.

"What have you done to your hair?" She finally commented on my shaved head. "You look like Kojak."

"Nothing. I needed a change."

We did not say anything else for several minutes. We just watched each other with distrusting eyes. I did not touch her again. I did not want to. As usual, she made the first move, slowly unbuttoning her blouse, and I stepped to her, kissing her, our tongues curling around one another. Her movements to the bed were halting, unsure, almost mechanical. But there was very little time wasted in removing the rest of her things as her fingers slid over buttons and zippers with an inhuman speed. Once naked, she sat on the bed, drawing the sheet up around her, keeping her gaze on me the entire time. When I got close to her again, I knelt at her side, running my fingers through her curly head of hair, bringing her face once more to mine for yet another kiss. I was lost in my lust for her. Her hand reached into my pants and caressed me. My dick twitched at her touch, so hard, so urgent. She inched the sheet away from her outstretched body.

"I love you, Xica," I told her, feeling the emotion deep in my heart. "Why do we argue so damn much?"

Xica shook her head, sitting there on the bed, all inviting girl flesh, her dark legs spread so I could see her fingers parting the lips of her soaked sex. That second mouth of hers nestled amid the tangle of glistening kinky hair. I marveled at my hardness, the first time in a long while this had happened without my hands around a woman's throat. Still, I wanted to stroke her skin, to run my hand over the satiny length of her, in spite of this urge. God, I wanted her so.

Soon I was naked as well. I could feel her eyes on me, burning, going over every contour of my frame.

"Eddie, see what you do to me," she said in her seductive voice. "I'm so wet down there. Here, feel."

This was how it always started, the touching, the slow arousal, the teasing. Sometimes she told me to treat her like a whore. Other times, like a frigid wife. Yet some occasions, she wanted me to submit to her whims, to her fantasies, no matter how twisted or bizarre. Once she begged me to let her whip me, which I did. Another time she ordered me to crawl on all fours to her, pleading for her to sit on my face, which I did not. She was mad for a week. On this day, I slid onto my friend's four-poster bed and inserted two fingers into her, moving them in and out gently, until her head tilted back and her eyes shut in bliss.

"I want you inside my mouth," she said gently. "I want you deep in my throat, while you're still hard."

Usually my hands would be already gripping her like the great beast mounting a lioness, going at her under the spell of something so wild and violent that it caused me to fear that I would hurt her. She said she liked it rough. This time was different. I didn't want to rush. I had never felt so . . . never felt anything like what I felt for her now. Suddenly, she pulled the sheet back up over her, motioning for me to kiss her again. I pulled her legs over my shoulders, my face now against her wetness, drinking in the perfumed musk. I kissed and sucked her through the cloth that was draped around her hips, feeling her swollen lips pulse against my mouth. Nothing could stop me until she convulsed with pleasure and cried out. I loved to watch women reach orgasm.

"You got a pretty ass for a man," Xica said after her breath returned. "Anybody ever tell you that?"

Sometimes she talked too much. She whispered she would be happy just to lay there with me, that we didn't have to do anything else, just snuggle. That went right out of the window once she saw the look on my face. By this time, she got the hint and started kissing me all over, my chest, my nipples, my navel, my thighs, my ass, even taking me into her mouth for a bit. Her hunger was upon her as was mine. It was so intense that neither of us wanted to wait.

"I love only you, Eddie," she moaned. "Only you."

I searched for her opening, for her clit, which was puffy and sensitive. Just touching it made her nuts with desire.

Her lips were near my ear. "Stroke it gently or I won't be able to concentrate. Let me get on top, precious." She swung over me and lowered herself down, her hips rotating sensuously. The juices rushed from her, and when she lifted, her movement produced a sucking sound, a hot Zulu rhythm to which she bobbed and bucked like a woman possessed. It was like our very first time together. She sat on it to the hilt, then raised up so she could see its full marbled length before plunging back down, panting with joy. Quietly, she shook and trembled, hitting her climax and then fell forward on me. I was still hard and able to go another round. It was electric. I experienced such happiness, such love with her that I covered her sweaty face with kisses. After the explosion, she lay in the crook of my arm, mumbling something before going to sleep. I watched her, listening to her snore lightly, curled up in slumberland.

Chapter 26

WHEN THE PIECES DON'T FIT

Someone moved in the darkness while I lay naked with my beloved, something evil crept through the apartment. This was what woke me up. I had a bad feeling about what was coming next. A match struck, torching the room with light, letting me see there was company present. The face could not be immediately recognized from this low angle. It was Zeke. He dragged a chair over to the nightstand, switched on the reading lamp, and let me see the gun in his hand before he said anything.

"Hey Lover Boy, what's happening?" You could tell Zeke had a few tricks on his mind by the way he asked me that question. Tonight was his night to star, to appear as the Gremlin, to play the heavy.

And I was ready for whatever was going to happen next. My entire life had led up to this showdown, how I was going to face death, whether I possessed courage or not. Pops always said I was going to punk out. Zeke leaned over, smiling at me the entire time, and pinched Xica's big toe. She was zonked out. The woman was so beautiful when she slept, all female, her soft skin still hot. Zeke loved watching me watching him watch my woman laying there naked. The gun pointed dead at me, no room for error. She stretched out her long arms like a tabby cat before she even opened her eyes.

Xica drew herself up and yelled at our former friend. "What the hell are you doing here, Zee? What is this?"

"You chose this piece of shit over me, this loser," Zeke shouted, walking over to where her blouse was folded over the back of a chair. He picked her blouse up, brought it to his nose and inhaled real deep.

Xica stood in the middle of the bed, hands on her hips, the defiant Amazon. She rolled her eyes. "Before I answer anything, you're going to tell me why you burst in here with a gun drawn while people are sleeping. Are you crazy, nigger? Whassup?"

"What does Killer here have that I don't?" He was back in the chair, more composed. "Tell me that. Is it how he smokes the ladies? Kills them?"

Moments like this transformed character. Either you survived them or you didn't. I looked around the apartment, the Ikea furniture, the cinnamon-colored Navajo rug, the faded photos of blues singers on the wall, the stacks of unread books on the floor, the clothes laid over chairs, the fold-out sofa bed. And the outraged glare of Xica's eyes. Another hide-out blown.

"Did you fuck him?" Zeke was directing the barrel of the gun at Xica, who quickly got down on her hands and knees.

She was a little shaken. The idea that this fool might really shoot her sobered her up real fast. *Mas rapido.* Nobody could guarantee that Zeke was not capable of trouble tonight. An idiot could have detected an element of real menace in his talk, rushed words and constant swallowing. He was bugged out.

"Xica, why do you treat me like shit? Why do you have to hop into bed with every man you meet?"

She was adamant about this point of serial cheating. "I was with Eddie first, Zee. You know that. He was my man before I ever got close to you. You know that. You think you own me."

"That's bullshit," Zeke said, knowing she lied.

"I hate men who try to control me. Just like a man, right, Zee?"

Now it was my turn. "Killer, don't you think she'd be the bomb if she got a big red rose tattoo put on her sweet ass, that left butt cheek I like so much?" he taunted me with this jive tone in his voice.

Zeke scooted forward so he could look deeper into her large brown eyes, squinting as if he was looking directly into the sun. Occasionally, the fool glanced at me to make sure that I was not going to surprise him suddenly. I wore my bravado mask for effect.

"What makes you such an expert on men?" Zeke spat at her. "Xica, you don't seem to stay with anybody for too fucking long. From one dude to the next. Why can't you choose one man and stick with him, baby?"

My beloved said nothing. She gave Zeke much attitude, like he was just another chump she had played to perfection. No words, no begging, no backing down. I was proud of her for how she met a crisis, all backbone.

"Your so-called woman's a whore, Eddie," Zeke said flatly. "Ask her who she was with for the last three days. Go ahead and ask her. Sweetheart, tell your man where you were."

Xica was mute. A honey with stitched lips.

"I'll tell you where the bitch was," he smirked. "She was with me all day, every day, kicking it. Isn't that so, sugar?"

Again nothing came from Xica. Her silence told me the entire story, every raw minute, every rotten kiss of betrayal. I knew everything. She was no better than this clown sitting in front of me. Neither one was worth a damn to me. Both were cut from the same cloth. At least, I had a code, believed in what I did, did it like an art form.

"You want to know what this gun is about, sweetheart?" Zeke went on with his one-man show. "I've got it because your boy here is a goddamn killer. He's the bastard killing all them sisters up here. The woman raped and killed in the Cloisters gave them your description, Killer, before she died. The police know it's you, beyond a doubt. It's just a matter of time."

I couldn't keep quiet any longer. "So they sent you to pick me up, right brotherman?"

"Don't smart-mouth me nigger," the clown said. "Remember who has the gun here."

"Is this about the ten large they're offering for the killer?"

Zeke smiled. "Could be."

"You're one sick boy," I said. "The cops have been watching me for the longest time. Believe me, if they had something on me, they would have been here real quick trying to arrest my ass."

Zeke didn't want to deal with that right away. "Eddie, does she let you hit the booty? Baby got back, much back. Does she toss your salad? Do you hit it doggy-style?"

"What are you trying to do?" I sat on the bed next to

Xica. The woman was as stiff as a statue, scared stiff, until he tossed her a bone. A chance to leave. To vacate.

"Xica, you can leave now because it's Eddie I need to deal with," he said to her without emotion. "I'll get with you later. We'll talk this out then."

She rolled over to me, watching my deadpan face. "Could you kill somebody, Eddie?"

"Yeah, I do it every day and twice a day on Sundays," I said it like I was reading letters from an eye chart, then started laughing like it was a joke while looking into her eyes.

"Eddie, I want the truth. Are you involved in this killer stuff? Are you killing these women?"

"Do you trust me, X?"

"Yes, sure I do." She said it cautiously.

"Do you believe me?" I put a cherub face on me.

"About what?" She knew what I was asking but playing dumb.

"When I say I didn't do what people say I did," I said. "What this chump says I did. I am on everybody's shit list."

"I don't know, Eddie, why are the cops watching you? What are you doing? Are you in trouble?"

I shrugged. "Listen to me. If I'd done what the gossips say, do you think the cops would let me walk the streets? They would have busted my ass by now. They would have been all over me like stink on doo-doo. You know that, X."

"I guess so." The expression of her face assured me of a direct hit. "Zeke, let us put on some clothes. This is messed up."

He said nothing. Xica reached over for her purse on the floor by the bed and the clown twisted his head so he could make sure that she didn't pull a gat from the bag. Instead, it was a pack of Newport, cool menthol, and she lit one for herself and one for me. Zeke frowned when she did that. Tobacco had never tasted so good. We smoked quietly, weighing the situation and the quickness of Zeke's reflexes, whether he could hit us both with one shot. It was in our eyes.

"Got any money?" Zeke asked us both.

We both shook our heads, no. In a way, I didn't give a damn about her screwing around now because I was cured in bed. I owed her something for that, something more than a pat on the back or flowers. Xica, the insatiable. I could still taste her, I wanted to be in her again. What did she see in this clown, damn high school dropout?

"You've got more down there than I thought you would," Zeke motioned with the gun at my crotch, shrugged and chuckled, then went over to the refrigerator. "What do you have in this fridge, Mr. Host? Don't do anything stupid."

"Answer him," Xica yelled.

"Eddie, they're on to you, they know you're the one offing all these women, man." His voice was muffled by the door of the icebox. He was all in the damn thing, relaxing his vigilance, his sentry duty. And for that, he would pay dearly.

"Whatever." I used the California Gidget-white girl voice he hated.

"They will get you, Eddie," Zeke said.

The same Valley-girl Barbie tones. "Whatever." It annoyed the hell out of him. He wanted to punch me out. I waited, biding my time.

Instantly, I leaped on him after two half-steps, banging the door against his empty hand and the other one lifted with a jerk and a shot went wild. Somewhere behind me, Xica screamed like frightened females do on roller coaster rides, really shrill, really long. My fist pounded him solidly in the face and chest until he folded over and the gun slid across to the other side of the room. He was mine. The clown swung a chair at my head while I was off-balance wanting to finish me off in some way, but I ducked it and the thing sailed past. Using a move I saw Sonny Liston do in old footage with Ali, I caught him with a strong shot in the nose, setting him back on his heels and followed up with an uppercut that made him bite his tongue. He fell back against the wall. I was on his ass in the blink of an eye, raining punches down on him before he could catch a breath, then wading in closer with a fast flurry of hard blows. The punk tried to push me off him, NFL strong-arm, tried to kick me in the liver, but no such luck. I was the stronger, probably because of those clove cigarettes he sometimes smoked, those things completely sabotage your wind.

Wisely, Zeke made the right choice and dashed for the gun. His body was on the other side of the over-turned chair, something for me to hurdle to catch the clown before he could pick it up. That was almost impossible. It was a no-win deal for me. I pivoted and ran back to the bed where I had stashed my piece. My .38. The whole thing reminded you of a TV game show, tick-tick-tick, beat the clock.

Our guns came up at the same time and we both fired. I didn't know I was shot at first. Most people say when you first get shot, you don't feel the bullet going in. It burned. One of the shots hit the refrigerator, ricocheting in a shower of neon yellow sparks, momentarily blinding me. I fired twice at him as I fell toward the floor, one shot whizzed into the wall above him, but the second round got him dead center in his throat, just as he pulled the trigger. His neck exploded in scarlet, splashing out in a geyser down his chest, making him grope like a baby learning to walk.

Xica screamed again. My attention was focused on the clown sprawled on the floor, him not her, unable to yell, dying on his back, choking on his own blood.

I felt no remorse. The punk should have killed me when he had the chance. Yakking can cost your life. If it had been me, I'd shot my black ass as soon as I entered the apartment. I put the gun up to his temple and watched him sweat before I put another cap into him. Chump. The other difference between us was that I didn't care if I lived or not. Not really. Shit, I died years ago back in that bloody living room with my parents and my sisters. I was dead and above ground.

When I turned, I saw Xica crawling across the hardwood floor toward the door. Her eyes were beet red from crying. "Eddie, let me go. I won't tell anybody . . . anything."

"I know you won't." I crouched over Zeke's body and went through his pockets, thinking about his car keys. No, a stolen car would be a dead giveaway. Xica gasped when I rolled him over with my foot so I could look into his face again. Cause and effect.

"Let me go, Eddie, please baby." She pleaded, her expression changing as she saw the blood flowing from a neat little bullet wound on my left side.

"Were you fucking Zeke the entire time you were seeing me?" I was serious.

She didn't bluff me. "Yes, but it meant nothing. He was just some beef. A dick. Strictly sex."

I felt crazy mad, enraged. Doped-up by the scene of blood in the room. Zeke's and mine. Thinking of his sightless eyes staring straight ahead, the death film on them already. "But you got with him, right? The fucker deserved what he got."

"Are you going to hurt me, Eddie?" She asked it in a resigned voice. Twenty-two years old and this was how it would end for her. I was twenty and I knew how this shit always ended up. With somebody dead.

"I'm afraid so." I didn't know my voice. Cold.

Xica was no fool. I would never let her go. And she knew it.

She looked at me through red, glazed eyes. A look of why. Like a cute puppy about to be put to sleep. For good.

"Bitch," I cursed her. Then I shot Xica, twice, but I didn't feel good about it. The word, *killer*, never left her lips; still I know it was the last full thought she had before the bullets found her. Two in the chest. I couldn't mess up her pretty face. One strange thing was that I wanted to hold her one last time before she kicked off. But all my real feeling for her died when she admitted to sleeping with the clown.

I stood over her, watching her die.

Everything was amok. From the floor, Xica watched me as the pool of blood spread from under her body. She looked at me like she was really seeing me for the first time. Bewildered. My side hurt like hell. It was not bleeding much. The bullet went straight through. I found a butcher knife in the kitchen and considered carving up the bodies, especially that of Zeke the betrayer. Clean up. Walk and don't look back, Eddie.

I kissed her on the forehead, listened to her gurgle, and shot her again, once in the pump, using Zeke's gun. Exhibit A. One dead bitch. She needed to be offed, she played herself, she never loved me. I was just a little dick on the side when the regulars were otherwise busy. When I finished that part of things, I put the gun in Zeke's hand and went to the bathroom to splash water on my face, washing up quickly to remove all traces of blood. Truthfully, I knew I couldn't possibly get away with this, too many loose ends. But I must try.

Damn, my side hurt. I tried to walk upright, but my legs were shaky. I bent over to catch my breath back. Had to go, quickly. The gunshots. Somebody probably called the police. My hands gripped the top of the kitchen table for support as my power started to fail me, then it passed. I was good again. Had to pull myself together. I packed up my shit, went to the door, looked out to see if anybody was in the hallway and walked down the stairs out the back door to the parking lot.

I thought about Zeke's car since I had his keys in my pocket but I knew if I took it that the cops would be tipped off to my involvement in the double murders upstairs. I wanted to buy as much time as possible. I was not thinking straight because I was shot. Ditch the keys the first chance I got. Damn the pain in my side. Instead, I walked over to where I saw a man putting oil in his car. He did what he had to do to keep the thing running, then he put the can in his trunk.

"Sir, I'd like to ask you a favor," I said, acting humble. "I was wondering if you could take me somewhere for a little money."

"Where do you want to go?" he asked, his bloodshot eyes on my face. He was about fifty and drunk. He slid into the driver's seat. I smelled liquor on his breath.

"Yonkers."

"How much do you have?" He wanted cash money.

"A hundred and fifty, that's it." My answer was interrupted by the sound of police sirens, two or three squad cars racing to get here. Somebody had called them after the gun battle in the apartment. I tricked the drunken guy. I know my grandma lived in New Rochelle but I told him Yonkers in case something went awry.

"You in trouble, brother?" the man asked.

"A little." I put on my innocent face, feeling the gun in my pocket. "Can we go? We can talk about the payment on the road, right? Anything you want, just roll up out of here."

The man nodded his head for me to get in, which I did, looking over my shoulder at the arriving cop cars. The law on the move. We drove right past them on our way out. I was safe.

Chapter 27

FOR HEAVEN'S SAKE

We were on the outskirts of New Rochelle, a suburb of New York City, close to Grandma Timmons's house where I could lay up for a moment and figure out what to do next. I convinced the man to take me further and he was generous. The car jerked to a stop after I smashed the man twice with a gun butt. He slumped over the steering wheel, bloody and unconscious but lucky to be alive because the blood urge was upon me. The last thing I remembered about the man was his putting his hand out, trying to take the money.

"I'm sorry, guy," I apologized for what I did. That was the first time.

Night. I ran quickly across a park toward a small hill, the breeze upon my face. Going up the incline, I fell hard on my ass, ripping my pants along my right leg and at the knee, and a wet sensation frightened me when I felt for the wound. The pain in my side was also getting worse, I was probably bleeding inside.

Behind me came a voice, a voice of concern and kindness. "Buddy, are you alright? Need help?"

I was still on the ground but gave a jerk of my head toward the shadow looming over me, mumbling that I was doing just tine. Just took a tumble, nothing serious. The man walked on, not bothering me any longer.

I got to my feet and looked around, clutching my side, my mind foggy, disoriented. The breeze stopped, just heat, suffocating heat. I must get to Grandma's place before I give out. Getting weaker by the minute, I staggered out into the street, trying to make it to the other side, the Big Bad Wolf on his way to Grandma's gingerbread house. Suddenly, a pair of headlights closed in on me and I'm going to die, but the car screeched to a stop and I wobbled to the far curb. Someone called me a "stupid NIGGER" from a car behind the one that almost killed me; still I didn't stop, no half-stepping, on my mission to get to Grandma's house.

Maybe all the night's hellish drama did was to keep me fired up, keep me focused, something going on all the time. What a wack night! Walking, aching, bleeding. Reminded me of that time when I flipped out as a kid in school, just after my folks got smoked. Couldn't stop screaming. Telepathic dissing. The other kids making fun of me. They got inside me, made me think the sick bastards at the hospital put a special transmitter in my head, placed that gizmo down into the wrinkles of my brain, sending me orders, teasing me about my dead folks.

I stopped at the crosswalk, looking back and forth, everything going from color to black and white, and then moving at half-speed like a film run too slow. I couldn't remember where Grandma lived.

The address? Kenmore. Redmore. Tidmore. Something more, right? Like Xica and that betrayer tonight. No more. You don't have to personalize fuck-ups like them to smoke their lives. Ever look up at a streetlight—no, maybe Kenmore was the right one. Four-eight-seven Kenmore. No. How long had I been walking on these dark streets, going around in circles, going nowhere. Redmore. Kenmore. The first time you kill sets something in motion, something you cannot stop. Follow, track, kill them. Them. You do not stop and dwell on what you have done, distract yourself, distance yourself. Never let the truth of what you've done hit you. Kenmore. Nine-eight-three Kenmore. No.

No, Xica. I never wanted to hurt her, never, not her. The cops were probably there right now, tracing all of it back to me. Needed an alibi, a strong alibi. Something more than an alibi. Grandma Tee, Seven-three-two Kenmore. Just keep walking, Eddie.

There were people watching me. They probably were thinking I'm just a harmless drunk, staggering his way to another drink and a dark alley. If they really knew who I was, they would be scared as hell. I am death. Shaking from the cold, I got Grandma Tee on the phone, her voice thick with sleep, my fingers barely able to hold the receiver. Who knew what time it was? I should have thought to call before. I had a tough time dialing the number.

"Where are you, Eddie? Are you here, in my neighborhood?"

"I guess so. Got a lift here."

"How far away?" She was starting to wake up. Her voice was stronger.

Silenece. I was trying to figure it out, where I was.

There was a gas station, a Texaco, up ahead, one of the all-night kind. I could see the attendant putting gas into a bright red minivan, a man and a woman laughing with him.

"Where are you exactly? I can tell you how to get here. Are you alright, Eddie? You don't sound like yourself."

"Yeah, fine." A lie. My knee was bleeding again. And I was probably bleeding inside too.

"What kind of gas station is that? What brand?"

"Texaco, I think." I needed a pep talk. She was good for that.

Grandma Tee was the only one who came to see me when I was locked down in the Nut House, Bellevue, the schizo ward. Inkblot tests, pills, questions, and more questions. On view like a caged Antichrist, just free associate Eddie, chant to chase the voices away. Three-seven-five Kenmore. I was close. I've got to remain clear, coherent, not twisted. Cannot let myself vanish away before my eyes. I'm so tired, Lord, my God who was always looking the other way. You never hear me, never. When was the last time I received mercy or grace?

"Where are you, Eddie?" she asked in a pathetic voice on the phone. She said something about it being late, after midnight. She was like the rest of them, all the niggers who made my life a hostile act.

"I need your help. I need to talk to you."

"What do you mean? What's going on Eddie?" She was becoming stern, putting that parent thing in her tone. "There's something . . . in your voice. Are you in trouble, baby?"

"No, ma'am." Yeah, I'm cool. Everything was cool.

She gave me directions once, slowly, a street at a

time. Talking to me like a mother would with a five-year-old. To an idiot savant. The guy in *Rain Man*, the Dustin Hoffman flick. Somebody you had to spell it out for because they'd mess it up. Or get lost.

A car went past, a cop car. The law shone their light on me in the phone booth. I ignored them, acting as if they were ghosts. Had to. Couldn't afford to get jammed now. Pinched. Kept on talking to Grandma Tee with the fools sitting there in the patrol car watching me for any misstep, any miscue. But I was cool.

"Did you get all that, Eddie?"

But I knew I wasn't normal, the voices and all, the visions, the evil deeds. I was an abnormal black boy. A living Freudian slip on both my good and bad days. How many of us are out there? A cruel remark from a God who cursed someone's life. Maybe the Law could see that from their car, written on my forehead. *Shoot the beast. Shoot the black boy, the NIGGER.* Who would miss him?

"I might stop for some ciggies," I said to the old lady.

"Don't make me wait up. Come as quick as you can."

The cops were still looking at me, checking me out. I fought down the impulse to do something drastic, some wack act outside of logic or rules. Something that would probably get me killed. What they did not know was that I still had a gat on me, a gun in my pocket. I couldn't guarantee that I wasn't going to erupt, do something rash. The turmoil in my head must have leaked into my speech because Grandma Tee asked me twice if I was alright, if I was okay or not. I lied and said yes. The eyes burned into me as I talked.

Sometimes I felt nothing, sometimes I felt too much. Sometimes I felt suicidal, I felt totally nuts, sometimes I felt like raw rage. Walking anger. Sometimes I didn't feel like I was alive. Like I was invisible. I was on the floor back in Harlem next to Xica, holding her in my arms, so dead and cold. I was in the closet, watching one of the gunmen feeling in my dead mother's panties after he shot her a third time. I was in grade school with two bigger boys forcing me to drink piss out of a Dixie cup. I was in a store with its white owner yelling nigger at me because he thought I was stealing when I wasn't. Sometimes I felt confused, sometimes I didn't know what to feel, three-seven-five Kenmore.

I was tired of hurting. I was tired of hurting others, I was tired. I am only twenty years old.

"Eddie, don't hang up. There's an all-night store two blocks from here. Could you get me some Pet milk, toilet paper, a box of grits, and the paper. The *New York Times*. I forgot to get one when I came in. Could you?"

"No, I'm broke. Completely busted. I've got just enough to get the cigarettes. I can go back out once I get there and pick up whatever you need."

What was it that Billie Holiday once said? Or was it Billie? Anyway, it went something like this: "If I had to live my life over again, I'd make the same mistakes —only sooner." Bullshit. Lady Day must have been doped up when she said that, if she did say those words. In ether. Zooted. Xica on the floor, dead. Wonder what she would have looked like in nylons. Moms used to wear stockings, nylons, with those great legs of hers. I remember Pops' thick hands on them, his fingers making an electric sound while going over their sheerness. Xica. She never looked cuter than she did on that Harlem floor, soft, juicy, and stone cold dead. I could still hear her pleading with me to spare her life, the begging, and I put my fingers in my ears. After the cops drove off, I limped toward Grandma's gingerbread house, leaking blood.

Chapter 28

TRUTH OR CONSEQUENCES

I stumbled my way to Granny's house. The bullet wound ached something fierce. When I was small, I remember reading a Red Cross manual about the care of wounds, not gunshot wounds but surgical wounds, a Red Cross manual that my Aunt Jill kept hidden behind her bed with her "nasty" books, vibrator, douche stuff, and two pictures of Sidney Poitier with his shirt off. The Red Cross book talked about rest, limited movement, proper nutrition, wound cleansing products, drain sponges, cloth tape, ointments, disposable rubber gloves and watching for pus or smelly drainage around the injured area. Why was I thinking about this now? The pain kept bending me over, clutching my side, the bullet felt like it was still in my body rotating, over and over, cutting up flesh and bone.

But I made it to Grandma Timmons's crib, staggering through the sweltering heat to the Sears and Roebuck style house with the large rose bed in front. Two cop cars passed me on the way there, again slowing down to get a better look at the nigger. I kept on stepping, feeling the wound bleeding again underneath my shirt. The light was on in the living room, a sign that she was still up, and I could see two figures through the windows walking back and forth.

Had the old bitch called the police? Was it a trap?

For a moment, I stood at the door looking up at the white glow from the moonlight, an eerie vision. I hesitated before ringing the bell, nervous and gripping the gun in my pants pocket, but she yanked the door and hugged me.

I winced from her touch. My body felt so strangely hot and cold at the same time. It was important for me not to pass out before I could get to the bathroom.

"Are you alright, Eddie?" she asked, watching my face. The whole house smelled of flowers, that sweet perfume of living things. Their aroma leaked into the house from the small converted greenhouse attached to the main residence, something she added about a few years ago for her flower business.

"Yeah sure, can I use your toilet?" I asked, careful not to grab my side although it was killing me. Hurt like hell.

She was dressed in her gardening outfit, which was unusual because it was so late, the soiled apron, knee pads, and gloves. In one hand, she carried a pair of sharp garden scissors. No doubt she had been working late on an order, preparing to ship out some of the prize product. On the way to the bathroom, I could see boxes of blooming tulips, all colors, the result of care and love.

Once inside the bathroom, I stripped off my jacket and shirt to inspect the wound. My shirt was soaked with blood. I was surprised at how much weight I had lost in the last few weeks, my ribs showed through my skin like a concentration camp victim. Even my face was gaunt, the bones more prominent, all angular, and when I glanced in the mirror, it didn't look like me. The ghoul.

I could hear a man's voice out there with Grandma Timmons, a deep bass voice. The cops? Quietly, I knelt at the door and put my ear to the wood, straining to hear all that was being said. The man was saying that I couldn't stay there, that the police should be called so they could arrest me. I stood up and fished in my pocket for my gun. So this was how it would end.

A knock at the door. "Are you alright in there, Eddie?" It was my Grandma Tee, no one could say my name like she could. Very sweet.

"I'm cool." I fingered the bullet hole. Some blood leaked from it and the skin around the entry place was tender to the touch. The pain came from deep in my body as if something has been smashed up inside.

"Do you need anything?" she asked.

"No, I'm cool." I repeated and sat on the toilet.

It had been two days since I moved my bowels. And nothing was coming now. But it felt good to stay here away from the world, from her questions, a moment of peace.

"Eddie, you can't stay in there all night," she said, interrupting my bliss. "Hurry up out so we can talk."

I could hear the man through the door again, saying something about me using drugs behind the locked bathroom door, shooting up, using the needle. Wrong. Never did the shit in my life. No way. I remember my shrink saying some stuff about me exercising some will power, controlling myself, making myself act in a certain way. I cannot. I can't carry out the orders I give myself. I have no will power. My shrink said I must learn how to support my will power, to strengthen it. Too much negative self-talk, she'd say. What good are words anyway? What does talk achieve? Not a goddamn thing. Isn't action always better?

"Eddie, you're worrying me," Grandma said to me through the door. The safe barrier. "Please come out."

"I will in a minute," I replied. "I got the runs."

Then suddenly there was a pounding at the door. It was the man pulling and twisting on the door knob, yelling for me to come out. I was still on the toilet when he yanked the door open and started shouting at me that I was a worthless junkie fuck. My hands covered my privates so he couldn't see them. I said in a low voice for him to get out and close the damn door, putting some menace in there to scare him off me. He left before he saw the bloody wound.

I stood up and pulled up my pants. The sound of the flushing toilet brought the sound of scuffling outside the door, like they were running for cover, diving behind sofas and whatever. I couldn't turn my mind down. It was too loud, saying rude things. Children can reflect what is going on inside parents. On the other hand, parents often blame children for all that has gone wrong in their lives. What was it Moms used to say all the time? What was that? Moms said she stayed in her horrible marriage because of us kids, her leeches, holding her in place. One day, I came home and there was a wet towel around her neck, a bright red welt angry against the brown of her skin. The old man told me she tried to hang herself after getting drunk but he kicked in the bathroom door when he heard her choking inside.

Another night, she sliced one of her wrists, then panicked, running through the apartment. Blood flew everywhere, blood on the beige shaggy rug, blood on my Dr. Seuss book.

"Eddie, come out of there," Grandma yelled. "Don't make me have to come in there."

I was on my knees near the door, the blood running down my side into the contour of my leg before dripping to the floor. My fascination with the red color was still there. No one told me that bleeding to death slowly was gentle, the waves of your life rolling out away from the shore, the pulsating peacefulness. The final cleansing of the soul. I wanted that calm that was lurking behind the draining of my life, but I had to face this now, if only to escape the Law.

I stood, flushed again and went out to face them after taping a sheet of paper towel and cotton over the wound.

Grandma watched me hurry past her with my jacket over the wound to a chair in front of the television, one of those big ones with a screen the size of the kind you find in a Cineplex. Large sucker. It must have been the man's bright idea, probably a sports fan. Because Grandma Tee didn't watch much TV. Hopefully she hadn't seen the blood. I sat where I could keep my eye on her.

"Why were you in the bathroom so long? " she asked. "Is your stomach upset or something?"

"No, I'm cool," I adjusted the coat over the stains. Where was the man, the owner of the male voice? Did he go outside to call the cops? I must be on my toes so I wouldn't be surprised.

"What's wrong with you, Eddie?" she quizzed me. "I worry about you. You don't seem to care about anything or anybody anymore. Not even about yourself anymore. Just out there wild. Now you're acting just like the rest of them, doing whatever you feel like doing, no matter how if affects anybody else."

I sat up in the chair as straight as I could. Give the old bat some attitude. "Right, no matter how it affects anybody else. Where is your man friend?"

"He's outside." She didn't like answering that question.

"Outside where?" I turned so I could see the door now, off to my left. No surprises.

"You keep on going like you're going and you'll wind up dead," she said. "I can't save you. Nobody can. You let the past swallow you whole. I warned you over and over about that, warned you so many times, and you never listened."

"Ain't nothing in life guaranteed," I replied snidely. My eyes scouted for the guy, just in case. "Who cares about me?"

"I care. You know I care." Her face said a lot more than her words. She was afraid of me but was doing her damnest to not show it. Like you would be cautious with a mad dog. Show no fear.

I was remembering when we lived in the Pink Houses in East New York when I was little, everything around trash and broken glass, pissy elevators, rats and roaches, stealing and killing, little kids cussing like grown-ups, rapes on the stairwells, and women selling themselves to make the rent. Real wack shit. I was so far away from that yet I never felt closer to all that than I did at that very moment.

"Grandma Tee, do you think I go off, get violent because of my father?" I asked her again for the zillionth time. "You know, something in the genes, bad blood?"

She played with her hair and kept looking at the door and then at me, real nervous like she was expecting the cavalry to arrive. To save her ass. Still, she kept up a pretty good front, acted as if none of this worried her. A killer in her living room, us chatting like to old biddies at a bingo game.

"I don't care what those white folks say," she said. "I don't think you were born that way. People don't come out of the womb ready to kill. You learn that mess, learn how to be violent. How not to care about taking someone's life."

"Was Pops violent, as violent as they said he was?" I needed to know.

So early in my life, people labeled me sick in the head, something wrong with my brain, the circuits. A severe neurological disorder with a biochemical imbalance. Whatever that was. Was my father the same way? Sick and too ashamed to get help.

"Your daddy had his secrets, many secrets," she said calmly.

"Like what? He always called me a punk, said I wasn't man enough for him. I was just a kid, what did I know about shit. I remember when Moms brought home my younger sister from the hospital. I heard the old man say she wouldn't have sex with him, always fidgeting around with the baby, used it as an excuse to keep from sleeping with him. He felt she didn't love him and probably he was right. One day, the baby was crying so he picked her up this time, cooing to her. Moms walked over and slapped the hell out of him. That was when the beatings really started too, him kicking her butt."

"She never told me how badly he was treating her," Grandma said quietly. "They both had their secrets, things only they knew."

"What was Pops' secret?"

"Eddie, did you know your daddy was married before? Did you know he shot his first wife? Luckily he didn't kill her."

"He never told me that." I looked down at the pillow, flipped it over and saw the blood. It seemed like the wound had stopped bleeding. Seemed that way but I was wrong. It leaked into the pillow.

"He was secretive, very secretive." She saw the pillow and the blood.

"Did Moms know?"

"Yes, she did."

"And she married him anyway. I don't get it."

"Yes, she married him anyway. She said she loved him. Married him against my wishes. I told her he was no good."

For an instant, I recalled the nights when Moms would come into the bedroom, late on sticky hot summer nights, and lay next to me completely naked. All sweaty. I could feel her breasts against me like big soft balloons. She was always humming some Motown tune under her breath, crying and hugging me all close. He had just whipped her ass probably. I was like seven or eight.

Grandma was in her own zone, back in the day talking about Pops and his defects. Trying to turn me against him. "Your daddy used to tell you if somebody did something to you, you had to strike back. He told you violence was the only way you solve anything. I hated to hear him tell you that, warped your little mind. He'd slap you when you were little, make you put up your tiny fists, yelling BE A MAN! He put you down all the time, said he didn't want a punk in this house. I remember the bastard telling you right in front of me, you were no more than six, that if you had a gun you should shoot first because if you didn't you would be dead. The Law of the Jungle, he'd say. Then he'd add that a real black man in the Hood couldn't afford to be soft, a punk."

"Why did he shoot his first wife?" I asked, still watching the door like she was.

"Caught her in bed with some fella. Another man."

"That was messed up," I added. "She slept around like Moms. Pops didn't have any luck."

Probably the reason why I couldn't totally hate my Pops was that there were a lot of times when he was alone with us, when she was out catting around, catting was his word for her bed-hopping, she'd be off with some dude in some motel, when he was alone with us and things seemed so normal. Like other families. It would be cool. Pops and us would have picnics with hot dogs and sodas in the living room where he could throw down a couple of blankets and a scary movie would be on, a vampire flick or a wolfman thing or some ghouls gnawing on some stiff's forearm.

Pops would sip soda with us from straws and cover his eyes when a monster got somebody. Or we'd go up to Prospect Park and toss a ball around or to the zoo in the Bronx. He dug the zoo. Sometimes he'd fix us breakfast, the best pancakes with strawberry jam and sausages, and sometimes he'd even go over our homework and tuck us in bed. Then I would smell the sour smell of crack coming from his room. But he'd be there, not her, and she'd be gone, in the streets for days.

She saw the expression on my face and walked over to the side of me, but not within grabbing distance. Watching me like a wounded leopard.

"Eddie, you spend all your time going over and over the past rather than trying to make something of yourself," she said. "I knew you'd end up like this when I saw you running around with those roughnecks."

I wanted to be down with the Hood rats, down with the style of the street. With the tough homies. Digging Newports, Tupac and Biggie, North Face jackets, smoking chronic, drinking forties, all of it. Nobody understood that. But Pops would have dug it. He was like the pictures of young George Foreman, not fat, just big. Saw him knock dudes out with one punch just like George, especially when they got funny with the cash money. Either bring back the product or some green. But he was a chump, really. Moms played him like a bitch. Once I saw her on the street down from Macy's with another guy, they were all hugged up and we all saw one another at the same time. I saw that she saw me. Later she told me that she'd fuck me up if I said anything so I didn't. But Pops was a chump.

Either a chump or a fool. Because Pops sometimes laughed when his buddies kissed and touched Moms in front of him. As if it had no effect on him. It confused me because I couldn't see him letting them do that right in front of him.

"Remember what Uncle Moye told you that time in Pittsburgh?" she asked me, breaking the spell, and I shrugged.

Maybe I shrugged but I remembered what Uncle Moye had said to me after I got sent home in the eighth grade after a fight in the cafeteria with a boy over a girl. "Listen, black boy, dark folks been suffering since the beginning of time," my uncle, the steelworker, told me. "God regularly kicks our ass because we tough as nails. He knows we can stand it. Make that heart pain work for you, boy."

I played dumb and Grandma Tee recited the now-famous

remark by my dead uncle. She was bugging me with this door watching routine and I thought about mentioning it to her but I didn't want to get her started on this killing business. The old woman knew damn well what I had been doing or at least she suspected something.

"I got a saying for you too," I shot back. "It goes: 'It is a waste of time hating a mirror or its reflection instead of stopping the hand that makes the glass with distortion.'"

"Who said that?" she asked with obvious surprise.

"Audre Lorde, a dead woman poet. Some teacher read it to me in high school and I never forgot it. Do you understand what it means?"

She nodded her head. "Yes, I do but I don't know how it goes with what we were talking about. It makes no sense."

"I think it does," I replied.

I smiled evilly. My mind was on this guy, Dupree, the one I caught riding Moms that night, that Friday night, when loud screams and moaning were coming from my folks' bedroom. I burst into the room to protect my mother from whatever was harming her. It was the fear in her voice. So I came into the room, only to get yelled at by Moms, who was shouting all kinds of mess, *get out, get out, this is adults' business*, and I was nearly out of my mind with fear for her. I didn't leave; I stood there until her new boyfriend got up and shoved me out. Moms did nothing, just giggled like the shit was funny.

Dupree was a rival drug lord to my Pops, a slick dude with a fancy Porsche, sweet clothes, plenty of honeys, and a crib on the swank East Side of Manhattan. He was loaded and totally hard core. Moms said she loved him, heard her say it one night. This was the same nigger that broke into our apartment with his crew and killed everybody. He spared no one. Including Moms and the little girls. I was thinking on that when I passed out on Grandma's sofa.

Chapter 29

THE RECKONING

I blacked out, I blacked out, I blacked out.

That was what I kept telling myself when my senses returned. I couldn't get into a position on the couch that would not hurt my side, my throbbing wound. My energy was leaving me, slowly I shifted on my side. Grandma stared down on me like a freak at a carnival. I don't think she really cared whether I lived or died at that moment. See, nobody cared about the pitiful, hurt nigger boy. I longed for more life. A chance. A change. Well, sinners had rights too. Like two crooks on the crosses beside Jesus. My mind was starting to go, unraveling bit by bit, probably from the blood loss, and my head would fall into my lap. And I'd be gone.

My eyes focused on Grandma's cigarette burning down close to her fingers, two yellowed fingers. I didn't know she was a closet smoker, never did I see her smoke in public. The only thing she ever did other than raise flowers was to read *Home & Garden* and and do the *New York Times* crossword puzzle. She gave me a pill and a glass of water, saying, drink.

"I watched you change from a happy little boy to this quiet angry thing who never speaks to anybody except to say get away," Grandma Tee said. Her face was a little blurry, like part of it was wiped away in a smudge of grease.

"Thanks," I smart-mouthed her.

"Did you ever mourn their deaths, your parents' deaths?" She put the cigarette out in a hiss in the ashtray.

Her eyes locked on my face as I lied in a stammer. "No, I've never been to the cemetery. I don't see why I should. They didn't give a damn about us kids, only about making cash money. Living large."

The man, whoever he was, was cooking in the kitchen, soul food by the smell of it, fried chicken, collard greens, yams and cornbread. That stuff. Maybe they didn't call the police yet. Maybe they would put something in my food. I won't fall for that. I thought you could survive without love in your life. I did it for a long time. If Granny had put me in protective custody years ago instead of palming me off on the Congressman and his outfit, then none of this would have happened. None of it. This Twilight Zone shit.

She was just like the rest of them.

"You're bleeding, sugar." She said it without any change in tone. "That wound looks bad. You should be at the hospital right now."

"No, it's alright. I'm cool." I knew they had not made up their minds what to do with me. Being shot had its benefits.

She was lighting another cigarette with shaking hands. "Eddie, don't be stubborn. Baby, you've got to let somebody tend to that wound. Too much blood lost."

"I know what I'm doing," I said softly. "No hospital.

You're always telling me that I must face the things in my life like an adult, so that's what I'm doing. No hospital, no cops."

With a quick motion, she turned the shade of the lamp on one of the two end tables toward me so she could see every blemish on my face. "What have you done? I want to hear it from you, not anybody else. The truth."

"You don't want to know. I've not been right in my head."

The man came from the kitchen, carrying a pair of garden scissors for the leaf-happy plants in her greenhouse. I guessed he was her boyfriend or something. He seemed awfully at ease in the house as if he belonged there. He said a trail of blood led from the bathroom to the hallway and the tub was full of it, blood everywhere. I turned to face him, woozy and wincing, holding my hand with pressure over the wound.

"If you don't want to go to the hospital, it's because you've done something wrong," the man said. "That looks like a bullet wound. We should call the police."

Now my vision was really messing with me. Nigger looked like a chocolate Seinfeld. Big nose and puppet eyes. I thought about treats, a hot bath, a Snickers candy bar, or a slice of peach cobbler, with cold vanilla ice cream on top. I closed my eyes and we, Grandma and me, were out in the greenhouse. I took a deep breath, taking in the comforting aroma of the flower blooms and most black earth. Through the frosted windows, I could make out the murky shadows of people on the sidewalk across the street and the darker outline of the houses and buildings in the distance. Grandma Tee smiled at me, very warm, the kind of smile that thaws you out. She stood near a tray of young buds, a watering can in one hand and a gnawed apple in the other. Golden delicious, my favorite.

I was startled back to the world with the sting of a slap. The old woman packed a punch.

She pondered the situation, a choice had to be made. After all, I was kin, family and all, blood, and blood deserved special consideration. Even if there was criminal activity involved.

"We've got to call the police," the man repeated, his stare glued on me. "If you don't report a crime, you can get into big trouble."

The old woman sagged back in her seat at the mention of trouble. "Eddie, what did you do?" she asked once more. "I want the truth, every detail. Don't leave anything out."

"No, you don't want to know," I replied. "And besides I don't say shit in front of him. I don't know him."

Frankly, she was irritated with me. I wanted to talk, I wanted to tell her everything, my side of things. Why I kill women. God never healed me.

"Did anyone see you come in here?" she asked. An odd question. Nobody would ask that without knowing some of the facts.

"No."

It was then I noticed the sound of her portable radio, in the corner of the room, much too loud. No one else seemed to hear it. Maybe it was so loud that only I could hear it, much like the high pitched squeal that only a dog could hear. The volume roared up, then it died out to a whimper before screaming back again. Perhaps what made me nuts even more, made me feel worse, was the scream of a female, yelling MURDERER. Murderer over and over. I glanced at it nervously. It was making me edgy.

"Look at me when I'm talking to you," she said nastily. "So what did you do?"

Some things were better off left secret and hidden. Below the surface. For the most part, men believe the worst about themselves and act accordingly. What beasts men are. Men are replaceable like spare car parts, this was what women really thought. The air in the room was steamy, sauna steamy, tropic. When was the last time I really laughed? Really felt happy?

"Do you believe in God?" she asked. "Eddie, do you believe in hell?"

"What kind of God would condemn somebody to live a life like mine? I've been getting my butt kicked all my life, no let up. What has God done for me but tell me every day what a worthless nigger I am? He's taken everything from me."

"Some people have it worse and they still believe."

"And they're fools. To God, I am the Other, the Thing, the Monster. Even the world has no place for me and other young people like me. We got the wrong complexion, wrong connections, wrong everything. Where in the hell do we belong? Who loves the black boys? Even our mothers don't. Nobody, that's who."

"Do you pray?" Her eyes were tearing up. She was somber.

"Hell no. There's no strong bond between me and God. He forgot all about me a long time ago. Look at what He did to my family, to my life. Look at all the kids who must live like I do. Check out what's happening to us. We're self-destructing like mad. There is no salvation, no redemption for us. People talk about us but not to us. God's got his foot up our butt."

I could hear the words in her head before she said them. "How could you do this, Eddie? To your own people. You're not killing your Mama, your parents, your pain . . . they say you're killing innocent women, innocent people. This is crazy. You're doing the white folks' work for them. Do you know that?"

What was I supposed to do with all this rage, pent up, all this frustration? Too many shitty things have been done to me. The Congressman and the Mrs. made me feel like this caged monkey trotted out for the voters' light entertainment. Eddie the Wonder Ape. I was tired of surpressing what I felt for so long. How do you break the act of killing someone down into parts? Hey, both my parents and the community must bear some responsibility for what I have become. Nobody said enough, not even Grandma Tee.

How could I be so evil if God exists? Where was His mercy in all of this? Hear this. That church shit doesn't work in the real world. Nobody respects kindness or tenderness. Show me where. They just say: *The Boy Went On A Killing Spree.* Too much time alone, too much time to mope, to brood. To form bad thoughts. Somewhere along the way I know what happened. I just snapped.

"These people, these women can't be scapegoats for what happened to you," the old woman said. Classic Grandma.

The gun was on the table between us. I was so out of it, that thing had been there the whole time. It must have fallen out of my coat. Grandma Tee saw me glance at it, flinched, but didn't move because she knew I would go for it, if she did reach out. The seeds for this end were already sown. I want to sleep without dreaming. I want life without the barbs.

Grandma, can you fix me? What can you do to make me whole again inside? How can you remove my pain? Can you give me my childhood back?

"Society would fall apart without rules," the man said, walking through the room, not looking at me. "And Rule Number One is that you can't kill people."

Before Grandma Tee could blink, I snatched up the gun and placed it in her wrinkled hands, laughing a dry sarcastic laugh. A look mixing fear and disgust came over her face. I wrote on the table with a bloody finger, *8, 7, 6, 5, 4, 3, 2,* glaring at her. The voices were there the whole time, *SHUT THE BITCH UP! SHUT HER MOUTH!* I put the finger on the trigger, letting out a war whoop, and put my forehead to the barrel of the gun. Pull the trigger. I was already dead, I didn't give a shit anymore.

"Two mornings ago, I got up early to watch the sun come up and it's a joke," I snickered. "Remember this, Granny. They made me into a monster."

"Don't play crazy, Eddie," she said. "Stop this! This isn't a game. Somebody could get hurt."

I finally cried out. "You shoot me, shoot me now or I'm going to fuck both of you up! I mean it. Kill my sorry ass." I pushed the barrel to a spot right above my right eye. But she wouldn't pull the trigger.

My voice had something in it that made the man stare at me in fear. Raw fear. It was in his eyes. That gave me a quick thrill, his eyes. He said something about not waiting anymore, calling the police right now, to hell with Grandma's opinion. The bastard went for the cordless phone and started backing into the hallway, out of range. But I wasn't having it.

"Here, give me this thing before you hurt yourself with it," I said to the old woman in a ventriloquist's whisper, taking the gun back from her. I was a kid when my parents were butchered. I saw myself at that second, in my mind's eye, as that kid again. Grinning, I pointed the gun at the retreating man and fired twice. *BLAM! BLAM!* Gun was loud as hell. A short yelp. There was a dark running blot of blood and something else on the far wall and the man's body slumped back into the hallway. He fell with a dull thud like a bag of potatoes dropped down the stairs.

"I couldn't let him call the police," I said to her in a completely serious voice. "He was going to ruin everything."

Yes, they might catch me, take me down, what they won't understand is who I am and what made me this way. Nor will they care. At school once, the girls teased and taunted me about my folks dead, laying on the floor spread-eagled like corpses, like lifeless bodies, and I cried for five weeks straight, tears so cold that they froze on my cheeks, but one day the wetness turned to steam. The rage started burning me up from the inside.

"Don't hurt me, Eddie," Grandma Tee pleaded. "You don't have to do this."

"Are you afraid?" I asked.

"No." She was proud. And from the Old School. All Guts.

"Well, you should be. I kill people."

"Eddie, you must turn yourself in. Stop this."

I shook my head. I struggled to my feet, smiled, and went over to check on Seinfeld. He was dead. No pulse anywhere. Good head shot. I fished in his pocket and found his cigarettes, lit a match and fired one up. Inhaled as deeply as I could. It relaxed me right away. I was the kid watching Pops grind my Easter eggs to a yellowed powder under his heel. I was the kid locked in my room without toilet privileges. I was the kid sitting starved in the kitchen, staring at four locks on the refrigerator door. I was the kid slapped hard in the face in public by Moms for burping after chowing down one of her greasy burgers. I became that kid again, so alone and angry, but with a gun in my hand this time. In control. Total control.

"And the whole world is unfair to poor little Eddie," Grandma said, making fun of me. Bad move. Just like the rest of them.

I couldn't think of anything to say right then, so I kept quiet. She fell forward with such force that the floor shook when her body hit. I started toward the kitchen where one of the pots was burning on the stove, dark smoke, charred odor. The whole city probably wanted me dead. She wanted me dead. Out of the way, Grandma, you lied to me. You betrayed me, abandoned me like the rest of them. You didn't keep your word, neither did I. *SHOOT THE BITCH AGAIN!* Grandma, you were trying to get into my head. I couldn't let you do that. I remembered what she said once: Your mother and your father were never interested in what made you kids tick. You were just something they had to feed and keep dry like puppies. The girls and you. I couldn't believe what I had just done, none of it. Shot them. Incredible. I felt crazy, really crazy for the first time.

Behind me, the bathroom door suddenly closed. The radio came on again, the lady screaming at the top of her lungs, *MURDERER MURDERER*. She said a lot of hurtful things about me. My hearing was going in and out, like when you channel surf from station to station, so it was freaking me out.

I heard her talking behind the door. Talking low and fast. I tried the doorknob, twisting it back and forth, but it was locked secure. Instantly, I stepped back, drew a deep breath, and rushed the door, smashing it down with a running start and a shoulder.

". . . Come quick . . . everybody . . . everybody's dead . . . my grandbaby done killed us all," she said in a strangled voice. Suddenly, before I could touch her, she pitched sideways to the tiled floor, with the cordless phone still in her bloodied hand. Damn.

I kneeled before her, reached up for a towel, and wet it under the faucet. When I got it moist enough, I set Granny Tee up with her back against the toilet, and wiped the blood from her forehead with a corner of the towel. Wiped her face clean. I stared at her, so dead. I killed her. I put my hand on her damp, cool cheek. My eyes got misty a little bit but I wiped it away quickly. No remorse.

It was me or them. I kissed her soundly on the lips once. It was my way of saying I was sorry, my way of saying good-bye. My hand found a brush on the sink, a fat wooden one with stiff brown bristles, and slowly I ran it through her white hair. Maybe I brushed her hair for a couple of minutes. Finally, I applied lipstick, a dark red color, to her twisted mouth, another two minutes, then I got up and straightened out her legs so she looked like a little girl sitting on the floor playing with her dollies. It was hard for me to leave her there because I wanted her arms around me once more, telling me that the world wouldn't get the best of me.

But I left her. I walked to the bathroom door, glanced back at her once, and quietly closed it behind me. Strangely, I felt so calm. Like I was high on some shit. I was alone now, completely alone. A minute later, I sat back in the chair, sitting very still, thinking back to what Uncle Vincent told me a year ago, that he knew I was doomed even back in my mudpie days. In my kiddie days. I closed my eyes and saw Grandma Tee: she reached out to hug me and told me how much she loved me. I expected to see her stand up and scold me for bringing death into her quiet suburban home.

When I opened my eyes, I remembered she was still dead, dead as a fork. I love you, Granny, I love you very much. I didn't mean to fuck nobody up. The gun went off by itself. Really it did. I didn't blame her. I would have called the cops too. It still felt like the tropics in there. I was drenched in sweat. And blood.

For a fleeting moment, I thought about loading the gun if there were more shells. The thought occurred to me that I was going into a thick, dark forest where there were no known paths or guidebooks on how to get back home. But I was the only one left. I alone survived.

At least, I had the joy of that and nothing could take that away. At least I had that. I leaned back in the chair to watch her Chihuahua run around in a frenzied circle in the middle of the carpeted floor. The only time he would stop was to scratch at the closed bathroom door. The dog's name was Boy.

The police, of course. Of course. They probably had the house covered from every angle by now. SWAT teams. Snipers on the roofs. Bradley and his crew monitoring it all from the van parked down the street. Didn't mean it, Granny Tee. Forgive me, please. I pulled the gun closer to the table. Company was coming. More police sirens yowled in the distance. There was some time left.

I thought about going to the bathroom to open Grandma Tee's eyes. Her dead doll-baby eyes, so she could see what happened next. What the fuck have I done? My finger bent around the trigger and I pointed it at my head. Strangely, I felt calm, peaceful, serene. Like the feeling I used to get as a kid after I prayed. I flashed on some of the people I'd killed during my spree, real quick, like colored slides rushing fast before my eyes, their faces. Just their faces. I placed the gun into my mouth and pulled the trigger. Nothing. Nothing but hollow clicks. Empty. I thought of my father holding my head down in the dirty toilet as he flushed and my mother slapping my face over and over in public. And perverse pleasure rushed through me. If I had just one bullet. Company was coming. Maybe now somebody will care about what I feel. Moms, just maybe.

Chapter 30

IN THE TWILIGHT

Immediately, I saw the police helicopter circling overhead, its spotlight scouring the yards, alleys, and streets, but it was looping wide of its mark. I ran through several backyards, hid behind some dumpsters, and behind a few parked cars before I could walk casually. The neighborhood was full of sirens, flashing red lights, prowling detectives and cop cars. I had borrowed a shirt from the man I killed, took it out of the dresser, and bandaged the wound again before I put it on. Yes, more bullets in my pants. Three. I stopped to load my gun.

It started to rain, first drizzling, then it picked up in a constant downpour. I tried to remember the direction I came from the highway, kept forgetting the street names, so I gave up. I just wanted to avoid the cops. After I cut through an alley, I came out on a fairly busy street, cars whizzed past on the wet pavement, and I decided to stick out my thumb.

A truck passed, another car turned at the corner, and finally a battered Trans-Am drove toward me. I stepped off the road, near the curb, and waved at the driver. The rain was coming down, drenching my skin through my clothes.

The Trans-Am pulled over and stopped. I trotted to it, chilled to the bone from the wetness. The car windows were steamed up but I could see there were four black men inside, all dressed in thug gear. The blunt smoke was thick enough to cut. Two of the brothers drank from forties, maybe Colt 45, and puffed away on reefer.

"What the fuck are you doing out here this time of night?" the driver asked.

"Trying to get the City," I said. "You headed that way?"

"Yeah, we cool," the driver, steering one hand with the other tackling the blunt, said. "This here is Lord Sabu, DJ Ghost, King Zouk, and Smoked Satin. I'm Rah Twista. What's yours?"

"Eddie," I replied. This was a motley crew. Lord Sabu looked like Dumbo, the Disney elephant. DJ Ghost had a pale, sickly look. King Zouk, well, you could tell he was full of himself. Super cool. I couldn't figure out Smoked Satin. He wore two earrings and I could see that he had a stud in his tongue. They were passing around the bottles and the blunts.

"Smoked jus' got out of Rikers yesterday, been to see his Mama, and now we having a celebration," Lord Sabu said in a rush of words. "He finished his nickel and now he's back to the world."

I looked at Smoked, his cheek held a smudge of red lipstick where his mother kissed him. He stared at me, like we were of rival gangs. I meant him no ill will. I just wanted to get out of here and onto the highway before the cops discovered the bodies. King Zouk offered me the blunt and I took it, knowing the dope would make me stupid.

"What did you go up for?" I asked Smoked, blowing

reefer smoke out both my nostrils. I figured he was about nineteen or twenty, not much older than that. He was around my age.

"I raped a women and robbed her," he said proudly.

I knew Rikers, that rock on the East River, with its twisting puzzle of concrete hallways, locked steel doors, brutal bulls, and razor ribbon. When Pops had a short stint, we used to go out there on the bus, going across the bridge with the guards and the guns.

"I was telling you the story, niggers attacked me with shivs and tried to make me give up my sneakers, my Jordans," Smoked said. "I kicked this asshole's teeth out, gold teeth at that. And I waited, bided my time until I got this nigger in a choke hold, put him to sleep. If the guard hadn't come up on me, I'd have croacked the muthafucka."

King Zouk laughed. "The nigger sick."

"You did time, Ghost?" Smoked asked, keeping his eyes on me.

"Yeah, a trey." DJ Ghost was smoking a Newport.

"What for?" King Zouk asked.

"It happened to me when I was in Louisiana." DJ Ghost flicked the ashes between his legs. "It was a hell-hole, right in the middle of the Mississippi Delta in Tallulah. I hated that place. The Tallulah Correctional Center for Youth. Fights would go on all the time. I had more black eyes and broken noses than I can count. The meals wasn't shit. I lost a lot of weight."

"What were you in for?" I asked.

"Three counts of attempted murder," DJ Ghost smiled. "I was 14."

"Damn," I said. These boys were the real thing.

A cop car rushed through the light, siren and red light flashing.

"They always talk about rehabilitation and shit," Rah Twista moaned, turning the car onto the ramp to the highway. "They send you up, let you do hard time, and then kick your butt out. No job, no schooling, no nothing. So you out here and you don't know your ass from your elbow. You jus' lost."

King Zouk livened up and pointed to the trunk. "We got the shit, the real shit. We got enough guns to hold up Fort Knox. I'm serious."

He proceeded to tell me that they had two cartons of guns in the trunk of the car: Accu-Tek Model 9mm, Colt Python .357 Magnum, Glock 9mm, Phoenix Arms Raven .25 cal–6 shot, Smith & Wesson, Ruger GP-357 Magnum, and Beretta 92 FS 9mm. What an arsenal! Man, if the cops pulled us over, that would be it. Gun trafficking. He said they were making a delivery in a housing project in the Bronx, doing a favor for a pal Rah Twista knew.

"What did you like about the joint?" Rah Twista asked Smoked.

"Booty, boy pussy," Smoked grinned. "I got a lot of that. What are you staring at? I don't like how you're looking at me."

"Hey, he's our guest, right?" Rah Twista said.

I nodded. Smoked kept on glaring at me. Then the nigger put his hand on my leg, moving up to my crotch. I palmed his wrist and bent it backward. He winced from the pain.

"I'm not going to be no bitch," I said firmly. "I just want a ride. That's it."

Smoked grinned again, feeling his wrist. He felt under his jacket and that was when I pulled my gun and placed it at his temple. The driver slowed the car, pulled over and stopped by the road. Rah Twista and King

Zouk pleaded for calm. No man, we don't have to get that way. Peace, brother. Put the gun away. Let's be friends.

"A punk is a punk is a punk," I snarled at the thug with the plucked eyebrows. I was waiting for him to make his move.

There was big time tension in the car. Everybody had that funny look in their eyes. The itchy trigger fingers. Traffic wasn't bad at this time of night but it was busier than the usual. And the rain was still coming down.

"Let's play nice," Rah Twista said, leaving both hands on the steering wheel. "Now why don't you, my brother, put away your gun?"

DJ Ghost used a lighter on his cigarette. It glowed in the darkness. "Hey, the brother didn't mean anything by his hand on your leg. He was just funning."

Scowling, Smoked laughed. "I ain't a faggot."

Alive or dead. I knew when he wouldn't look at me for that second. He was making his move and I beat him to the punch, splattering his brains against the window. Everybody stopped in shock and surprise.

"Fuck, he croaked him, he croaked Smoked," the driver yelled as he drove off into the highway traffic. "Deal with this nigger. Deal with him. Fuck him up."

"Punk-ass nigger," DJ Ghost pulled his 9mm, got off some shots, very wild shots. In the tight space of the car, it seemed like everybody was drawing their gats and squeezing off shots. The car blazed into another lane, drawing a chorus of blaring horns. I shot King Zouk in the neck. He was slouched down in the far corner on the back seat, a neat bullet hole above his Adam's apple.

Rah Twista jammed his foot to the floor, overtaking a car and a truck but the Trans-Am slid into another vehicle, a Jeep, sending off a shower of sparks. Another series of shots, DJ Ghost and me, trading slugs, and he went back into the door, two horrible wounds to the lungs. I tried to dive for the key in the ignition but the driver swooped the car from side to side. Furthermore, my arm wouldn't stay up, couldn't lift it.

"Pull this fuckin' car over," I yelled.

Tires squealed. I got him in a choke hold, and we fought like madmen, hands around his neck and eyes, then he tried to slam on the brakes. At some point, DJ Ghost shot me in the shoulder and under the armpit. Blood was everywhere. He put up his hands over his face, screamed like a bitch, the car hurtled through the air and rolling over and over, and a crushing sound, the hymns of shattering glass and twisting metal and darkness. I was thrown from the car, which was burning with the guys still in it, except Smoked with his plucked eyebrows. He was still dead under another car. Two cars and a truck were overturned. Drivers ran to the crash. I crawled, part of my face missing, bleeding from my mouth, and leaking from a deep gash in my neck.

I tried to speak. But nothing came out of my mouth. I saw a lot of shit. I caused a lot of shit. It was too late to grow a conscience now . . . shit got really fucked up. My body went into spasms, or maybe seizures . . . Grandma Tee would be proud of me . . . I remembered my prayer . . . *Our Father . . . which art in Heaven . . . give us this day . . . as we forgive our debtors . . . lead us not into temptation* . . . fuck it . . . I'm not going to Heaven . . . maybe I won't even go to hell . . . Hands lifted me up on a stretcher . . . God gave me a really bad hand . . . dead is dead . . . I grinned and then I quit.

Hell, I quit life and living.

Grab These Other
Dafina Novels
(mass market editions)

Check Out These Other
Dafina Novels

Look For These Other
Dafina Novels

If I Could
0-7582-0131-1

by Donna Hill
    $6.99US/**$9.99**CAN

Thunderland
0-7582-0247-4

by Brandon Massey
    $6.99US/**$9.99**CAN

June In Winter
0-7582-0375-6

by Pat Phillips
    $6.99US/**$9.99**CAN

Yo Yo Love
0-7582-0239-3

by Daaimah S. Poole
    $6.99US/**$9.99**CAN

When Twilight Comes
0-7582-0033-1

by Gwynne Forster
    $6.99US/**$9.99**CAN

It's A Thin Line
0-7582-0354-3

by Kimberla Lawson Roby
    $6.99US/**$9.99**CAN

Perfect Timing
0-7582-0029-3

by Brenda Jackson
    $6.99US/**$9.99**CAN

Never Again Once More
0-7582-0021-8

by Mary B. Morrison
    $6.99US/**$8.99**CAN

Available Wherever Books Are Sold!

Check out our website at www.kensingtonbooks.com.